THE LAST
Guy

ILSA MADDEN-MILLS
TIA LOUISE

The Last Guy
Copyright © Ilsa-Louise Books, 2017
All rights reserved.

ISBN-13:978-1546910091
ISBN-10:1546910093

Cover design by:
Shanoff Formats

Photography by:
Wander Aguiar
David Wills, cover model

Interior Design & Formatting by:
Christine Borgford, Type A Formatting

For best friends, lovers, and true believers.

And RuPaul.

One

REBECCA

SCRATCHY PINK TULLE hits me square in the face, and I jerk away as a shrieking tornado of blonde curls bolts past me. I am in hell, more specifically *pageant* hell, the deepest and darkest level.

"Petal Boo Bishop! PETAL BOO BISHOP!" A large woman stomps after the child, shoving me as I dodge to avoid being tackled. "Get back here and put your tutu on this minute!"

My camera-guy Kevin snorts as I regain my footing. He gets a brief, snappy glare. Let him try interviewing tiny humans in the middle of chaos.

Clearing my throat, I smile and hold the mic down to the four-foot beauty queen I'd been addressing before the interruption. "And what will you do if you win Miss Planetary Princess, Kaitlyn?"

She pushes her helmet of golden-brown hair away from her face. It's bigger than her head and strong enough to withstand any climatological distress. My hair, by contrast, is completely wilted and flat in the Houston humidity that blasts through the room every time a door opens.

"First, I wanna eat chicken nuggets then pizza with pineapple and a Coke—oh, and some taco bells. I haven't had a taco since I was three years old. Mama says tacos are bad for business."

Mama gives Kaitlyn a warning look.

"That sounds like my kind of fun!" I laugh, giving her a fist bump and then winking at the camera. The wink is my trademark, along with my pencil skirts.

Kaitlyn's mama charges me, putting her hand on the mic alongside mine and giving it a tug. I tug back—while pretending I'm not—as I smile through clenched teeth. I refuse to let go, and she hunches in front of me to speak.

"After we win here, we're heading to Little Miss Galaxy at the San Francisco Zoo," she states. "We'll go straight to catwalk training and poise. The girls in Little Miss Galaxy come from all over the country, you know. Their bodies are streamlined and toned—no baby fat. We're on a healthy but strict diet."

I blink in horror as I absorb her speech. *Think about the anchor job, Rebecca. Smile.* "Wow. That seems rigorous for a five-year-old."

Mama rakes her eyes over me. "I'm sure you wouldn't know anything about it."

I jerk the mic away, ignoring her body shaming. "Kaitlyn, how do *you* feel about being Miss Galaxy?"

"*Little* Miss Galaxy," her mother corrects.

Huge brown eyes gaze up at me. "I'll be Princess Leia!"

Mama bursts out laughing. "With that honey-bun hair! You are *not* Princess Leia. Except for maybe those chubby cheeks, but we're working on that."

The child's eyes land on her shoes, and I swallow the knot of anger in my throat. I might be a hard-boiled newswoman, but I'm fighting a deep desire to steal this little cutie and give her a normal childhood—tacos and all.

Looking straight into Kevin's lens, I do the wrap. "There you have it, folks. Miss Planetary Princess is just the latest preschool pageant feeding into the Miss USA circuit. Catch all the taco-worthy drama tomorrow night at eight, right here at the Houston Expo

Center. I'm Rebecca Fieldstone, KHOT News."

I hold the smile a beat longer until Kevin gives me the signal. "We're clear."

He lowers the camera, and my shoulders drop. This assignment is soul sucking.

I need to get back to the station and edit the story, but I can't help sneaking a last look at Kaitlyn. Her shoulders are also slumped, and her mom steers her in the direction of the Channel 8 news team set up in the corner across from us. I hope she gets a taco soon.

"You ready?" I tuck the mic under my arm and pick up my bag.

"Miss? Excuse me, miss?" The large woman who had almost knocked me down earlier touches my shoulder.

I don't stop walking.

The woman keeps my pace, breathing heavily as she jogs. "Sorry about earlier, but you haven't talked to Petal Boo. We'd really like to have her on camera for her résumé."

Not another one, I groan inwardly. "I'm sorry. I can't guarantee what goes on air—"

The lady shoots out a hand and grips my arm, stopping me. "Oh, you'll want to talk to Petal. She's not like the rest."

My eyebrow arches, and she releases me. Still, her face is pleading. "Just take a look. Please?"

Something about her gives me pause. Maybe it's the sweat lining her brow—I can totally relate. As per usual, it's a steamy late-September day in southeast Texas, and I left my blotting papers back in the news van. I'm sure my face looks like a red Solo cup right now.

Giving Kevin a quick nod, we follow her. My mic is out, the light goes on, and Kevin points the camera at a fluffy little girl in a white-blonde wig styled with long ringlets around her oval face.

"Hi, there," I say with a smile. "What's your name?"

She throws back her shoulder and tilts her chin. "My name is Petal Boo Bishop, and I'm from Meridian, Mississippi!" She's practically shouting in her clipped country accent, but her execution is polished. "I got started in the pageant circuit after I won the Beautiful Child competition. You've probably heard of the Beautiful Child pageant. It's famous."

"I'm afraid I haven't—"

"From *To Kill a Mockingbird*? You haven't read *To Kill a Mockingbird*?" Her tone is astonished disapproval.

The camera trembles with Kevin's suppressed laughter, and I smile, knowing good footage when I see it. I bend down to her level, sucking in my gut. From this angle, it's more of a challenge to hide the extra few pounds I've picked up these last couple months.

"It's been a while," I say, and she charges on.

"It's been voted one of the greatest novels of all time. It concerns the evils of racism."

"You're a smart girl, Petal. How old were you when you won Beautiful Child?"

Her face snaps to the camera. "I was four years old when I won my first contest. After that my mama said I could win a bunch of money in pageants, so we hit the road. We've been to Atlanta, Tampa, Nashville, Baton Rouge, and now we're here in the great state of Texas to claim Miss Planetary Princess." Her arm goes straight up, victory style, and she says it all without even pausing for breath.

"Okay, then." I stand, taking the pressure off my back. "Good luck to you, Petal."

"Thank you, Miss Fieldstone."

This kid knows my name? "How old are you now?"

"Seven and a half. I'm right slap in the middle of the playing field." She does a little hip-cock—as much as possible in her fluffy pink dress. "This is gonna be my year, just you wait and see. I'm gonna take home the tiara."

Her mother rocks back on her heels, arms crossed, beaming with pride.

"In that case, I'll be watching for you, as will Houston tonight at six and ten. Do you have a special message for our Channel 5 viewers?"

"You bet your butt I do." She looks into the camera. "People of Texas and the world, don't settle. You deserve the best, just like me. Work as hard as you can and have some fun too." She gives the camera a thumbs-up. "Y'all take care now!"

I watch her prance off, tutu flouncing with every step, and I confess, I'm a little envious of her confidence. That's *exactly* the kind of attitude I need when it comes to getting the weekend anchor position. It's been on my radar ever since Maryanne announced she isn't coming back from maternity leave. She wants to start a family, and her decision is my chance to get off this underpaying, exhausting reporter's beat. *Please, God,* I pray silently. *I need that anchor job.*

Back in the van, I flip down the visor and lean forward to check my appearance as Kevin races us to the studio. We've got exactly forty-five minutes to get this package together for the six o'clock news.

"My nose looks like an oil slick, and I've got mascara specks under my eyes." *Shit!* My gaze cuts to Kevin. "Why didn't you say something?"

Kevin takes a loud slurp from his Big Gulp. With frizzy brown hair and two-inch thick glasses, he's the consummate tech geek, wrinkled shirt and all. "I didn't notice. Petal was more interesting."

I groan and dig through my oversized purse, pulling out a small compact of pressed powder to blot my face. *Why didn't I check the mirror before that stupid segment?*

Marv, our overbearing news director, could catch a speck of pepper in your back teeth. I'm dead. Glancing out the window, I wonder if we could possibly get back and do a re-shoot . . . Who am I kidding? No telling where Petal Boo is now, and depending on the downtown traffic, we barely have time to get to the station.

"You look fine, Becks." Kevin takes another slurp. "You're always too hard on your appearance."

I glare at him, and he shrugs, keeping his eyes on the road. *Fine* doesn't cut it these days. You have to be young and pretty much perfect to land an anchor gig. They're the top-paying, most visible spots in the broadcast-news food chain.

We're finally at the studio, and I dash to the editing booth to pick the video clips and put the story together. Most of Kaitlyn's interview ends up on the cutting-room floor in favor of scene-stealer Petal Boo. It's sad, but I can't help grinning as I realize Petal might be the one bright spot of my week. Even though I look like a disheveled mess standing next to the tiny, spray-tanned beauty queen, I don't mind so much. She's got loads of personality, and she's definitely one to watch.

I record my voice-over and layer it on top of B-roll of little girls teasing hair the size of Texas and twirling around in thousand-dollar sequined evening gowns, bedazzled cowgirl boots, and glittering one-piece swimsuits. The entire package is ready to go as the Channel 5 theme music begins.

"Becks! I need that story now!" Vicky, our executive producer, waves at me from the end of the short hall where the editing booths are located.

I punch *Save* and give her the thumbs-up. "It's on the server ready to roll!"

Leaning back in my chair, I think about the old days when a kid with a cart full of tapes would run the stories to the control room. It's so much easier now that digital has replaced film.

Standing, I don't even bother tucking my white blouse into my skirt. Hell, it's too tight anyway. My shoes are in my hand, and I collect my jacket and purse ready to call it a day. I've been at the station since nine, just in time to catch the morning show wrap up before heading out on my assignment. I'll stop by my desk and check my emails before I leave.

Of course, my path takes me right past the sports den, a newly renovated space consisting of desks and computers arranged in the shape of an octagon, *like an MMA fighting arena.* I don't even try to suppress my eye roll. Still . . . the one thing that stops them rolling is our new sports director.

With wavy dark hair and steel-blue eyes, Cade Hill has been here less than three months, and already he's revamped the entire department into a slick, SportsCenter-style man-paradise.

He's an ex-NFL superstar, son of a millionaire, and infuriating as hell. After retiring from the Atlanta Falcons, where he was the starting quarterback before blowing out his knee, he came here and was immediately put in charge of sports. He has zero experience, and he thinks he's a newsman. *Please.* It takes more than a sexy physique to tell a story on air.

Lucky for me, he's bending over a co-worker's computer, giving me the full, amazing view of his tight ass. I have two weaknesses in life: a muscular backside so toned you could bounce a quarter off it and Mexican food, and I'm sure not thinking about guacamole right now.

As if he can sense my eyes on him, he turns and catches me staring. My cheeks heat, and he grins that infuriatingly cocky grin with those deep dimples that actually make my panties wet. He rises to his six-foot-four height, and I pick up the pace, hoping to avoid speaking.

Get it together, Becks. Cade Hill is the last guy I would ever let ruin my plans for stardom.

"Truly Earth-shaking reporting today, Stone," he says, stepping to the open doorway.

I summon my inner goddess and put my nose in the air as I continue to the newsroom. "Stereotypical male response to a fe-male-dominated profession, Hill."

The butterflies in my stomach do somersaults when I feel the heat of his body right behind me, but I don't slow down.

"Profession?" he says, and I hear that grin still in his voice. "What did I miss?"

"Charitable organization," I reply. "The Miss USA pageant awards more than 350 thousand dollars in scholarships every year."

"You know, we could use your hustle on the sports team," he says, and when I do stop, he extends a finger as if he'll touch my cheek. I inhale a sharp breath. "Picked up a little shine there."

He did *not* just mention my oily face . . . Oh, he did. "For your information, the humidity in downtown Houston was a thousand percent this afternoon."

"Funny, Pat's weather report said it was only ninety-eight percent."

"Pat wasn't there, and neither were you." My eyes glide down his blue cotton shirt, cuffed at the elbows to show off his muscular forearms, to his Armani slacks. "It's a good thing. I'm sure you wouldn't want to ruin that ridiculously expensive suit."

"Thanks for noticing." He veers off, heading in the direction of the control room and giving me another view of that ass, but for whatever reason, he pauses and looks back. "You seem upset, Stone. Do I make you uncomfortable?"

Yes. He'd brushed against me in the break room once, and the sizzle had nearly given me a seizure. Okay, I exaggerate, but I had spilt my coffee down my skirt, all the way to my brand new knock-off Louboutin pumps.

"I'm a professional. I am not uncomfortable around anyone."

Lies, all lies! Cade Hill is the sexiest, most intimidating man I know, with a beard I might have imagined between my thighs more than once. *Shake it off.*

He chuckles and continues walking. I step over to my computer, quickly scan my inbox, and decide everything can wait until to-morrow. The six o'clock news is done, and I'm ready to get home, whip off my bra, and kick back. I'm passing our news director's office when I hear Marv call me from inside his glass-walled box. "Rebecca! Can you step inside for just a moment?"

Marv is old school, and I give my disheveled appearance a quick survey. Shirt out, shoes off, makeup melted—I've had better days. Still, I've been at KHOT five years. These guys know me.

Dropping my shoes, I step into them as I stuff the front of my blouse into my skirt. "Just heading home . . ." I pause when I see Cade sitting inside the door, his back to the wall. He seems confused, but I put on a smile as I focus on Marv. "How'd we do in the lineup?"

"CBS led with the plant explosion in Texas City. NBC stayed with us and covered the cellular strike blocking up traffic on the north side," he replies, glancing at three big-screen televisions mounted on the wall—all tuned to our competing local affiliates.

"Thank God we didn't get stuck in that." I drop into a chair opposite Cade.

"It was a tight turnaround, but I appreciate your hustle." He takes a pencil off his desk and rolls it in his fingers. "Watched your bit. It was decent."

Decent? I'd rocked the hell out of a silly human-interest story, but Marv can be hard to please. I take his criticism with a nod. Working for the top local affiliate in the fourth-largest city in the U.S. isn't for the thin-skinned. "Viewers will love Petal."

He doesn't look as confident, and a prickle of misgiving zips down my spine. Petal might have been spot-on, but my appearance was iffy.

A noise of heels clicking outside the door captures his attention. "Vicky!" Marv shouts. "Could you step in here a minute?"

Vicky, too? Now my throat is tight.

"What's up?" Vicky steps in the door looking professional and cool in cream-colored slacks and a green shirt that perfectly compliments her red hair. "Hello, Cade." She looks around the office and adjusts her glasses. "Hey, Becks. Nice work with those little robots today."

"Future Stepford Wives," I quip, and she laughs. "Except for Petal."

A stylish lady in her forties, Vicky Grant and I hit it off my first day, and she's had my back ever since. We both share a vision of shaking up this football-and-oil-dominated city and shining a light on projects and organizations trying to make a difference . . . pageants possibly included.

"The consultants arrived this afternoon." Marv pulls our attention back to him. "They gave me the feedback on our six o'clock show."

My stomach sinks. Corporate sends a pair of "insultants" (as we call them in the newsroom) twice a year to watch our broadcasts and give "constructive feedback," which essentially consists of ripping the reporters to shreds from the way we dress to how we walk to the word choice in our tags. It's brutal, and I do not want Cade in here listening to whatever they said about me.

Marv leans forward on his desk, resting on his forearms. Gray eyes lift under his bushy eyebrows. Our gazes meet.

"Okay?" I shift in my chair.

"What other projects do you have in the works, Becks?" He's back to playing with that pencil, rolling it back and forth in his fingers. "Any outside gigs in the hopper?"

"Outside gigs?" I'm confused. I spend every waking minute at this station, including weekends if there's breaking news. "I don't have time for a cat, Marv."

"Hmmm. Any interest in joining the production staff?" He glances at Vicky, and I do the same.

I can tell she's caught off-guard, but she covers it. "Er . . . of course, we could use someone like Becks in production. She's smarter and has more experience than any of our reporters, but—"

"Great! That's great!" Relief breaks over our boss's face, and he leans back in his chair as if a decision has been made. "Don't you think, Cade? You're in management now."

My eyes cut to him.

"In sports," he says. "I don't have any say over the regular reporters."

"Still," Marv continues. "You know what the board wants. You have eyes."

Dread pools in my gut. "Wait . . ." I can't hide the panic in my voice as I quickly glance from Cade to Marv. "Did you just take me off reporting? You know I've been working toward that weekend anchor chair."

Cade's brow lowers, and Marv's moment of cheer flits away. "The consultants think you might do better *behind* the camera, rather than in front of it. But don't worry, it's not the end—"

"What the fu-*hell*?" I curb the profanity. He's still my boss, but I'm on my feet. "Why would they say something like that? They loved my piece on the dinosaur excavation last summer!"

Marv's Adam's apple bobs as he swallows. It's his tell that he's nervous—which makes *me* nauseous. "They think we need fresher faces. Someone who'll appeal to the . . . eighteen to twenty-five age bracket."

"You have *got* to be kidding me! Those aren't the people who watch the news." I pace around the room, propriety gone.

Cade clears his throat. "Marv, I'm not sure I should be—"

"They're thinking of the advertisers," Marv continues. "Viewers don't want to be scolded by their mothers on the nightly news."

My brain literally short-circuits, and I can't decide if I'm more offended by his use of the word *scolded* or his use of the word *mothers*. "I'm single! I'm not even dating anyone!"

"Well . . . perhaps you should."

My jaw drops. He did not just go there. "That's sexist! My personal life has nothing to do with this job."

"This is news to me, Marv," Vicky says, her voice infused with calm. "Maybe we should discuss this in private before we make a decision."

He shrugs, eyes fixed above my head. The ass can't even meet my gaze. "Maybe there are some steps you could take to improve your on-camera look. Something around the forehead to look less . . . angry."

"Botox?" I snap. "Are you saying I need Botox?"

"Now, don't put words in my mouth." He rises from his chair, holding out a conciliatory hand. "I didn't say anything about possible plastic surgery. Did I, Cade?"

"Plastic surgery!" My heart beats faster and my chest rises. I twist the handles on my bag. Shit, I might hyperventilate. "I just turned twenty-eight!"

Cade shifts in his chair, and Marv continues. "Now, Rebecca, even you have to admit you haven't been yourself lately." His eyes drift to my straining waistline.

I stiffen, standing straighter and trying to suck in subtly.

"You've been with us five years without a break." He scratches his nearly white goatee. "Maybe a little R&R . . . combined with some good, brisk walks around the park."

"Are you calling me fat?" My question is just short of a shriek.

Marv looks like he swallowed a goldfish and isn't sure how it's going to come out.

Again Vicky attempts to calm the situation. "It's been a long day. Why don't we all get some rest?" She takes my upper arm and leads me to the door. "Marv and I will get with Liz over the next few days, and we can talk more about it then."

"Good idea," Cade says.

I allow Vicky to lead me to the door, but I'm vibrating with anger and outrage.

"Just breathe," she says a notch above a whisper once we're in the hall.

"Oh, sure, quote classic country to me." I don't smile. It's easy for her to say. She can age all she wants in the control booth, but I have to remain eternally twenty-one.

Cade exits Marv's office and does a sudden U-turn when he sees us. I can't stop a tiny growl. "*He* should not have been in that meeting."

"I agree." Vicky's eyes narrow behind her glasses. "I don't know what Marv is thinking."

I'm still feeling sick. Production is where you work if you love TV news, but the camera doesn't love you. "Is he right, Vicky? Do I look like somebody's overweight, angry mother?"

"Of course not." She pats my arm. "I've got you covered here. Still . . . you could help me help you."

I halt and meet her gaze head-on. "What are you saying?"

"Stop frowning." Her eyes travel down and up my body. "Just make some changes on your end. You know . . . little things."

I grip her forearm. "Be brutal and pretend we aren't friends. Tell me what to do to stay in front of the camera."

Releasing a deep sigh, she crosses her arms. "Okay . . . but I'm only saying this because I care. You need to drop at least five pounds—at least. High-def shows *everything*."

Looking down, I see the seams straining on the sides of my skirt, and I tighten my lips. It's true. I've let things go a little bit. When my best friend Nancy had lived with me, she'd always been able to whip up my favorite Tex-Mex recipes with half the fat and calories. It had been her specialty—favorite foods with a healthy twist. Now she's at the Culinary Institute in New York chasing her dream of being on the Food Network, and I'm left with Doritos Locos Tacos from Taco Bell . . . and an additional fifteen pounds.

Of course, there's also the other thing.

"I guess I've been in a funk since James and I broke up . . ." I hope for a little sympathy. "It's hard to care what you look like naked when the chances of anyone seeing you naked are less than zero."

"You can increase those chances if you pay attention to your makeup."

I throw up my hands. "We busted our asses to file that pageant story on time. It was hot as hell in the expo center, and when I realized I'd left my blotting papers in the van, it was too late . . ."

Her expression changes, and my voice trails off. I know what she's going to say before she even begins.

"This is a competitive, appearance-driven field, Becks." She gives my arm a squeeze. "You can't slack off, even for a month, and expect to move up in the ranks. I'll buy you a few weeks, but you have got to show that you're making changes."

"I know." I rub my forehead. "You're right. I know you're right!"

"Get started tomorrow." She leaves me at the door and heads back to the control room to prep for the ten o'clock broadcast.

I throw my blazer over my arm and start for the door. A unisex restroom is just at the back exit, and I decide to make a pit stop before heading to my car and getting stuck in late-evening Houston traffic needing to pee.

Flinging the door open, my eyes land on the glorious backside of none other than Captain Sexy himself. He steps away from the toilet, and not only do I get an eyeful of that sexy tush in all its toned and lined greatness, he turns before his slacks are completely over his hips, and I'm treated to a view of his long, thick . . . member. *If that's at ease, what must it look like at attention?*

My jaw goes slack, and the horrible meeting is forgotten as my purse plops to the floor. Never in my life have I ever wanted to increase my chances of being seen naked again. Forget being seen—I simply want to be naked all over *that* . . .

It. Is. Amazing.

CADE

"DON'T YOU KNOW how to knock, Stone?" I finish buckling my belt, hiding my surprise at seeing the sexy blonde bursting in the door like a wild woman.

Her mouth opens, closes, and then opens again. "Your pants were down! I saw . . ." She swallows, her face cardinal red. "I can't believe you go commando in Armani!"

My lips twitch as I wash my hands and dry them. "It's called taking a piss, and I usually do it alone. Do you mind giving me some privacy?"

I turn to adjust my tie in the mirror, secretly pleased we have something to distract us from that bullshit meeting Marv pulled me into just now. He'd been dead wrong thinking I'd side with his sorry ass over Stone. I've had my eye on her since day one, with her laser focus and her utter disinterest in me. Part of me finds it intriguing—a woman not falling at my feet—while the other side of me is annoyed. I want to get to the bottom of it.

She huffs. "Well, you should have locked the damn door—and stop calling me Stone! It's ridiculous. Killer."

My jaw tightens at her reference to my old football nickname. "I see you've done your homework. Do you prefer Becks?"

"That's for close friends only."

"Rebecca?" I ask silkily, liking how the three syllables roll off my tongue. Our eyes meet in the mirror.

"No." She crosses her arms.

"Why don't you like me, Stone?" I arch a brow as I turn around to face her. "What have I ever done to you?"

"For starters, you should *not* have been in that meeting just now."

"Agreed."

I can tell she's stunned by how fast I answer. Her face shutters, and she pushes a strand of hair behind her ear. While her eyes are fixed on the floor, I take a minute to study her uninterrupted. Her rumpled hair is a deep honey color and perfectly complements her pale, creamy skin. She mutters something to herself.

"What was that?"

Clearing her throat, she says, "I said you also remind me of someone. My ex, James. He had the beard thing too." She waves her fingers toward my face, still not making eye contact.

"It didn't end well?"

"He was a douche." Her hair slides over one shoulder as she shrugs. "He left me three months ago for the coffee barista who used to wait on us every morning on the way to work. Now I can't even go to my favorite coffee place. Did I mention she's twenty-one? Right up your *Killer* alley."

"Are you saying he's my doppelganger?" That bothers me, imagining Stone in a relationship with my twin, not twin.

She sighs. "The beard and hair is the same, but you're—"

"Hotter?" I grin.

Her lips purse and she starts to say something but seems to think better of it.

I study her. "The truth is you've been mad at me since I started here. Why?"

A flash of determination glints in her irises. "You want to know?"

"I wouldn't have asked."

"It's annoying—no, maddening—that you breeze into the best

station in Houston without a journalism degree and suddenly become *the* sports guy, all because you were a decent quarterback and your dad happens to own half the city."

I smirk. She's trying to get under my skin, and I like it, but I can't let the football slight pass.

"Decent quarterbacks don't score Super Bowl wins. I'm one of the best."

She thinks for a moment and nods. "Fair enough. But you insist on having that . . . that hair on your face when everyone else on camera is clean-shaven. Heck, your beard even gets fan mail!" A long exhale comes from her mouth. "Everyone loves you, and you didn't earn it."

"That's it?" I tuck my hands in my pockets.

"Mostly."

I shrug. "Cool. I can live with that."

She cocks her head and gives me a quizzical look. "It doesn't piss you off when I say you're skating by on your ridiculous beard, past talent, and family name?"

"How do you skate by, Stone? What's special about you?"

Her lip trembles, and I immediately want to yank the words back. *Shit.* Usually she's up for the snarky banter, but after that brutal meeting . . .

I scrub my face. "Er, what I meant was—"

She holds a hand up, seeming to find her equilibrium. "First off, I don't have to skate by. I have a bachelors in pre-law and a masters in journalism—"

"Couldn't get into law school?"

"And six years experience in front of a camera—"

"So do I. It's called the NFL—"

"Get into law school?" she repeats. "As if I want to be stuck in a stuffy office all day reading briefs and clocking billable hours."

"Good point. I probably wasted my time in law school."

Her eyes widen. "What? Where?"

"Leland, top of the class."

"You're lying."

"I thought you did your homework?" I smirk.

"Why are you smiling?" she demands with a little huff, and my slow grin widens.

"Because I'm *not* the dumb jock you think I am. I deserve this job. I've worked for it just as hard as you—only in a different way."

She dips her head. "You're probably right." Her voice is defeated.

No. I don't like this. My jaw grinds, and I'm pissed at Marv for blindsiding her like that. Stone is *never* this easy to best, especially in a verbal sparring match. I let my eyes cruise over her, scrutinizing her wilted shoulders and the way she holds herself as if she might break, and shit—her face scrunches up.

Wait.

Is she crying?

No, Jesus, please. Not here. Not now. Not with me.

She is. Her shoulders tremble as she sniffs and wipes her nose with her hand.

Fuck me.

Helplessness rolls over me, and my eyes roam around the room. Seeing the tissues on the counter, I grab a handful and press them into her hands.

"Shit, Stone. Did I hurt your feelings?"

She takes them and cleans her face. "God no. It's not you. Sorry for this. I never cry. It's been a long, craptastic day."

"Right." I pause. "Do you want to talk about it?"

"Not with you."

Thank fuck. I don't know how to talk to women. I've spent most of my life in a locker room surrounded by men.

Against my better judgment, I ease closer to her. "Look, I know we don't know each other well, but I've been told I'm a good listener."

She blinks up at me, emerald eyes glistening with tears. "Of course you are. You're Mr. Perfect, right?"

"I'm far from perfect," I murmur quietly. "In fact, I'm drawn up in a knot right now because you're crying."

She smiles a little. "Really?"

I nod.

She gathers herself as she dabs at the mascara under her eyes. I watch her intently. The truth is I'm a bit fascinated by Stone. I blame it on her lips. They're a deep pink color—naturally—with a lush bottom lip that begs to be tugged in a soft nip.

And her breasts are fucking incredible, perky and full, and I may have pictured my face there a few times—

Don't touch those tits, I remind myself sharply.

Don't mess with your co-worker when you're beginning a whole new career.

Voices echo from out in the hall, bringing home that we're two people in a one-person bathroom—which could be construed as inappropriate. Marv and I do not see eye to eye, especially when it comes to Stone, and I don't want to give him any more ammunition. Since the moment the board agreed to give me free reign of the sports department without his influence, he's been a little bitch.

She's still unsuccessfully fighting tears, and I rake a hand through my hair and pace around her. *Screw it.* Feeling uncomfortable, I go with my instincts and walk over to her, wrapping my arms around her loosely. It's a slight hug, sort of like I'd give a sister if I had one.

"Fuck Marv," I say gruffly. "Want me to kick his ass?"

Her head is buried in my shoulder and moves from side to side in a *no* motion.

We huddle together in the small space, and I wait patiently as she takes deep breaths, seeming to calm herself. After a bit, she leans back from me, straightens her shoulders, and looks around the room as if orienting herself. "I'm sorry for barging in on you."

"It's nothing," I say softly. "We can get out of here and have a drink if you want?" My eyes land on her full lips.

She stares at my beard, meets my eyes, and then flushes a deep red again. "No . . . no, I can't."

I heave a sigh of relief. I don't know what crazy part of me even offered that.

She says a hurried goodbye, scoops up her purse, and practically runs out the door. I hear her bump into someone in the hallway and apologize. It sounds like the fresh-from-college reporter Savannah.

I stand there and wait for the hallway to clear as I run the last few minutes through my head. Rebecca Fieldstone has seen my cock, told me off, cried on my shoulder, and then apologized. It's the most personal interaction we've ever had.

I make my way back to the den and into my private office. The contractors had just finished it a few weeks ago. Whole new offices were part of my requirements for coming onboard at KHOT. The board had agreed—not the usual for a sports guy—but then not everyone is Cade Hill. I could have gone anywhere I wanted, even SportsCenter, but Houston and this station are exactly where I want to be.

I shut the double panel door quietly and stalk toward the plate-glass window that overlooks the parking lot. I want to make sure she gets to her car without any trouble. Our office is in the nice part of downtown but there have been a rash of muggings in parking garages lately. From witness reports, police think it's the work of the same guy or the same group of guys.

I watch her stomp out into the September night, legs flashing under her snug pencil skirt. She's tall in her heels, about five feet eleven and curvy in all the right places, just how I like a woman.

And I'm a fucking hypocrite for thinking about her like that. I push it down. I have better shit to focus on. Like work. I need to run through the line-up for the college football games tomorrow.

Still, I stand at the window, my eyes following her.

With a fast pace, she clutches her brown bag against her chest and moves toward her little green death machine, an electric Prius.

People in Texas drive trucks or SUVs, but not Stone. Nope, she's entirely different.

She flings the door open and throws her stuff inside. Then with a quick spin, she turns back to face the red building and flips the bird with both hands.

I laugh. I'm sure it's for Marv . . . and the fucking *insultants*.

Hell, maybe it's for the whole damn system.

She climbs in her car and cruises out into traffic quiet as a mouse. It's not the tire-squealing exit I'm sure she wants, but at least she's saving on gas.

From behind me, my office door opens.

Two things happen at once: an irritating giggle meets my ears and floral perfume assaults my senses. I turn to see Savannah standing there. Pretty, blonde, and bouncy, she's been sending me signals that she's available for a quick fuck since she was hired. She's forever popping in here for some inane reason—without waiting for me to tell her to come in.

"What?" My voice is sharp as I settle back in my chair and bring up the agenda for tonight on my computer.

"Oops, sorry, Cade." Another giggle. "I can't seem to figure out this door. It just flies open." She pauses and clears her throat. "Your fiancée is in the sports den asking for you."

My head rises slowly. I don't have a fiancée, but I do have a slightly crazy ex. She has a habit of saying we're engaged whenever it suits her. I frown. "Skinny platinum blonde with an attitude?"

"Bingo." She comes closer to my desk, her hips sashaying in a pair of tight black pants. "She says she isn't leaving until you talk to her."

I rub my face. "Fuck."

Savannah gives me a view of her cleavage as she scoops up an empty coffee mug. "She said you might say that. She also said to tell you she's going to be at your father's dinner tonight."

My jaw tightens. Baron, my father, thinks Maggie Grace is perfect for me, especially since her elderly aunt is on the board of directors at Hill Global, our family's investment company. With Maggie Grace set to inherit her aunt's shares, she's part of his master plan to get me settled down with a society wife and fully ensconced in his business as in-house counsel. I also own shares of Hill Global, but I want no part in the day-to-day of the business world. Football is my life, and being the sports director is as close as I can get right now to staying in the game.

I am not Baron Hill, and I never will be.

"Want me to tell her to leave?" A glint of glee lights Savannah's eyes.

I smirk. "Carry on, Savannah. I'll handle this."

"Fine." She shrugs, her gaze roaming over my shoulders before she quietly shuts the door.

I exhale, button my jacket, and stand up from the desk.

I've learned the hard way that when it comes to my dad and Maggie Grace, it's best to meet my problems head on.

Three

REBECCA

"OH, GIRL, NO. They did not pull that ageist shit on you!" My best, technically male friend and new room-mate, the fabulous Chas-say McQueen is on the couch holding a pink Cosmo in her large brown hand, pinky finger out. "That's why you should never do anything with kids or pets. First rule of showbiz."

"Last summer when I interviewed that professor and his thou-sand year-old bone, they couldn't compliment me enough," I grum-ble into my wine glass.

"Mm . . ." Chas sips, dark doe-eyes circling around our small apartment. "A thousand year-old bone. I wonder what that's like."

"Don't. Make. Jokes," I snap. "I'm pissed."

"You're getting there." Chas is in full drag-queen makeup, a large blue hibiscus over her left ear. "I watched the show. Those little girls were tight. Why didn't you at least put a little powder on your nose?"

My eyes go wide. "I didn't have time to check a mirror! We were sent late, it was blazing hot, and Kevin didn't even bother to tell me I looked like I'd just stepped out of a fucking steam room."

"Kevin wouldn't know his ass from a hole in the ground. Who's your makeup artist?"

I level my gaze. "You know it's me."

"Well, there's your problem right there." Setting her drink on the side table, Chas goes to her bedroom, and I listen as she rakes hangers across the metal bar in her closet.

She bounces back in the room with a blue-sequined dress in her hands. "What do you think about this? Too Cher?"

"Where are you going?"

"Jazzy claims to be sick." She rolls her eyes, "So I'm filling in for her tonight at the Pussycat Club."

"Oh." I sink back into the couch taking another long sip of Chardonnay. "Who are you doing?"

"RuPaul André Charles, of course!" Chas turns with a flourish, and with the makeup and wig, it's pretty hard to tell her from her drag queen idol. "You should come. Wallowing is not good for your complexion."

My nose wrinkles, and I pull my knees closer into my chest. "I'm not in the mood for drag."

"That is the most ridiculous thing I've ever heard. Don't you know drag was invented to shake off those blues? It's about embracing the comedy in life, and flinging your burdens away in a manner that's larger than where you are!" She throws her arms wide, and at her height, with her wingspan, it's quite the exclamation.

"You've been reading *Fiercely You* again."

"I'm becoming the me of my imagination. And you should too."

"I'm becoming the me who finishes this drink and goes to bed. Partying is not going to help with my crow's feet."

"Girl, at this point only one thing is going to help with those crow's feet." Chas laughs, and I narrow my eyes. "It ain't all that squintin', either. You need the joy of life lighting up your face."

She disappears back into her room, and I stare at the oversized television above the space heater. It's our joint splurge. Chas is as big a fan of the small screen as I am, although her favorite shows fall squarely in the reality-TV zone, which is what she'd been watching when I arrived home in a funk.

I sit silently observing the reality series she has on mute. One of the Kardashians is lounging on her couch, wrapped in a fuzzy blanket. Her dark brow is lined, and she's clearly talking about something distressing her. She holds a glass of white wine like me, and her sister K in the kitchen listens to her intently. It makes me think of Nancy and me.

We were like sisters, and while Chas has always been our big brother-ish in a sort of twisted-sisters-from-another-mister kind of way, I still miss Nan so much. She would probably make me a clean, healthy meal right now, force me to bed early, and be sure I attended my Pilates class in the morning.

The show continues with a very animated discussion where Kitchen K throws her hands up and waves them around as she shakes her highlighted head. Couch (Kouch?) K is clearly upset. She blinks rapidly, and the camera zooms in as she wipes an invisible tear away with her fingers. I gasp when she barely misses taking out an eye with those acrylic nails.

The next cut is the two Ks wearing slinky dresses and sky-high heels as they dance among the flashing lights in a club. They both hold skinny flutes of champagne, and guys and girls twist and gyrate all around them. Everyone is smiling and joyous and shaking his or her hips, and I blink at the screen a few times. In that moment, I make a decision.

Setting my wine glass on the end table I stand like a woman taking control of her destiny. Petal was right. If I want something, I have to go get it. I am not sitting home tonight and wallowing about being fat and wrinkled and possibly losing my job. Not when there is alcohol to be drunk, and I still have dance moves in me.

"Chas!" I call out. "What time are we leaving?"

A dark face topped with a huge platinum wig pops around the corner. "Whenever you're ready, baby girl!" The rest of my roommate emerges, draped in blue sequins and skinny feathers. "I'll do your eyes."

Four

CADE

I'M TENSE AS I stalk out of Luigi's Italian Kitchen and into the warm night air. Behind me I hear the clacking of Maggie Grace's heels as she hurries to catch up. I don't wait for her but stride to the black and white uniformed valet and ask for my car.

My father is still in the restaurant talking to an old oil crony. At least my monthly meal with him where we discuss my inherited holdings in Hill Global is over and done. Of course, he'd insisted on sticking to our regular schedule even though this meeting falls on my younger brother Trent's birthday.

My thoughts turn to Trent. He loves to celebrate, and there's no telling where we'll end up tonight. Last year he'd rented out a warehouse and organized an all-night rave for his twenty-fifth. I can only hope tonight will be on a smaller scale. I scoff. *Who am I kidding?* Trent never does anything small.

I love the shit out of him. Too bad my father doesn't.

And just like that, familiar anger rushes to the surface.

Growing up, Trent had been a soft-spoken kid who'd loved acting and music. He didn't have a shot playing football with his slender frame, plus he couldn't run for shit. Still, my father pushed him, signing him up to participate in anything athletic. Trent rebelled his senior year—by announcing he was gay to my parents. In the middle of my senior year as quarterback for the University of Texas, I'd dropped everything to come home and be the buffer for the drama between him and my father.

It hadn't worked.

Dad demanded that if Trent wanted to live under his roof, he had to attend a camp where they *got the gay out of you.* That didn't fly at all. I'd delved into my savings and paid for Trent to have an apartment close to home and attend an online high school.

Now it's eight years later, and any mention of Trent makes my father clam up.

I shove those memories away. *Forget your father.* Focus on the birthday boy—who should have texted me by now with where he is with his mob of friends.

As if he reads my mind, my phone pings with a text from him.

Done eating with the Old Dragon? In a bad mood yet?

Yes and yes. What's the plan, birthday boy?

He'd assured me earlier it was going to be low-key.
I don't believe him.

Pussycat Club on 959 Highland Street in one hour. Leave your suit at home and bring some dolla bills.

Pussycat? It doesn't ring any bells. I picture a blinking neon sign outside with *Girls, Girls, Girls* flashing.

This a strip club??

I'm not necessarily opposed to a strip club, but now that I'm a sportscaster who delivers news to a mostly conservative audience, I have to think twice about where I make public appearances.

He sends me a long string of the laughing/crying emojis. Even better. Drag show. Strip clubs are for jocks and straight men.

Fucker. I grin.

Why do I need dollar bills? I type.

In case you want to tip your bartender. Get your head out of the gutter. Drag queens are classy.

I bark out a laugh. I'm not sure about this place or if I should even go since I have to work tomorrow, yet part of me is amped up and ready to do something. Maybe it's the run-in with Stone. I keep picturing her flouncing across that parking lot in her heels.
Stop thinking about her.
Right.
I heave out a sigh, weighing my options for the evening. Trent is going to keep me up late, and there'd be copious amounts of alcohol involved. Maybe I should pass on the clubbing tonight and just chill at my place.

A long slender hand curls around my bicep, and I gaze down at Maggie Grace.

Tonight she's dressed in a black lace cocktail dress and high heels. Her white blonde hair is swirled up in some fancy style and her lake blue eyes are studying my face.

I assume she's reading my stony *What now?* expression because she sighs. "Look, I've already apologized for crashing your dinner. But I happened to be in town for the day and your dad called me." She pauses and stares at the ground. "And . . . I didn't want to miss an opportunity to see you, Cade. It's been weeks since we ran into each other at the polo match—"

"We're not getting back together, Maggie Grace. You're just lonely because you broke up with someone." Yeah. She'd been dumped a few weeks ago by some senator's son.

She blinks rapidly and a shimmer of tears appears. "We had a good thing. I miss it."
Fuck, what is it about me and women crying today?
My mouth tightens as I remain firm at the sight, not wavering— which is clearly not what happened with Stone in the restroom

earlier. Interesting.

My eyes bounce off her and stay glued to the road and the missing valet. *Where is my goddamn car?*

"We spent a year living together, Cade," she says, a pleading tone in her voice. In typical Maggie Grace style, she's not giving up.

My teeth grind together.

She blots at her eyes with a tissue she pulls from her clutch. "I'm set to inherit Aunt Anne's shares at HG. We're *going* to see each other at some point. I can't help how I feel—"

Frustration erupts, and I can't stifle my groan. "Just stop orchestrating us bumping into each other. We are over. Go find another guy—or better yet, find yourself."

She inhales a sharp breath. "There's a part of you that still cares about me, Cade."

I *had* loved her, but when I'd blown out my knee, things had gone haywire and within a few months of me being retired from the NFL, she'd left.

I give her a hard look. "You walked out on me three years ago when I needed you the most."

She bites her lip and shakes her head as if the memory of it hurts. "Fine. I made mistakes. I was young and stupid, but I've grown up since then. I know that everything isn't about *me* anymore. Can't you forgive me?"

I exhale, close my eyes, and then open them. I don't want to encourage her, but . . . *fuck* . . . in the end, her ditching me *had* been for the best. The girl I want in my life isn't anything like Maggie Grace. I want someone who doesn't give a shit that I can't run down a football field anymore.

"Cade?"

I rock on my heels, considering her.

Maybe she needs closure.

Anything to get the hell out of here.

"Yes," I say finally. "I forgive you for getting on with your life when you obviously weren't happy. There. Is that what you want to hear?"

"And we can be friends?" Her eyes are wide and hopeful.

"Of course." I nod rather absently, already checking my phone again to see if Trent texted me. "Friends."

I shift and ease myself away from her as I see the familiar headlights of my black Escalade. I step to the curb, ready to dart inside as soon as the wheels stop turning. I send her a small wave, feeling more magnanimous now that my escape route is here.

"Look it was . . . nice . . ."—*fuck, that's a lie*—"seeing you, but I have to go."

"Call me sometime," she yells out as I walk away.

I tip the valet a twenty as he opens the door for me and I slide inside. Heaving a sigh of relief that this part of my evening is over, I give her a nod and pull from the curb, headed to my penthouse a few blocks away.

After parking in my reserved spot in the basement, I catch a ride up in the elevator to the twentieth floor.

Because it's been a stressful evening, I pop in the shower to relax. I'm just getting out when my phone pings—Trent again.

HELLO? Where did you go? The show is on in half an hour. It has five stars on Trip Advisor. A "must see" in Houston.

I grunt and type a reply. *Bob's BBQ has 5 stars and gave me food poisoning. Nearly put me in the hospital.* I add a puking emoji.

His reply is instant. *This isn't some redneck food joint, and you won't be eating, you'll be drinking. IT'S MY BIRTHDAY.*

I stare at my phone, pondering what to do. Trent has a way of making everyone around him happy, and after the shit dinner I'd had tonight . . .

Maybe I need to let loose, even if it is a drag queen show. For the past few months, I've been working my ass off at KHOT. Things are finally falling in line like I want. I crack my neck and roll my shoulders, feeling how tight I am. No doubt about it, I haven't let myself have a good time in a while.

Besides . . .

What else am I going to do? Sit around and watch TV? Think about work? Call Mom?

And that thought makes me pause. Here I am thirty years old and contemplating calling my mother. *Dude.*

I come to a decision. *Fuck it.* This is my only brother, and if he wants to throw down at a drag queen club, my ass is going to be there to cheer him on.

I reach for a pair of jeans.

Pussycat Club, here I come . . .

Five

REBECCA

THE LARGE, FLAT-SCREEN TV above the bar in the Pussycat Club is silent, but it's set to KHOT. I cringe knowing the pageant story will rebroadcast in less than an hour.

"Was it really that bad?" I take a long gulp of my gin and tonic (with cucumber, of course—nods to Christian Grey).

"You were un-powdered in a mob of infants, and the lighting was horrifyingly bad. What do you think?" Chas holds a fresh Cosmo and levels her brown eyes on me. "You know what would take your mind off it? *A big* O."

I snort into my drink and cut my eyes up. My roommate towers over me in full drag, and I suppose at that height, she can be a little intimidating. I know her too well to care.

I smirk. "When you wave your arm like that, everybody looks at us."

"Let them look!" Chas punctuates each word with jazz hands. "You're too young to be working your life away. When's the last time you got laid?"

"James."

"Oh my *God!*" More hand waving. "Don't even say his name.

I hate him."

I agree, smoothing down the front of the beige sequined micro-mini dress Chas insisted I wear. If I reach too high, I'll flash the world, since I'm only wearing a nude thong under it. Still, with my taupe sling-backs accentuating my toned legs (my one body part still holding onto muscle memory), my ego is somewhat bolstered. Every now and then I get an appreciative glance, which in a room full of queens is saying something. At least someone values my new curves.

The bar is filling faster as word gets out my roommate is performing. Chas has been making the rounds on the drag circuit since we graduated college, and her RuPaul impersonation is legendary. The Pussycat is actually a very upscale club, complete with a mirrored dance floor, laser lights, a disco ball, and retro dance music blasting. Polishing off my drink, I signal for a refill as Chas continues her tirade on James. She has *never* liked him.

"It's no wonder he left me." I take a long pull from my fresh G&T. "We never saw each other. My schedule was ridiculous. I was never home."

"So that's what it was?" Chas's tone is pure skepticism. "I always assumed it was his lack of ambition and cheating with the chippy at the coffee shop that drove you apart."

"I guess we didn't have much in common," I sigh. "He didn't give a shit about my schedule as long as I fucked him regularly."

"Girl." Chas shakes her head. "That's all he wanted."

I take a bite of fresh cucumber. It's possible I'm a little tipsy. "You're right," I say, nodding. "It was all pot and porking."

"You did not just say *porking.*"

Our eyes meet, and we both explode with laughter. My eyes water, and I sniff a few times, calming down, growing serious. "I had the dream again."

My roommate sits on a barstool, putting us closer to the same height. At the mention of my dream, all mirth is gone. "The one about the tall, dark, and handsome man?"

Nodding, I drink more. "That's the one."

"The stranger who shows up at your door in a hot as hell suit and takes your hand in his so passionately?"

"Yes."

"The one who says he's never seen anyone as gorgeous as you, but he's waiting to hear back from an exclusive, top-secret NASA program?"

More gin, more nodding.

"Then after he gives you the greatest orgasm *of your life*, he finds out he was accepted into the program, and he's leaving immediately to go to Mars for five years?"

My forehead wrinkles. "Do I tell this one a lot?"

Thick false lashes bat at me for several seconds. "Honey, that dream is your problem right there. You're a commitment-phobe!"

"That's not how I see it at all," I sniff, taking another sip. "It means my dream guy—my perfect man, who is handsome and intelligent and ambitious and great in bed—is an impossible dream. He doesn't exist."

"Commitment-phobe!" Jazz hands. "Does this impossible dream-man even have a name?"

"Chris."

A loud group of guys bursts through the door, and we glance in their direction. It's mostly young, fashionably dressed hipster types, but one taller than the rest sticks out in the crowd. I have to do a double take. *Cade Hill? GAY? With a dick like that?* Figures.

"Chris?" Chas is still ranting about Dream Man. "As in Pratt? Chris Pratt? Star-Lord?"

I'm sneaking another glance at Cade when suddenly his steel blue eyes hit mine. Heat floods my core, and I snap my head back to my roommate. She doesn't miss a thing.

"What was that?" Her voice is too loud.

"What?" I try to act clueless, but Chas isn't buying it.

"That right there. Who is he?"

"Proof I'll end up marrying a gay man if I'm not careful," I grumble, taking a longer drink. I'm almost ready for number three.

"That's why I'm here to guide you. That sexy straight man is staring a hole through you."

"What?" I chance another look, and Cade *is* staring, only now that cocky grin is curling his lips, creating those dimples. It's like a lightning strike.

Asshole, I remind myself—only, now I'm not so sure. He was actually really nice in the bathroom earlier after the whole Marv thing . . . after I saw his heavenly package. I have to squeeze my thighs together.

"Stop looking at him!" I hiss. "That's Cade Hill, the sports director at KHOT. I walked in on him in the bathroom."

"Wait . . . What? You did *what?*" Chas finishes her Cosmo and sets it down quickly.

"Tell Mama what you saw."

I squeeze my eyes shut. I know what's about to happen. "I saw his penis."

"WHAT!" Chas shouts.

I cringe. "And it is gorgeous . . . and enormous."

We both burst out laughing. "Girl . . ." My roommate sighs, catching her breath. "Now I just want to rub his beard. Do you think he'll let me rub his beard?"

"I'm not talking to you anymore."

"That's right you're not. I have to do my set." Chas is off the stool and rising to her full height. "Remember the *O*."

We air-kiss both cheeks. "Break a stiletto!" I call.

"I wouldn't dare!" She scampers away, and I'm left feeling very alone and exposed.

Turning to the bar, I try to make myself small. Of course, at that very moment, the television starts running my Planetary Princess story. My face fills the screen, and I shrink. I really do look like I'd just run four blocks before filing that story.

"Oh, God," I sigh, polishing off my third gin and tonic. I signal to the bartender for another just as a deep voice rolls through my insides.

"It's not that bad," Cade is at my side radiating heat.

Fuck a duck. The man is so close to me I can smell his citrusy aftershave and my traitorous body leans in for a better whiff. He props an elbow on the bar, and I give him a brief glance coupled with a nervous smile. After I'd left him standing in the restroom, I'd practically run to my car to put some distance between us. Comforting, concerned, protective Cade is dangerous.

"So you don't agree with the insultants?"

"To put you behind the camera?" His tone draws my eyes to his. His brow is lowered and he actually seems angry. "Marv is a nitwit if he agrees with them. You're one of the best reporters we've got."

Oh. I blink. He's being kind . . . again. For a minute, I only smile. His suit is long gone, and he's dressed in jeans. The light blue dress shirt remains, sleeves still rolled up, muscular forearms still on display. Dark hair curls around his ears and *ugh!* I bemoan the fact that he is impossibly hot.

"Unexpected praise coming from you," I tease . . . *not flirt.*

Cade is my coworker. *I do not want to bone him.*

Oh, yes I do!

"Of course, it's nothing like the sports desk," he says, and my eyes roll. *There it is. The swagger.*

"What are you having?" He nods to my drink.

"Gin and tonic with cucumber."

"So you're a Hendrick's girl?"

"He is the most influential rock guitarist of all time." I try to joke.

"First, Jimi Hendrix is psychedelic, second, Stevie Ray Vaughan is the most influential rock guitarist of all time, and third, he's a Texas man."

"Is that so?"

"It is so. His contribution to Bowie's 'Let's Dance' modernized the sound of a legend and gave Bowie his first Top 40 hit in a decade."

My jaw drops, and I can't help but laugh.

"What? No comeback?"

"I-I was only teasing," I confess. "I don't really know that much about rock guitarists."

The gloat on Cade's face dissolves. "Oh." He turns to the bartender and gives him a wave. "Now I'm just embarrassed."

At that I really do laugh. "I never knew you were such a music nerd. What would the boys in the sports den say?"

"You can be a real pain in the ass sometimes, Stone."

I cover my mouth with my hand, but more laughter snorts out.

"That's attractive." His grin is teasing, and he hands the bartender a ten. "So what the hell are you doing here?"

Clearing my throat, I take another pull from the tiny straw in my cup. "I could ask the same of you. I would never have expected KHOT's chief jock to be hanging out at the Pussycat."

He does a little shrug and all traces of annoyance are gone. "It's my little brother's birthday. He always gets a kick out of taking me to his most *fabulous* hangouts."

"Your brother?" I turn back to the group of young guys. "Which one is he?"

I feel Cade gesture beside me, and an attractive guy with blond hair and similar eyes and jawline perks up and waves back. I do a little wave.

"I would think going to a drag bar would be a hard limit for someone like you." I take another sip.

"Hard limit?" His dark brow furrows and he glares down at me.

"It's a *Fifty* . . . It's a book reference."

His eyes drift over me. "Into that BDSM shit, Stone?"

I flush. "No."

Silence. He's watching me intently.

"Are you?" I ask.

His face is smooth as glass. Not one iota of an expression is there—his reporter's mask. "For the right girl, I'd do anythi. g."

I swallow and pretend I don't hear him, but I can't deny my heart is pounding a hell of a lot harder since he sat down.

He polishes off his scotch. "Anyway, back to my bro. He had a tough time growing up gay. Our dad is not the most . . . forgiving. Hell, *Texas* isn't forgiving."

"I take it your brother isn't into football."

That gets me a laugh, and I'm surprised at the warmth it spreads across my stomach. *Don't forget he's an asshole! Or is he?* I'm getting mixed up.

"Our father doesn't believe in gays."

I pull up short. "Doesn't believe in them? He's a gaytheist?"

Another laugh. "Good one. Gaytheist." He signals for another drink before returning to me. "No, he says *fags*—his word, trust me, not mine—are either perverts or psychopaths, and in either case, they should be institutionalized."

"Oh my God." The words are out before I can stop them. "That's . . . That's . . . ."

"Pretty disgusting," Cade says under his breath, dimples gone. "Growing up, everything at our prep school revolved around sports, and if you weren't good, then you'd better hope you were smart and funny. At least Trent's funny."

He smirks. "I'm kidding. He's also smart as a whip. He's . . . flamboyant, always has been, and Dad, well, he never took to it. Mom, though, she's the one who loves us unconditionally."

"What the hell is going on over here? It looks like an undertaker's convention!" An arm is thrown over each of our shoulders, and Cade's brother charges between us.

"Trent, I'd like you to meet my coworker, KHOT's very own Rebecca Fieldstone." Cade motions to me, and his brother steps back.

"Rebecca Fieldstone!" His voice has taken on the volume of someone celebrating. "That piece you did today on the mini beauty queens was *fabulous!*"

"Is that so?" I say through a laugh. "You should call my director and tell him."

"Although, girl, you need to FIRE your makeup artist. That bitch let you down—ouch!" Trent jumps back, and I can only guess Cade gave him an elbow. "Well, anyway, it's my birthday! Shots! Shots! Shots!"

His entourage soon joins his chanting, and the bartender is quick to comply. Six shot glasses are lined up in front of us.

"Oh, no," Cade steps back holding up both hands. "I don't have the flexible hours you keep. I have to be in the office tomorrow."

"Bullshit! Stop being a workaholic and live a little," Trent shouts, and a shot of Fireball is shoved into my hand. "IT'S MY BIRTHDAY!"

Trent and Co. all lift their glasses and shoot the cinnamon whiskey, leaving only Cade and me staring at each other.

"He does have a point," I note.

"You're a bad influence, Stone. I'll drink, but only if you do."

"Do it! Do it! Do it!" The group is shouting.

Cade crashes his shot glass against mine. "*Skal!*" We both throw it back at the same time.

"Ahh!" I squeal as the cinnamon burns my throat. I've barely caught my breath when another shot is put in my hand. "Oh! I don't know—"

I'm cut off by the loud blast of trumpets. Candi Staton's "Young Hearts, Run Free," begins, and it's the start of Chas's act. I quickly toss back the shot and cheer, twisting my hips and dancing as I rush to the stage.

A silver metallic curtain flashes open, and out prances my roommate in a white mini, white lace bustier, white opera gloves, and thigh-high white tights. Eight-inch white stilettos make her even taller, and Chas has replaced her RuPaul blonde wig with an enormous white afro. Pleated metallic fabric is attached at her shoulder blades and wrists to form silver "wings," and her dancing consists of hip shaking, arm waving, and silver metallic glitter falling from the ceiling. It's like an angelic Mardi Gras rave, and we're all invited.

I scream and jump up and down, clapping as she leads the celebration, and Trent is right at my ear. "Do you know her? I saw you having drinks."

Leaning into his ear, I shout back, "That's my roommate!"

Trent jumps back, and his eyes are so big, I can see the whites. His mouth is equally huge, and I lean forward laughing. The whole group of Trent's friends and Cade along with the crowd has swept in around us, and it's as if we're all caught up in a tsunami of joy. A third round of shots filters through the group, and we scream and dance right along.

Another round of Fireball, and I can't feel my face. Chas is onto her next number, "Let's Hear it for the Boy," by Deniece Williams, when a pair of strong arms circles my torso, turning me so I'm face to face and chest to chest with the man I not so long ago thought was an arrogant prick who looked way too much like my ex.

"She's great!" he says, leaning a little too close to my face. I'm pretty sure Cade is as drunk as I am. "How the hell did you meet?"

I feel both heavy and light. I laugh and rest my cheek against Cade's collarbone. "Chas was my date to the prom."

"What?" He shakes me so I lift my head and look at him again. "Why?"

With a shrug, I shake my head and let my mind wander back through the years. "I wasn't going to go. Chas couldn't go—at least not how she wanted—but she said we were *not* missing senior prom. So we went together."

"Why weren't you going to go?" His tone is so intense, it causes me to study his mouth. I've never noticed until right this second how perfectly defined his lips are. I want to trace them with my fingertips.

"I thought proms were stupid."

Those perfect lips curl into a smirky grin. "You didn't have a date."

Irritation heats my body. "I didn't want a date! Proms are stupid."

"Only people without dates say proms are stupid." His strong arms hold me, and my fingers curl on his biceps. I notice how rock hard they are.

Chas terminates any further discussion as she launches into her grand finale, "Proud Mary" by Ike and Tina Turner. She's full-on Tina-dancing, hip shimmy and all, and I scream with the rest of the crowd in front of the stage.

The production ends with a huge flourish, deafening applause and cheers, and my roommate blows kisses at everyone. When she spots me, I get a thumbs-up and a dramatic nod that even in my inebriated state makes me blush.

Cade's arm is tight around my waist. My back is pressed to his chest, and I hate the idea of moving. Still, the number is over, the house music is on, and I have no reason to continue standing in such an intimate way with him.

"That was a helluva show," Cade says, giving me a flash of his perfect teeth.

"She'll be out in just a few minutes if you'd like to tell her yourself."

He nods, and when Chas comes out, Trent and his group of friends scream like it's a Beatles concert. I laugh, and again, strong arms circle over mine.

"Trent is really happy," Cade says behind my ear in my hair. I can't stop a shiver.

"What is this?" my roommate exclaims, eyes wide and blinking. "I have a fan club?"

Cade still has me in his arms, and I watch as my roommate dances a few measures to "Dancing Queen" by ABBA with the group. Her eyes light on me, and all six-foot-one-hundred-inches of her in those platforms prances up to us.

"Well, hello!" Chas says, holding her hand toward Cade. "And you are?"

"Cade Hill," he says in that polished, sports-director voice of his . . . although I do detect a slight slur. But what do I know? I'm a bit slurry myself.

"Chris?" Chas's eyes roll around to me. "Did you say *Chris*?"

If I had better balance, I'd kick my roommate in the shins. As it is . . .

"Um . . . no." Cade is confused.

"Oh, no matter!" Chas waves a hand. "It's clear you know my friend Rebecca."

Cade gives my waist a squeeze, and I melt a little more against his firm chest. I want to tear my dress off and press my body against his.

No, Rebecca!

Yes, Rebecca!

No!

Wait . . . whose side am I on?

"We work together," Cade says.

Oh, right.

"Oh my *God*, that's perfect!" Chas emphasizes the words as if it's a dispensation from the pope. "Would you possibly be able to do me a *huge favor*?"

"Of course." Cade smiles.

"I've just been invited to a party that will probably go all night. Rebecca and I came here together, and I really don't want her going home alone—what with all these muggings and all." She lightly touches Cade's arm. "Would you possibly ease my mind and be sure she gets home safely?"

My mouth falls open, but I close it quickly. *Sneaky bitch—we took an Uber here!* Cade glances at me, and I see uncertainty on his face. *Oh no . . .*

"Sure, no problem. I'm glad to help out."

"You really don't have to," I say, shaking my head.

"You are such a lifesaver, Chris!" Chas exclaims. "You are literally *out of this world!*"

Now I do consider kicking my roommate. "Cade is only being nice—"

"It's not a problem," he tells me. He arches an eyebrow. "Unless you don't want to be alone with me?"

I lick my lips and look around. "I was planning to call an Uber—"

Chas interrupts me. "You think I trust Uber alone with you? Have you seen that meme? Gary the Uber driver who looks just like Ted Bundy? Here . . . I'll pull it up."

"That won't be necessary," I catch her texting hands.

Her eyes go round, dramatically serious. "I would never forgive myself if some skeevy Uber driver took you to the desert and stole your kidney!"

"Good God, Chas, this isn't Brazil!"

Cade laughs, a low, rich vibration, and my roommate's eyes dazzle. "Oh, *yes!* Did I mention I won't be coming home tonight? It's getting late. You two should run along. Don't you have to work tomorrow?"

"Jeez, here's your hat and what's your hurry," I grumble.

"Goodnight, my love. I want to hear all your thoughts tomorrow." Chas leans down and air-kisses me on both cheeks.

I begrudgingly air-kiss back, and join her in the standard RuPaul "Byeeeee!"

Six

CADE

*W*ITH PLANS TO return early the next morning, I leave my SUV at the Pussycat Club and order an Uber. I'll drop her off then head home. *Alone.*

The car arrives, a small black sedan, which will be hell for me to fold my large frame into, but I go with it.

We crawl inside, and it smells like stale French fries and leather. I ease to my side, playing it cool, but my peripheral gaze eats up the toned legs of my companion as she gets settled. Her dress rides up and I see a flash of inner thigh. I tear my gaze away and stare out the window.

"Stupid seat belt," she mutters as she clanks the two pieces together unsuccessfully.

"Here, let me help." I lean over her and reach for her straps. It takes me longer than it should because I've had too much to drink, but I finally click it together. Still, I hover over her a few seconds more. She smells so fucking good, like coconuts and sunshine mixed together. I lower my arm, and my hand brushes against her breast.

Fuck.

I sit back and adjust my own belt.

The car is quiet as a church on Sunday as we pull away, and I imagine she's wondering how the hell we ended up in a car . . . alone . . . together.

My mind goes back to the club and how we'd been pressed up against each other. Like a couple.

What the hell had I been doing back there?

Flirting, asshole.

Yeah. With prickly, uptight Rebecca Fieldstone. Now what?

Drop her off at her place and then go home. That's the sensible thing to do.

But part of me doesn't want to be sensible. I want to throw Stone's legs over my shoulders and fuck her brains out.

I bite back a groan at the image in my head. Not doing that. I clasp my hands in my lap and stare out the window. Again.

She clears her throat and plays with one of the beads on her dress. Without the rambunctious crowd and loud music backing me up, I'm without witty comebacks and apparently so is she. To distract myself, I reach down and grab two bottles of water the driver has left in a small basket on the floor. I twist the top off one and offer it to Stone. She murmurs a small *thank you* and takes a deep drink. I watch the smooth glide of her throat as she swallows, her full lips tight around the bottle.

Her lips . . . my cock . . . swallowing.

Stop.

I shake myself mentally.

I rub my temple. God, should I still be calling her *Stone*? It fits. I like it because it's different.

Why am I attracted to her?

Those goddamn lips.

Her tits.

Those snappy comebacks.

I grab another bottle of water for me and chug it down in hopes of sobering up.

Too late to hydrate, my brain says. *You're fucked.*

I watch the clock on the radio in the front seat. Exactly two minutes since we've spoken. It feels like two hours.

I glance at the driver, a young guy in a baseball cap. "How much longer till we get there?"

He glances at the GPS he has mounted on his dashboard. "About five more minutes."

Fucking forever.

Why doesn't she say something?

Better yet, why am I acting like a young buck on his first date?

Finally I give in, take her hand and just go with my gut. "Hey. Thank you," I say.

"What? Why? For dancing with you?" She looks a bit disoriented as she glances at our hands and then up at me. I bite back a smile. Stone is cute as hell when she's trashed. I resist the urge to push an errant curl behind her ear.

I shrug. "For just having a good time with us and introducing Trent to Chas. The truth is my brother likes pushing my buttons. I was prepared to be the butt of all the jokes tonight. Literally and figuratively." I let out a laugh. "I almost didn't come, but I had this crap dinner with my dad . . ." my voice trails off and I sigh. "Nevermind, it's not anything you want to hear about."

"You're really sweet to your brother." Her thumb rubs the top of my hand, almost absently, as if she's unaware of the caress. "I'm glad you came. I-I had a great time with you."

"Me too."

She smiles, and I like how genuine it is, not like her on-air smile which looks real to the viewers but isn't. "Tell me about Trent."

I nod, relaxing. "He spent a lot of time blaming himself for our parent's divorce, but my mom's better off without my dad. And Trent . . . he's the only sibling I have. When I busted my knee, he showed up at my apartment and took care of things. I mean, you saw him partying, but he can be serious when you need him."

She nods. "Chas is the same."

"Do you have any siblings?"

It feels like small talk, but it isn't. My brain registers that I really want to know more about her.

Plus, we're holding hands.

God.

We're fucking holding hands!

What am I doing?

Moving nonchalantly, I remove my hand from hers and rake it through my hair.

She frowns but continues to talk. "No, but my best friend Nancy is like a sister to me," she says. "She moved to New York—hence the fifteen pounds I gained this year."

Her voice is cryptic, and it riles me up.

"I like your curves."

Her eyes catch mine. "Oh. Why's that?"

"It fits your personality. Plus, you're a tall woman and the overall image is . . . well . . . hot."

Her face flushes.

"You've got something special on camera. Don't let Marv or anyone else tell you different."

Her face is soft as she gazes at me. "That's the sweetest thing anyone has ever said to me."

I get warm all over.

It isn't from my buzz.

The car has stopped, and I'm relieved to have her home. After telling the Uber driver to wait, I get out and cross to her side to open her door, but she's already out and stumbling on the curb. She giggles as I steady her. "I've had *waaayyyy* too much to drink tonight. We can't tell anyone, right?" She holds her index finger to her lips and makes the *shhhh* sound.

"Cross my heart." I grin. "Come on, let's get you inside." I take her hand and wrap it around my bicep as I lead her to her building. We stop at her entrance, and we're standing so close, I can see the freckles on her nose.

"Do you want me to walk you upstairs?"

"There's a doorman for that if I want." She shrugs.

"Okay." I'm disappointed, but it's for the best.

I glance around. "You know, our buildings aren't that far apart. I'm just a few blocks from here."

She bites her lip. "That's cool. Maybe we can hang out some time."

"Yeah."

The seconds tick by as we stand there staring at each other. I focus on her mouth as her eyes sweep over my shoulders, drifting down to my crotch before flying back up to my face.

She clears her throat. "You know, it's only twelve, and I'm still feeling a little hyped up from tonight." She hesitates as if thinking it through. "You want to come in and chat? Have a cup of coffee?"

I want to.

But I don't need to.

"Kinda late for coffee."

"We're *just* pals," she says rather brightly. "Plus, I want to hear more about growing up with Trent—and what it's like to be in the Super Bowl. I'm actually a big college football fan."

I rub the back of my neck. "Ah, I don't know—"

The Uber takes off from the curb, and both of us gasp as we watch him speed away.

"Well, damn." I laugh. "Looks like I'm stuck with you now, Stone."

"You can Uber another car."

"True."

"Do you want to?" Her voice is breathless.

We study each other, and the air thickens. "No."

"Are we going to stand out here all night then?"

I grin as I tuck my hands in my pockets. "Is the offer for coffee still open?"

She gives me a short nod, and it's all I need to escort her inside and get on the elevator.

"Damn!" I exclaim, entering her apartment a few minutes later and taking in the magnificence of the flat screen television as if it's a sacred relic. "It's huge . . ."

"That's what she said," Stone says with a giggle.

"Is that eighty inches?" I touch it reverently.

"According to the box."

"I thought only guys bought shit like this. You just moved up on the cool scale."

"Biologically, Chas does have a penis," she reasons. "But I also work in the medium."

"And look good doing it."

She winces. "Except for today when my oily face and laugh lines were in high-def for everyone to see."

She mentions the coffee again and tells me to get comfortable in the den, but I follow her instead. Part of it is because I like watching her ass swing in that short-as-fuck dress, but the other is I don't want her to feel shitty about today.

"It wasn't that bad." My voice is gentle.

She pauses as she puts a mug in its place and drops a pod in the coffee maker. "It was pretty awful."

I tug on her shoulder, turning her around until we're face to face. "You're gorgeous, Stone."

"You need to run to the optometrist because you need glasses."

I smirk. "Can you imagine me with glasses *and* my beard? The ladies would go nuts."

She scoffs and pops me on the arm. "You're so full of yourself."

I may be cocky, but really I just want to make her laugh. "Admit it. I look good on camera."

She rolls her eyes. "Never."

I take her hand in mine and lead her back to the den. I don't know what I'm doing—oh hell, I totally do. I'm going to fuck Stone and fuck her good.

We get comfortable on a loveseat in the den. "What made you want to be a reporter in the first place?" I ask as my arm slides around her shoulders and my fingers find the nape of her neck and rub.

She sighs and closes her eyes as I massage her with deeper strokes.

I imagine my hands in other places.

"My first producer said I had a nose for news."

I touch the tip of her nose lightly. "It's cute. I love the freckles."

"Oh," her eyes drop.

We're quiet a moment. The crash of the ice machine refilling in the kitchen breaks the silence, and I shift in my seat to ease the ache in my cock.

There's still time to leave, the voice of reason says. *Get out now.*

"What made you want to be a reporter?" Her chin lifts, and I'm pretty sure our faces are closer now than they were a minute ago.

"It wasn't part of the plan—that was to be a superstar quarterback—but I knew someday it might end, and if it did, I wanted to be in front of the camera at least talking about football. In prep school, I was the debate club president. Hard to believe, huh?"

She nods, her face drifting closer to mine. "Why law school?"

"Basically, I love rules—and I needed something hard to keep me occupied after football."

My hand lowers until it's resting on her back. I let my fingers trace her spine as I study her face, taking in the classic straight nose, the arching brows that are a shade darker than her hair.

I want to kiss her.

"I remember the day you arrived at the station in your suit. Your toned ass was absolute perfection. I didn't think you'd last a week."

"You think my ass is perfect?"

She covers her mouth. "I can't believe I said that."

I chuckle, pleased. "I remember the first time I saw you, too. Your shoes were off and your shirt untucked." My eyes roam over her hair. "You had your hair twisted up with a pencil at the back of your head. You looked exactly like I thought a news reporter should . . . hard working and caring less about appearances and more about the story."

Her bottom jaw drops. "I really made an impression on you?"

"Mhmm . . ." My fingers make small circles around the top of her shoulder. I slide them underneath the strap of her dress, pushing until it falls down. Her creamy skin is exposed. "You seemed so smart . . ."

"Nerdy?" Her chest is rising rapidly.

"No." My fingertip rises to trace the line of her jaw, and she shivers.

"I thought you were way out of my league."

She blinks. "I think you underestimate yourself."

"Do I?" I lean forward until our lips are a breath apart.

Seven

REBECCA

I HAD BEEN focused on Cade's perfect mouth up until this point, but when my eyes flicker up to meet his, a charge of electricity races from my chest all the way to my core. In the space of a breath we're together.

His mouth covers mine, and both hands are in my hair, holding my face. A little moan escapes my throat, and I push into him, kissing him back. I grasp his broad shoulders and climb onto his lap in a straddle, the hem of my mini-dress rising up my thighs.

The beading scratches my skin, but Cade's warm palms smooth the irritation as they venture higher. I'm kissing and lightly biting his luscious lips when his thumb traces a line down the center of my crotch. Electricity races through my pelvis, and I rise up with a moan.

"Oh, God!" I gasp, holding his cheeks.

He quickly jerks my thong aside, and it rips, falling away. Long fingers stroke my slit moving up and down, causing my legs to shudder. I lift my chin to exhale another noise and his mouth covers my throat. He's sucking and biting when one long finger dips inside.

"Fuck, you're so wet," he groans, his breath hot against my skin.

I quickly reach behind my neck and unfasten the button on my top. It falls away, revealing a pink lace demi-bra. Cade shoves the thin cup down with his mouth and gives my nipple a hard pull.

I gasp. I'm going to orgasm right on his lap at this rate.

Another long finger plunges into me, and he's massaging my clit, priming my core. His mouth comes off my breast as his other hand snakes to the back of my neck. With a pull, my face is back to his, and he kisses me, tugging my lips with his, giving me nips with his teeth.

"I want to fuck you," he groans. "I want to sink my cock into your clenching pussy and have your cream all over my balls."

Oh shit! A shiver crosses my shoulders with the light touch of his hand. "What a dirty mouth you have, Mr. Hill." I drag my tongue along his bottom lip.

"You with me?" His skilled hand moves to my ass, holding me flush against his torso as he stands.

My legs go around him, and I'm holding his neck, kissing along the line of his scruffy jaw to his ear. "I want to ride you hard then come all over your dick."

"Mm, that's my girl."

A little thrill flashes through me. I've never been good at dirty talking, but for some reason, it comes naturally with him.

"Next door," I say, just before I kiss the shell of his ear. "That's right. This is mine."

He kicks the door shut and without even turning on the light, he tosses me on my back on the bed. I prop up on my elbows. My dress is up around my waist, my bra is wet from Cade's mouth, and my nipples are pointing right at him.

"Damn," he rasps, and I watch, mesmerized as he reaches behind his neck to pull his shirt over his head, leaving his hair a sexy mess.

The light of the full moon blasting through my window covers him in a silvery glow. My stomach clenches when I see the lines of his muscles deepened by the shadowy light. My God, he's gorgeous. He looks otherworldly.

"We really shouldn't do this . . ." My voice is breathless.

"Agreed."

He strides toward the bed, his eyes never leaving mine. He's focused, determined, and I watch as he unfastens his belt, the top of his jeans, his zipper.

"This is a terrible idea."

"Yes," he murmurs, cupping my face. I sigh and lean into his palm, letting the sizzle between us electrify me. *If* I do this . . . *if* I go through with boning him . . . it's going to be the best sex of my life, judging by the tiny raised hairs all over my body.

I scoot to the foot of the bed so I'm right in front of him and my head is level with his waist. Looking up, I slide my palms to his sides, pushing his jeans lower. He's standing in front of me in black boxer briefs. I slide my palms up and down against the hot planes of his pelvis, teasing him, tracing my fingers around the straining bulge of his erection. "We're gonna regret this."

A long shudder comes from him, and his eyes are heavy-lidded as he watches me. "I don't think so, Stone. Not in a million fucking years." He leans down and his lips capture mine, his tongue sweeping inside my mouth, exploring, owning me.

Using my fingernails, I catch the edge of his briefs, and drag them down his thighs. His incredible cock springs free, a drop of precum on the tip. I curl my fingers around his thick shaft, smoothing my thumb over it.

Breath hisses through his teeth, and his large hands move to my face, fingers curling into the sides of my hair. He wants me to suck him off, but I've found building up the anticipation is such sweet torture. I blink up at him as I trace my fingernails along his inner thighs to his sack, lightly scratching him.

"Jesus." His brow lowers, eyes burning with desire when I finally flick my tongue out and around the tip of his penis.

"Fuck, yeah," his voice breaks, as I fist him, pumping his shaft as I suck at the tip.

Leaning back, I pick up the moisture with my hand and work him faster as I take him in my mouth again, pulling him farther to the back of my throat. Our eyes meet, and I can see he's on the edge. I feel his hips moving, picking up the pace. His lids are lowered, eyes glazed, and I'm sure he's about to shoot down my throat when he stops me.

Holding my cheeks, he moves me back. His dick pops out of my mouth and bobs at me as he leans forward, moving me onto my back.

"I want inside that sweet pussy," he growls, reaching down for my thighs and pushing my legs up and open. He blinks down and moves back, dropping to his knees and sliding his tongue from my center to my clit.

"Cade! Oh . . . oh . . ." My hips jump, and I'm gasping and chanting as his tongue follows a fast figure eight over and over my clit. That luscious beard scruffs and teases my inner thighs, and I'm winding tighter with every pass. I'm so close to coming. "Oh, yes . . . oh, *yes!*"

He leans back, and a cool breeze drifts over us before he plunges into me with one swift drive.

He's thrusting fast and hard, bigger than any guy I've ever slept with, and it's a deliciously erotic stretch I've never felt before. He's hovering over me, and I hear his breathing. I see the bead of sweat glistening on his cheek, and I want to lick his entire body. Instead, I gently push his shoulder.

Our eyes meet in a flash, and it only takes him a moment to understand. My legs go tight around his waist, and he cups my ass, rolling us over so I can be on top. He's lying back on the bed, and I'm sitting straight up, brazen in the moonlight. My knees are on the mattress, and I start to rotate my hips, circling like a hula dancer.

I'm on my knees grinding my clit against his body with every rotation, faster and faster. My eyes flutter shut, and my entire focus is on the orgasm building in my core.

Cade thrusts up, and I throw my head back as the pressure explodes in my belly. My pelvis clenches into a burning, tight ball, and I call out, my voice breathy and broken.

Imaginary metallic glitter falls all around us as my body shakes and clenches through a mind-erasing orgasm. Cade's large hands grasp mine, our fingers clasped as I ride it out.

It feels so good, it's almost painful. I never want it to end, but just as fast, Cade snatches his hands out of mine.

"Oh, fuck!" He scoops me by the ass up and off his dick, resting me back on his thighs.

I'm still shaking, and I reach down to rub my clit as he pumps his cock with his fist, groaning and bucking his hips as he comes, the thick white liquid landing on his stomach and my thighs. Another shimmer of orgasm moves down my legs, and I reach forward to cover his hand with mine, moving slower as his orgasm tapers.

Our eyes lock. We're facing each other in the moonlight, panting hard, covered in sweat. I've never felt more satisfied. Cade is gorgeous in my bed. The muscles across his stomach flex, forming a six-pack as he sits up, facing me where I'm straddling him.

Holy shit.

"I didn't have a condom," he says apologetically. "I wasn't sure if you were on the pill."

"I am," I sigh, with a smile, resting my forearms on his shoulders.

"Still, I figured it wasn't polite to come inside without a condom." He turns his face and kisses my arm. "I mean, without the proper conversations and paperwork."

"You're very considerate," I tease. "I think we violated all safe sex standards when I put your dick in my mouth."

"Fuck, that was a stellar blow job. I almost shot right down your beautiful throat."

My lips curl in a smile. I even chuckle. "It's the foreplay, the teasing . . ."

"You're so tight. You felt like a virgin on my dick." He moves his lips to my jaw, kissing the side of my neck.

I lean my head to the side. "You make a habit of fucking virgins?"

"Mm." He runs his mouth up behind my ear, and tingles flow through my insides. "We all have our first."

"I suppose you're right." My eyes start to close. My nipples are taut and tingling, and I want him to suck them. I want him to make me come again, but for now, we're both covered in the product of our last orgasms.

"We should shower," I say, and his head rises.

Strong arms wrap around my waist and he lifts me, sliding us to the edge of the bed. Once again, he's carrying me, my legs around his hips.

"Tell me the way." He grins, and my soft tits press against his rock-hard chest.

We both smell like faded cologne, sweat, and sex mixed with the faint lavender scent Chas likes to spray around the house.

"To the front, opposite hall."

He's walking quickly through the dim apartment, following my directions.

"That thing you did with your hips—"

"It's a shimmy—"

"Blew my mind."

"We can do it again." Resting my forehead against his shoulder. I feel light and buzzy. "I used to take a belly dancing fitness class."

"I've never felt anything like it."

We're in the bathroom, and I push back, lowering my legs to stand. Facing the shower, I lean forward to turn on the water and test the temperature. I feel the heat of Cade at my back, and I'm suddenly aware my ass is pointed right at him.

"Oh!" I moan as his long fingers slide between my thighs, cupping my pussy, testing inside.

"You're still wet," he groans.

"Yes . . ." My back arches slightly, and I hear him make another low noise just above the hiss of the water.

He slides his fingers forward and over my clit, circling that sensitive little bud faster and sending waves of heat through my lower stomach and thighs. Closing my eyes, I press my palms against the wall of the shower, and I feel the shifting at my backside.

His hand moves to my hip, and he's pressing his cock at my entrance again. I buck against him, wanting him inside me, and without hesitation, he sinks, balls-deep into my throbbing core.

"Fuck!" he shouts, gripping my hips hard with both hands.

I use the wall for balance, and he jerks my ass hard against his pelvis, hammering fast and deep into my core. I don't want him to pull out this time. I want us to ride this building orgasm all the way to the end.

His hand snakes around the front of my thigh to find my clit. My legs spread wider so he can rub me off as he pounds into me from behind.

"Oh, yes . . ." I'm whimpering and bucking, rising on my tiptoes with every hit.

He's still moving, still massaging, and I'm so close to the edge. Every muscle in my core tightens, draws up, ready to burst. His palm slides over the skin of my ass, and without warning, he gives me a firm *SMACK!* It's like the strike of a match to my insides.

"OH!" I cry, as my orgasm explodes through my stomach.

My knees buckle, but he catches me, pulling me back up, continuing to pump his cock in my spasming pussy.

"Fuck, yeah!" He shouts, and I feel his orgasm start.

I'm flush against his body, and we're matching each other pulse for pulse. My eyes are squeezed shut, and I'm not sure I can move at this point. I'm wondering if these electric waves of pleasure will ever subside. I hope they don't.

Warm arms wrap around my chest, lifting me so that my back is against his torso. I'm firm against his body, and his mouth is right at my shoulder, kissing my skin, moving into my ear. "So good," he murmurs.

He's smiling, and I'm flush with heat. We enter the shower, allowing the spray to cover our bodies. I reach for the cloth and pour the lavender-scented body wash on it. Without a word, I smooth the foam over me then turn and smooth it over his pecs. Making my way down the hard ripples of his abs, I allow him to take it before I rinse.

My body feels boneless and deliciously satisfied . . . and utterly exhausted. I step out of the warm spray, lift my towel off the rack, and wrap it around me. Reaching in the narrow cabinet, I pull one out for him. He takes it, and we exchange a smile. Leading us to my moonlit room, everything feels soft and lofty as I drop my towel and push through the sheets, resting my cheek on my pillow.

I'm drifting on a cloud, floating in space when pressure on the other side of the bed tells me Cade is here. He slides closer and pulls my head onto his chest, wrapping a strong arm around my shoulders. It's delicious.

"Remember that Beatles song 'The End'?" I ask from my fluffy pink cloud.

"Um-hm." The vibration of his voice tickles my ear.

"Do you think they meant you should make more love so there's more for you to take? Or you should take more love so there's more to make?"

"Mm."

I lift my head and see his eyes are closed. Pushing against his side, I repeat the question. "Make more love or take more love? Positive or negative?"

He exhales heavily and rolls toward me. In the process, he turns me so my back is to his chest. "I'll fuck you again," he says through a thick layer of sleep. "Just give me a minute."

"No, that's not what I . . ." His breathing is more rhythmic, and I hear a slight snore. I let it go.

I'm exhausted, and everything is warm and cozy—yet I can't fall asleep. Marv's words today keep repeating in my brain. He wants me to give up my dream. The idea makes me sick, every molecule inside rebelling at the thought. Houston is where I started . . . it's where I've built my reputation. It's my home now. How many people get to build their dreams at home? Not very many, that's how many.

Cade's arm tightens around my middle, and I decide the answer is taking.

Maybe I should take more love and ask questions later.

I'm not sure.

I need to think about it more . . .

I'M CURLED UP like a kitten, still in my pink, gauzy heaven where pastel-rainbow mermaids swim in glittery lavender seas. Rainbows drift in hazy beams all around me, and I'm just about to eat a sparkly cupcake when a loud, nonstop *BUZZ! BUZZ! BUZZ!* Shatters everything—including my head.

I sit up quickly to stop the horrifying noise, when, "OH!" I moan.

I've just been hit with an invisible sledgehammer, and my skull has shattered into a million pieces. The sun is blasting through the window like a prison interrogation lamp, and I slap the clock across the room and cower into my pillows, pulling the blankets tight around my head.

"Oh, God," I whimper, tears of pain wetting my eyes. "I'll never drink again . . . Never never never! I promise this time! Please, please just let me die now. Please put an end to this suffering!"

A groaning sound comes from my left, and my insides freeze. Unexpected warmth is near my leg, and I carefully, cautiously slide my foot to the side until it encounters . . .

"What!" I sit straight up.

The blankets are tight around my head and over my ears, as I turn carefully to see . . .

My brain scrambles.

Cade Hill is in my bed! Cade Hill is lying on his side, eyes closed, and . . . my eyes drift down . . . completely naked!

Oh, shit! Oh, shit! It wasn't a dream!

I move again, and I feel deep in my core the ache of every time we had sex last night. I remember our first glorious time before we got in bed, then our second mind-altering time in the shower . . . and then somewhere in the early morning hours, it seems like my ass got too close to his erection, and he instinctively grabbed my hips, sinking that enormous cock deep into my pussy and pounding out a quickie. My whole body flushes with heat.

That erotic flashback is quickly replaced with panic. "No . . . no . . . no!" I whisper, scooting away to the opposite side of the mattress.

What have I done?

Why did I do those shots? Dammit!

As gently as possible, I slide out and crawl to the towel lying on the floor where I dropped it last night. Scooping it up, I wrap it around my naked body and scurry out of the room, across the hall to Chas's closet where I can borrow a robe.

Hanger after hanger, it's all satin and feathers and rainbow colors. A low groan of pain from my bedroom causes me to grab the next one I touch. It's black with white feathers all around the collar and cuffs. *I've got to triage this crisis . . .*

I take a deep breath and go to the door, pulling it open to find Cade standing in the hall in his jeans and shirt. It's unbuttoned, and his lined torso is on full, glorious display. His dark brown hair is a sexy mess, and his blue eyes go wide when he sees me.

"Jesus! What is this place?" Just as fast he groans, reaching up to rub his forehead. "Fucking shots."

"You're . . . at my apartment." Nice. He doesn't remember a thing. Maybe I can work with this.

"You wear that around your apartment?"

Looking down, I pull the feathery lapels closer. "I-I needed

THE LAST *Guy*   63

something to wear. It's my roommate's."

"Right." He nods. "Sasha Fierce."

"Chas-say McQueen."

"I gotta go."

He's across the room faster than I expected he'd move. Maybe his hangover isn't as uproarious as mine? I haven't budged, and he's scooped up his shoes, hand on the doorknob when he pauses.

"Uh . . . about last night. I—"

"You don't have to say a thing." I hold up both hands like he's got a gun on me. "Shots. Lots of shots. Big mistake. Huge. What happens in the apartment stays in the apartment."

Something passes across his face I don't understand. Confusion? Disappointment? Regret? His forehead creases as he studies me, then he nods, a short, brusque nod.

"I'll see you at work."

With that he's out the door, and I collapse on the spot with a moan. "Oh, God! Now I really do need to die."

Eight

REBECCA

*V*ICKY IS WAITING for me when I arrive at the station at three. I'm usually in by nine, but I was vomiting in my toilet at nine.

"I spent the whole night thinking about this," she says, following me as I walk.

I'm in the newsroom with my sunglasses still on. I've managed my headache with several ibuprofen, but the harsh fluorescent lighting isn't doing my puffy eyes any favors—another mark against me in Marv's book.

I nod.

"Marv is a spineless bastard. He should have fought for you," she continues. "But . . . if you're weekend executive producer, just think of the power we could have . . . over story selection, guest interviews—"

"I'm not interested in production. My contract as a reporter isn't up until December thirty-first."

"It's late September." She's looking at me with those clear blue eyes. "Just think about it," she says, before striding down the hall.

She has a point. If we want to make a change in the priorities of this city, one of the best ways to do it is take over the highest rated news station in town. Still, I thought I'd be doing it from behind the anchor desk.

Glancing down at my tight skirt, I think about how I should have gotten up and gone for a jog this morning. The mild nausea is back at the very thought. Exhaling a sigh, I start up the hall when Cade emerges from his office, and our eyes meet. Lightning strikes my already clenched stomach, and I take a step back. His perfect lips tighten into a thin line, and his eyes dart away as he heads into Marv's office.

Oh, God . . . I force myself to start breathing again. Going to my desk, I shake my mouse to wake my computer. The screen pops up, and I look over my schedule for the day. Continued coverage of Planetary Princess . . . *No*, I shake my head. I just can't.

Snatching up my phone, I punch Vicky's number. She answers on the first ring.

"You've come to your senses?" I can tell by her tone she's annoyed with me.

"I think I've got a stomach bug." It's true. I'm a coward. "I've got to go home. Savannah can take day two of Planetary Princess."

"Savannah's covering the wastewater treatment plant."

"She'll owe me one."

I hang up, thinking about the perky twelve-year-old reporter Marv hired over the summer. Okay, she's twenty-three. Still, Vicky's been giving her shit stories (literally) in the name of "paying her dues." The truth is I'm the one getting shat on. With her size zero waist and perky little breasts, Savannah will be in the weekly anchor's chair, the very top spot next to Cade, by year's end. Another jolt of nausea wrecks my beleaguered stomach, and I make a straight line to the door.

Chas is home when I arrive, curled up on the couch eating popcorn and watching Wendy Williams. Wendy Williams has a show.

"What are you doing home?" Her legs pop out and she trots over to me.

I drop my purse on the floor where I stand. My roommate's eyes flicker from my sunglass-covered face to my purse on the floor and back.

"Come sit on the couch with me. Wendy's debuting her Janet Jackson poncho."

"Uhhh . . ." I moan, following my bestie to the couch.

"Did you wear my black Kim K satin robe?"

I drop on the couch and flop over on my side, burying my face in the faux-mink throw pillow.

"I don't mind," Chas continues. "I just need to know if you spunked it up. That is dry clean only."

"Nooo . . ." My face still in the pillow.

"What's wrong, sugarplum?" I feel Chas's long hand stroking my side. "Chris the astronaut couldn't get it up? Girl, y'all were throwing them back last night. I'm surprised you're moving."

Another wince and a moan into the pillow.

"If you're not going to start speaking English, I'm taking Wendy off mute."

I turn my face so my mouth is uncovered. "He got it up," I say in a mournful tone. "Several times."

"Yes, he did!" She's shouting and clapping like she just won *Drag Race*. "That's my girl! You go!"

I pull the faux-cashmere throw off the back of the couch and over my head. "Please stop screaming. I'm about to die."

"You know when my aunt LouVerne worked at the Libby glass plant in Little Rock, she got totally wasted one night and slept with both her bosses at the same time—"

"Cade is not my boss. He's the asshole sports-director."

"He didn't seem like an asshole to me!" Chas is too excited about this. "Anyway, Aunt LouVerne ended up pregnant and had no idea which one was the father."

I confess, I'm piqued. "What happened?"

"She took my advice and went with the one who wasn't in her

ass, of course!" she laughs. "And they were married twenty years."

My face crinkles. "I can't believe she told you that. How old were you?"

"Oh, honey, don't do that with your face. Marv won't even want you in production with that puss."

Slapping the pillow, I sit up. "I don't want to work in production! I want my own show!"

"Toddlers and Tiaras!" Chas calls, one hand cupped beside her mouth. "Someone's missing from the set!"

"I'm sorry," I sigh and collapse on the comforting pillow. "It's hard to accept when your dreams are over."

The room falls quiet. Wendy is on our enormous television twirling in her poncho. I want to make an Urban Sombrero joke, but I'm not really in the mood to laugh. What I really need is a good long cry.

When Chas speaks again, her voice is softly serious. "Why haven't you ever told me this before?"

"What?" My voice is sad as I trace my finger along the lines of the faux mink.

"If your dream is to have a show, you need to pursue it. You need to take the steps to make it happen."

"It's too late." I'm not pouting. I'm simply stating the facts. "Marv thinks I'm too old, too fat, and I don't want to move to another station."

My phone starts to buzz, and I lift it. It's the station. I don't want to talk to Vicky or Marv, so I send it to voicemail.

"I'm going to lie down. I'm not feeling so well."

"I've got a show tonight at the Tick Tock, so I'll be late again. Will you be all right recovering alone?"

"I guess," I say, pushing off the couch. I skulk to my bedroom thinking of perky Savannah and hoping those little princess brats make her look at least twenty-five.

Chassy frowns. "Cheer up, Bee. If you can't love yourself, how the hell you gonna love somebody else? Right?"

I force a watery-eyed smile. "Right."

IT'S QUIET WHEN I open my eyes again. My headache is significantly diminished thanks to the wonders of ibuprofen, but I feel like I swallowed a gallon of sand. Tossing back my blanket, I scoop Chas's Kim K robe off the chair where I left it this morning. I don't even care that the white feathers lining the collar tickle my nose. The black satin is soft around my aching body. Speaking of ache, with every step my cheeks heat at the ache deep in my core.

"Oh, God!" I whine softly under my breath as shame flashes down my spine.

My arms go over my head. I slept with Cade right here in my house . . . so many times . . . and it was sooo *good*. Shivering, I grab my phone and hit the Door Dash app. Alone in this apartment, I can't face what I've done without tacos.

"The New Rebecca Revolution starts tomorrow. Tonight it's Doritos Locos Tacos. Ooo! Cool ranch!"

I tap the menu items to add them to my cart. My eyes linger on the Cheesy Gordita Crunch, but before my worst nature can kick in, I hit "complete order" and toss my phone on the couch. It helps that I know *gordita* means *chubby girl* in Spanish.

The New Rebecca Revolution might start tomorrow, but I can't enjoy a "chubby girl" thinking of Marv scowling at me the whole time while he's giving my dream job to Savannah. Doritos, on the other hand, are allowed in this final wallowing session.

My comfort food arrives in less than fifteen minutes—I love modern times! I don't even care that the pimple-faced, chicken-chested guy delivering my salvation looks at me like I'm a demented Norma Desmond in Chas's satin and feathered robe. I take the food and go straight to the couch, bouncing in place as I crunch through my little pile of heaven.

"Tomorrow," I reassure myself. "I'm setting my alarm for seven, and I'm going for a jog around the neighborhood before I get ready for work."

Hangover food consumed, belly nice and round, I take a quick shower before heading to bed at a reasonable time. I don't linger in the shower, thinking of how I smoothed my lavender-covered cloth down those chiseled ridges of his abs . . .

Much.

And I definitely do not pull the pillow Cade slept on to my face and sniff it repeatedly, searching for any leftover traces of his cologne . . .

More than once.

I responsibly set my alarm, click out the light and close my eyes. I do not slip my hand between my thighs and rub one out while fantasizing about him gripping my ass or the feel of that massive member stretching me in the most erotic way or the low vibration of his voice as his soft, full lips traced a burning trail up the side of my neck followed by the scuff of that beard . . .

I do not have a mini O dreaming of the bigger, more enormous O I had last night with my sexy coworker.

I go straight to sleep.

IT'S A TRUTH universally acknowledged that every wakeup alarm created for the iPhone sounds like the screaming bells of hell.

"Why? Whyyy?" I cry, slapping the face repeatedly to make it stop.

My eyes are still closed as I drag New Rebecca out of bed and across the room to the drawer containing my sorely neglected workout gear. If God had wanted us to run this early in the morning, he wouldn't have invented pancakes.

Jog-bra on. Ultra-tight spandex running pants that support

ass and supposedly improve stamina in place. Too-tight tank top that makes me look like a sausage also in place. Running motivation . . . still asleep in bed, most likely burying face in pillow searching for final traces of delicious Cade-scent.

I force myself to think of those motivational posters Nancy always quoted and not *If you see me running, call 911.*

"Sweat is fat crying," I say, not even pausing to look in the mirror on the way out the door.

My old two-mile route with Nancy used to take us from our loft on Texas Avenue east to Minute Maid Park. We'd do a couple laps around the stadium then head back home. For whatever reason, today I don't want to do the old route. Maybe it's just too depressing being alone.

Instead I head south then east to Discovery Green and around the jogging trail there. It's in the more posh part of downtown, and I'm on the sidewalks more than I should be on my way back. The morning traffic is heavier on this route.

"Should've gone the other way," I mutter to myself.

I'm heading up McKinney when I spot a woman walking what looks like a herd of dogs in all shapes and sizes. They're taking up the entire sidewalk, and I look around frantically to see if I can cross in the middle of the busy intersection.

"Shit!" I swear through a labored breath.

Cars are everywhere, and I'm directly in front of One Park Place, one of the most expensive apartment complexes in the city. I'm wavering on whether to go left or right. The mob of dogs is getting closer, and it's clear they're pulling the woman holding the leashes rather than the other way around.

My eyes strain for a break in the traffic when I see a man coming out of the revolving doors at the front of the historic building. The brass doors turn, and all six-foot-awesome emerges, complete with dark waves, beard, and steel blue eyes. It's Cade Hill, and I want to die. I'm covered in sweat in my sausage shirt, and I just know little hairs are flying out of my ponytail.

As I'm panicking, I see a perky blonde is right behind him. She runs up to him, catching his arm. He stops, and she turns into his chest, sliding her fingers into his dark beard and pressing her lips flush against his.

It all happens so fast, I forget to hide. My eyes bug, my jaw drops, and I'm frozen in place across the street watching the man I'd ridden like a pony two nights ago kissing a young, blonde stick insect.

"What the hell?" My voice is louder than I intend, and I'm surrounded by dogs. The herd is on me, and it's all leashes wrapping around my waist, around my legs, combined with frantic yapping.

"I'm so sorry!" The sweaty dog walker raises her arm in an attempt to untangle them.

"Ow!" I duck as she clocks me in the forehead. "Oh no!"

A shaggy gold dog jumps up, putting his paws on my shoulders. He's licking me right in the mouth, and I'm spitting and shaking my head, trying to get him off.

"Down, Buster! Heel!" The woman shouts.

YIP! A loud noise from the smaller dog I just stepped on makes me jump out of my skin. "I'm sorry!" I cry.

I'm stepping and struggling, and my mind is screaming *Run! Hide! Get the hell out of here!!!* I glance back across the street, and I see Cade. His brow is clutched, and he looks pissed.

A traffic signal must have just changed, because a barrage of cars pours down the street between us. I'm finally free of the leashes and all five million dogs, and I'm reeling from the fact that it took less than forty-eight hours for him to replace me with a new blonde bimbo in his bed.

I hiccup a breath and do the only thing I know to do. I take off running full-speed, around the corner, and back the way I came. All the way to my place.

Nine

CADE

A WET NOSE pokes at my closed eyelid, and I know it's my rebound-after-Maggie-Grace-left-me cat. I open my lids and she gives me her *wake up and pet me* stare. White and fluffy with pale blue eyes, she's the prissiest damn cat I've ever seen. The moment Trent, Mom, and I had spied her at the pet store, they'd insisted I bring her home.

"Morning, Killer," I mumble as I stretch out in my king-sized bed. She purrs and pushes her head against my hand. I pet her while she curls up next to my bicep, her paws tap dancing on my muscles.

"If only all bedmates were as easy as you," I say.

Stone is on my mind . . . the hot sex we'd had . . . and the way she'd shoved me out her door the next morning.

Flashes of the night come at me, and I scrub my face.

What the hell had I done?

You boned Stone, asshole.

YOU BONED STONE. Three times to be exact.

I heave out a sigh. *What must she be thinking?*

She regrets it. Wasn't it obvious?

Fuck.

Scooting Killer carefully out of the way, I jump out of bed and crank up some Stevie Ray Vaughn on my speakers. I push all thoughts of Stone out of my head as I get in the shower.

It's nine by the time I'm dressed in a slick Tom Ford suit. I pull out a green tie, thinking the color reminds me of Stone's sultry gaze. But I stop. Nope. Not going there. I whip it off and go with the sapphire blue—which matches *my* eyes.

After making sure Killer has her mouse toys and her food dish filled, I give her a final pet, exit the penthouse, and take the elevator door to the lobby.

The door swooshes open and I step off—right smack into Maggie Grace.

She takes a step back and I reach a hand out to steady her, easing her to the side to let the other passengers get off.

"Cade! Oh good. I was trying to get up to the penthouse, but apparently you have to have a key for that. Your doorman tried to call you but you didn't pick up."

Thank God.

"I'm starting to think you're stalking me," I say in a curt tone. I want to go off on her. I want to tell her to get the fuck out of my face and maybe check into getting some new meds, but I don't. She's a female, and my mom raised me to treat ladies with a gentle hand, so I grind my teeth together instead.

She straightens her shoulders. "Actually, after seeing you the other night, it got me to thinking—"

"What?"

"It's been forever since I saw your mom, not since her breast cancer, and you may not know this, but my sister was recently diagnosed, and part of me just needs someone to talk to. My sister . . . they caught hers late . . ." she pauses and her forehead puckers with a line of worry.

I exhale and my anger deflates. Her attire is softer today, a yellow sundress, and her hair is down and curling around her shoulders.

"I'm sorry about your sister."

My mom had been diagnosed a year ago and had just finished

her chemo and radiation treatment. She's clear for the moment, but I know the emotion Maggie Grace and her family must be going through.

She nods as she watches the people come and go in my building. "I don't have her new address or cell since she moved—so I thought I'd pop by and ask you. She was always so easy to talk to. Do you think she'd mind if I came by and brought her some flowers for her garden? I know how much she loves to mess with plants." She exhales. "Honest to God, Cade, this isn't about you. I just want to get in touch with your mom."

My gut says no, but I see the uncertainty that flits across her features. She grimaces. "My sister . . . she may not make it. I'm scared."

I sigh, knowing that feeling all too well.

I tell her my mom's address and cell while she types it into her phone. We walk out of One Park Place to a sunny day. We say our goodbyes, and I turn to head to the coffee shop before getting my car.

"Wait," she calls.

I pivot and pop an eyebrow. "Yeah?"

She walks toward me and before I can stop her, she grabs my jaw and stares into my eyes. "You're the best damn thing I ever had, Cade. I wish I could go back and redo what happened between us." Then she plants her red lips against mine, her tongue begging entry to my mouth.

I freeze. My ex is making out with me, and I let her.

Maybe I kiss her back—like out of some kind of caveman Neanderthal instinct—but I don't mean to.

After a few seconds, I push her off me, glowering at her.

She stares into my eyes a bit sadly, smiles, then turns and walks away.

God. Women are fucking crazy.

My scowl grows when I catch sight of Stone ensconced in a mob of dogs just a few yards away.

What the hell is she doing here?

But before I can say anything, she turns and sprints in the other direction.

AFTER STOPPING OFF for coffee and a bagel, I arrive at work and immerse myself in preparing for the six and ten sports reports. With the weekend coming up, we're working on football game times and who the big rivalries will be.

It's after lunch by the time we're done, and I head to the conference room for our daily editorial meeting.

I slide in and like a magnet my eyes are drawn to Stone. She's been avoiding me all morning. She must have gotten here late judging by the half-eaten bran muffin next to her notebook full of doodles. Her hair's up in a messy bun, and she's thumping her pen on the table and swinging her heeled foot back and forth rapidly.

Someone is antsy.

I grin in her direction and when our eyes meet, I get hot. My lids go low, remembering her pussy clenching around my cock, and she seems to see the place my thoughts have gone because she blushes. A few seconds later, she shakes herself, her gaze turning chilly. She turns her back to chat with the two weeknight anchors, Matt and Lorie.

My lips tighten as I swoop past three empty seats to take the one next to her. There's no way I can let this . . . this thing between Stone and me go—not with this much chemistry between us.

Plus, even though I'd been trashed, I recall every single mind blowing orgasm she had. She wants me.

Feeling confident, I ease down into my seat, straightening the crease in my slacks as I do so.

She's glaring at me when our eyes meet again. I lean into her space and take a whiff of coconut. "Morning, Stone. Didn't know you liked to run. We should go together sometime." It's a statement, not a question. I smirk and reach over to grab one of the powdered donut holes in the middle of the table and pop it in my mouth. I chew for a few minutes, eyeing her carefully. I'd give up all the donut holes in the world to know what she's thinking.

"Don't hold your breath." Her face is blank and cold. "Now, if you'll excuse me, I was chatting with Matt here before you interrupted."

And then she turns back to talk to Matt.

Fine. She's still upset about the hook up. Or it's because she saw Maggie Grace locking lips with me. Hell, it's probably both.

I want to explain the situation with Maggie Grace, but Marv and Vicky arrive together and shut the door. They read off the headlines for the day and the on-air reporters perk up. We go through the various options, and the anchors, myself, Marv, and Vicky pick and choose what will make the six and ten show.

I tune them out, distracted by Stone's body heat. I feel ramped up. I need to get her alone. Maybe the bathroom again—

I come back when I hear my name.

". . . . of course, he won't be the one to say it, but Cade's volunteer work in the inner city schools would be a great feature story. He coaches and you should hear him talk about those kids," Lorie says, shooting me a big grin.

She's one of the sweetest people in nightly news. Her husband is a big Falcons fan, and I had been to their house for a couple of dinner parties.

Vicky considers me. Nods. "Might be good for the lull we expect around the holidays."

Marv gives me a narrowed look. "What's so great about being a coach for kids? Wouldn't it be better if you sponsored a fundraiser instead? Those schools need money."

Savannah pipes up. "We can do a bake sale for them!"

I hold in my eye roll.

Stone stops tapping her foot, and I feel the weight of her eyes on me, but this time, *I'm* playing hard to get. I refuse to glance at her.

"You're absolutely right," I say, speaking to Marv. "I'd like to plan a charity event someday, but I'm just getting started."

"Which schools do you go to?" Savannah asks.

"Deadrick's the main one," I say. "Academically, it's been the lowest performing high school in Houston."

A few reporters nod. I hear someone say *right*. They cover this city. They know the areas where these schools are located. It's crime-infested and hard for a kid to break out.

It's Stone who speaks next. "So you just waltz over during the day—*in your Armani suit*—and show them how to throw a ball?"

Marv smirks.

I don't *just* volunteer. Sure, on paper, I coach in my downtime, but I've donated over a hundred thousand dollars this year alone for new helmets and food for the kids to eat before practice. I want to do it for all the schools, but Deadrick is where my former teammate Hart coaches.

I turn to Stone and my gaze brushes over her, lingering on her lips before taking in her shirt buttoned up to her throat. "I go on Saturday mornings and help the regular coach out. He used to play with me in Atlanta."

I glance at Lorie. "If you decide to do the piece, I suggest you focus on the kids and the struggle they face—not the guy who shows up on the weekends. Those kids . . . they're amazing . . . they just need someone to tell them."

Stone lets out a little sound like she's surprised.

Marv purses his lips. "It's an okay story and since you're *you*, people will tune in. The question is do we really need another story about some athlete—"

"It *is* interesting," Stone interrupts, her face brighter than it had been when I'd come in. She looks like a reporter after a story. "Honestly, I'd like to know more, like how many hours does he spend with these kids? Does he get to know them on a personal level? Does he feel like he's making a difference?"

"Why don't we revisit this closer to November," Marv juts in, silencing her.

She huffs under her breath and presses her pen into her notebook. She doodles a taco with a frown on its face.

"Let's move on." Marv looks at Vicky. "We got anything live and hopping for tonight?"

Vicky adjusts her glasses and checks something on her phone, picking back up with today's news. We're constantly getting updates from social media, emails, Reuters and the Associated Press wires. "The new petting area at the zoo opens to the public at three. They're really doing it up big with a mix of exotic animals, plants and flowers, a waterfall, that kind of thing. It's supposed to be gorgeous. One of the Bush cousins had her wedding there." She checks her clock. "We've got plenty of time to get a reporter there for the live ribbon cutting at six. A few of the more famous local artists are unveiling murals."

"Stone, you should take it. You'd be great," I say to her softly. It's an impulse remark, based mostly on the fact that she's been down. I picture her in a garden with flowers, a waterfall . . . I stop that train of thought.

Marv perks up. "Yeah, you take the petting zoo and Savannah can head to the Courthouse for the verdict on the Smith case. They're saying the jury is close, but they'll have the verdict by five."

Stone flinches. "Smith case! Marv, you didn't mention the verdict in the rundown. I'll take it. I've interviewed the lawyers on both sides. I know more about it than anyone here."

He waves her off. "Already decided. You get the zoo. Thank your friend Cade here for suggesting it."

I stare at him, my brow furrowing. "I didn't know about the Smith case or I wouldn't have said—"

"Already. Decided. Meeting adjourned."

I seethe quietly, but my fists are curling under the table. I want to punch his sharp, squirrel face.

I turn to Stone, and her expression is tight as she gathers her things.

"Look, I'm sorry about getting you the wrong story," I say. "I was trying to help."

"Thanks," she bites out as she stands. I rise as well, not wanting her to leave before we hash this out.

"He was hanging on to the Smith case for the end. You can't blame me for that. Marv has his own agenda."

She makes an exasperated noise, and I can tell she wants to get past me, but I block her way to the door.

"Look, about the other night . . ." I lower my voice. "I want to talk to you. Will you come to my office?"

Most of the room has cleared out, but there are a few lingering, and I don't miss that Savannah's one of them. She cuts her eyes at us as she picks up her notebook and phone.

Stone stuffs the wad of bran muffin in her bag and glares at me. "Sorry. I need to get busy on the petting zoo."

And with a twist of her hips, she brushes past me, bumping me to the side as she marches away.

I watch her the entire way out the door, her cute little nose in the air.

Damn, I like her.

Ten

REBECCA

VICKY HEADS UP the hall to the control room as soon as the meeting ends, and I take off after her. My insides are all messed up from Cade's expression after the meeting. He actually wants to talk to me? Like I didn't see him kissing another woman less than five hours ago—less than forty-eight hours after covering my body with red marks from that sexy beard and blowing my mind with his enormous . . . perfect . . .

Not going there.

More importantly, he opened his big mouth and got me stuck covering baby animals instead of the Smith case. Granted, a prison inmate suing a doctor for malpractice isn't as sexy as immigration reform or police brutality, but it's a human rights case. It enhances my image as a serious newswoman—as opposed to preschool beauty pageants and petting zoos. It will also keep my mind focused on serious, work-related matters, and not having drunk monkey sex with that . . . player.

"Vicky!" I call, hustling in my navy pencil skirt. This one has a slit up the front, allowing me to move faster. "Hey, Vicky?"

She turns and gives me a smile, tossing her red hair over her shoulder. "You look better today. I hope it means you're taking my advice?"

"I went for a two-mile jog this morning." *That ended in a half-mile sprint home*, I silently add. "Have you had a chance to chat with Liz?"

Our station manager Liz Chapman started out in Marv's position before she was promoted two years ago. She's pretty much the only person with the power to veto his sexist, sizest, ageist attempt to demote me.

"Ah." She nods and continues walking once I'm by her side. "Not yet. She's in Barbados for her sister's wedding. As soon as she gets back next week, I'll schedule a lunch."

My shoulders droop. If Liz is out for a week, it'll be more like two weeks before she has time to talk to anyone. News piles up faster than compost on a dairy farm. She sees my response and gives my arm a pat.

"Keep up the good work, and keep nailing these stories."

"A petting zoo?" My voice drips with skepticism.

"You're better than that. Local artists? Exotic animals? A ten-foot waterfall? You can make this human-interest story relevant. Give it depth!"

Taking a long breath, I nod. "Okay. And thanks . . . for your help, I mean. I appreciate it."

She nods and veers down the opposite hall. I turn, and I'm standing directly in front of the sports den. Cade is facing the wall of flat-screen televisions, and I allow myself to linger a moment admiring the way his tight ass fills out those slacks so perfectly. My entire body hums, and my fingers curl at the memory of touching him, tracing my fingers over those lines in his abs in the shower . . . *Damn him.*

"Shit," I whisper, blinking away fast when he turns and catches me.

"Stone?" His tone is low, and the rich vibration of his voice rattles my core. "Got a minute?"

I answer fast. "No!" Spinning on the heel of my nude pumps, I move away quickly. "I-I have to read." It's high and breathless, and I sound defensive.

He's right with me, moving with far more grace in fast-motion than I am in these shoes. *Damn athletes.*

"Okay, thirty seconds." Large hands close over my shoulders briefly, stopping me, flooding my panties with heat before moving away just as fast. "It's about this morning."

My jaw clenches, and anger—*not* jealousy!—gives me the strength to meet his panty-melting blue eyes. "You don't have to explain yourself to me. It is not my business."

"No, but I want to be clear. I did not invite Maggie Grace to my apartment. She just showed up."

In my peripheral vision, I can see my chest rising and falling quickly, and I force myself to calm. "Don't you live the charmed life? Women just throwing themselves in your bed, making out with you in the middle of Houston."

"It's not like that."

"Look, Cade, I appreciate your . . . concern." I reach out and almost touch him. Then I think better of it and pull my hand back. "It was nice of you to try and do whatever it was you were trying to do in the meeting just now, but I can take care of myself."

"I never meant to suggest you couldn't—"

"Marv doesn't need your help sinking my career." I won't even mention my sinking love life. "Next time run your ideas past me before you announce them in the middle of a meeting, okay?"

His brow cocks, and he takes a step back. "Sure."

"And about this morning, I didn't know where you lived, but I can assure you, I will never run past your building again." His jaw tightens, and my stomach feels sick. "What happened the other night was a mistake. I think it's best if we forget it ever happened." *As if that will ever be possible.*

Muscled arms cross over his broad chest, and sweet baby Jesus, it's like he grew two more sexy inches. Why are angry guys so fucking hot? I blink away, barely holding onto my survivor mindset. I really want to cry. I really want to break down and beg him to tell me why . . . *Why?* Why was he sucking face with some bitch named Maggie Grace of all things this morning? Didn't two nights ago mean anything? Wasn't it the best sex of his life, too?

Of course it wasn't, Rebecca Fieldstone. Grow up. Cade Hill is the Killer. He's the player, quarterback, superstar jock who goes through women like ratted-out tube socks.

"Anything else?" I don't miss the clipped tone in his voice.

"I don't think so." My voice wobbles, and I make a break for it. It's my last chance to get away with my dignity intact. Naturally, I bump right into Savannah lingering in the hall. "Oh! Sorry," I mutter, moving faster. I can only imagine she'll be the next blonde stick insect riding his lap.

I. Do. Not. Care! With a fortifying breath, I go to the news desk to collect the media kit on the petting zoo. It's finally a cool day. I'll read it in the courtyard and meet Kevin at the satellite truck. Cade Hill is my coworker, and that's the end of it.

TURNING TO THE window, I try again to adjust the built-in bra of my special "no-iron" shirt. "Stupid thing never fit right," I grumble, regretting my midnight impulse-buy. *Damn infomercials.*

A loud slurp fills the news van, and I give Kevin an impatient glance over my shoulder. He's holding another soda cup the size of his head.

"You're going to get diabetes if you don't stop drinking those." I give my blouse a hard yank, trying to get the bottom of the cup under my left breast. Finally, it feels like it's sitting properly.

"Don't be bitter because I can have all the calories I want." I turn in my seat to face front, and his eyes drop then immediately go huge. "Holy shit!"

"What—oh shit!" I look down and see my top button has popped off, exposing a clear shot of my cleavage. I grasp the sides, pulling them together. "I must've ripped it . . . Give me a safety pin!"

He only gives me a wolfish grin and waggles his eyebrows.

My brow lowers. "In your dreams, Big Gulp. Now give me a safety pin."

"What do I look like? Wardrobe?" He takes another loud slurp, staring straight at my boobs.

"My eyes are up here, asshole." *Of all the ridiculous things to happen . . .* I grumble as I dig through my bag, searching for anything to fix my blouse. "I can't be around a bunch of little kids like this."

"It's supposed to be exotic, right?" Kevin laughs. He keeps glancing to the side, and I scoot around in my seat to face the window again.

The seatbelt increases the level of difficulty trying to stay covered while also trying to find something to fix this malfunction. Finally, my fingers land on small, thin metal in the bottom of my purse.

"Ah-HA!" I whip out . . . A paper clip. "Shit," I hiss.

"What kind of shirt is that anyway?" Kevin says, now crunching on Cheetos and still slanting his eyes in the direction of my chest.

"Just shut up." I mentally curse my haste this morning.

This is what I get for trying to get in shape. First, I'm attacked by a mob of dogs. I'm Frenched by a Golden Retriever. Then I see Cade making out with some blonde bimbo right outside his apartment. My chest hurts, but I grit my teeth fighting those feelings with anger. Cade "Killer" Hill is not my focus. I'm focused on that anchor position.

Pulling the paper clip apart, I push one end through the fabric where the button used to be and the other through the buttonhole. Giving it a firm twist, the sides of my blouse slowly close together. I sit back and straighten my shoulders . . .

"It worked!" I rotate in my chair to face Kevin. "Check me out. MacGyver'd it!"

My camera guy actually makes a disappointed face. "I liked it better the other way."

"Yeah, kiss my ass." I've got my phone out, quickly scanning the press release sent over by the zoo's public relations manager. "It says they're bringing over a few baby animals today only . . ." I read. "Looks like we'll get some good B-roll here. Stacy Kulcheck is organizing the whole thing. I'll talk to her, and you get shots of all the highlights. I want the murals, this Venus flytrap, and the baby monkeys. Oh! They have a baby giraffe—we definitely need that."

"Another giraffe?" The van bounces, and I look up to see we're entering the parking lot.

The window goes down, and he shows our press passes to the guard. The uniformed lady smiles and waves us through. We're able to park close to the entrance, and I turn the narrow gold watch on my arm as I slip out of the van. It's five fifteen. We've got plenty of time to get set up and get a few interviews before live coverage of the ribbon cutting starts at six.

Kevin is right behind me when I show our credentials at the gate. The attendant runs out to take a selfie with me, and I'm feeling pretty encouraged by the time we reach the new wing.

"Oh my goodness!" My jaw drops, and I grip Kevin's arm. This is no ordinary petting zoo. This place is breathtaking, like something out of Disney's Animal Kingdom. "Be sure to get those shots I asked for."

Stepping into the large, open-air facility is like stepping into a jungle. Huge palms surround us with red succulent blooms rising from their centers. A net-roofed area is filled with tropical birds of all colors and sizes. Children shriek and run across roped footbridges suspended over ponds containing alligators and turtles, and smaller pens separate different types of animals.

The animals for petting consist primarily of the usual farm variety, including miniature horses, goats, chickens, and pot-bellied pigs. It's a whole wilderness safari theme.

"You must be Rebecca!" A female voice greets me, and I turn to see a woman with shoulder-length brown hair and bangs, wearing a thick, white tank top and khaki shorts walking toward me.

"Stacy?" I ask.

"That's me! Where would you like to start?"

"This place is amazing! I'm so glad I came."

"Well, we're glad to have the coverage. We've spent a lot of money on all this," she laughs. "I didn't have time to get it in the media kit, but we're in the running for Top U.S. Family Vacation Destination and 'Ten places to take your kids before 10' by *Parents Magazine*."

"That's huge," I agree, jotting notes quickly on my steno pad.

"The climate is perfect for this type of facility. With the awards and coverage, we're making a major impact on the Houston economy."

"And you're not oil or football!" I squeeze her arm, thinking how I owe Cade a big apology when I get back to the station.

Stacy gives me the tour of the different "learning areas," as they call them. She shows me the indoor reptile exhibit and we visit the bird shelter. Kevin is back with us, and I'm able to ask her questions for the ten o'clock package about school trips and future plans for the facility. The time passes quickly, and she waves over my shoulder.

"We're getting ready for the ribbon cutting. Are we going live?"

"Yes!" I stop at a metal bench where Kevin has set up the satellite box with its tall antenna. "We'll send the feed from here."

Steps away, I see a man in a white shirt with a badge and epaulettes. He's also wearing khaki shorts like Stacy, and he's holding a small, brown monkey with a little pink bow on her head.

"Oh!" I cry. "She's so cute! Do you think I could hold her?"

"What a fun idea! Let me ask." Stacy walks to the platform where the man is standing.

Behind him on the elevated platform, sit the mayor, a few members of the city council, and the zoo president and CEO. Their information is listed on the press release Stacy sent us, and Lorie will read it over the B-roll Kevin shot earlier. He'd sent it back to the station, and Vicky picked out scenes.

While Stacy chats with the monkey man, I turn to Kevin. "Let's set up the shot so we're ready."

"Becks? Can you hear me?" Vicky speaks to me from the control room, and I nod as I adjust the small headphone in my left ear.

"Loud and clear." I look into the camera and smile.

"You look great from here," she says. "What have you got for us?"

"Have Lorie ask me about the *Parents Magazine* awards. It's two new things, not on the press release. I'll say something about how they're hoping to make a major impact on Houston tourism."

"Sounds great." I know Vicky is making notes as she speaks, and she's clearly impressed.

I adjust my shirt, making sure the paper clip is holding steady, and this time I have my compact to powder my nose and forehead. I smooth my hair, and I've just reapplied my lipstick when Stacy returns with the man and his monkey.

"Rebecca, this is Albert Jones and Pixie."

"Hi, Pixie!" I scrunch my nose and hold out my hand as if she's a baby. "Is it okay if I hold her?"

"Sure." Albert has a distinct, flat accent.

"Are you from the Midwest?" I ask as he hands over the small primate.

"I studied at the University of Wisconsin," he says.

"Oh!" My grip wobbles, and Pixie immediately grabs my neck and shoulder, pulling hard on my shirt. "She's heavier than I expected . . . and strong!"

My earpiece lights up, and Vicky is speaking fast. "Ready, Becks? We're leading straight in with you at the top of the hour."

Kevin is behind the camera, and I'm doing my best to loosen Pixie's death grip on my throat.

"She doesn't seem to want to let go," I say with a nervous laugh, looking to Albert for assistance.

He's focused straight on the camera lens, hands behind his back, no smile.

"We're ready in five, four, three . . ." Kevin points out the last two numbers in the countdown, and I've finally managed to relocate Pixie's ridiculously strong paw . . . hand?

The red light goes on, and I lift the mic for the tease. "It's a big day here at the J.P. McGowan Children's Zoo. I'll have all the highlights when we return!"

I do my signature wink, and they cut away for Lorie to announce the other top stories in tonight's broadcast. Pixie jerks and once again has a hold on my precarious blouse. She's climbing around on my waist, her monkey toes cutting into my hips, and I have less than five seconds to rearrange her before we're live again.

"She's like an octopus!" I look to Al for help, but he's a deer in headlights.

"Coming back to you, Becks," Vicky says fast.

"It's a beautiful day for a ribbon cutting." I hold my smile steady as the monkey climbs me like a tree. "Get ready to have your socks knocked off, Houston, because this new facility is truly top notch!"

They cut to the B-roll Kevin shot of the different areas, the succulents, the waterfall, and Lorie reads the text I sent over to go with it. I've finally got Pixie situated on my hip, and I look down into her little face.

"You gotta work with me here, Pix. Okay?" I smile, and her round eyes move over my face then down to my blouse. Naturally, the silver paper clip catches her attention, and she picks at it. "No no!" My voice is high like she's a baby. "Don't touch that."

"Pixie is too young to understand language." Albert has finally rejoined the circus. "Once she's weaned, she'll learn more—"

"I'm sorry?" I'm still looking at Albert, eyebrows up, when I realize Kevin is pointing the countdown to me. My mic is in my hand, and I'm balancing a curious monkey-baby on my hip.

Lorie speaks again in my earpiece, and I know this is all live. "So Rebecca, I hear the zoo is up for a few awards?"

"Yes, we just found that out today, Lorie—Oh!" A monkey hand is inside my blouse. It is on my boob. The monkey is gripping my boob, and I push her body with the mic. "No no!" My voice is still high, but like some freakishly strong nightmare-baby, Pixie won't let me go. She's pulling my shirt apart.

"Stop, Pixie!" I yank her primate wrist while still jabbing her with the mic. "Stop!" My entire boob is on display for all of Houston to see, and the monkey won't let me go.

"Oh, my word!" Albert grabs Pixie around the waist and lifts her off me.

I have just enough time to jerk the material over my exposed breast before the segment ends. The camera is shaking violently with Kevin's laughter. My hair is wild around my head, and I'm blinking fast, trying to remember my name.

"Well, that is exotic!" Matt's voice is in my ear, and in the background, I can hear Lorie's snorts.

My face is hot as a firecracker, but I'm a professional. I clear my throat and do my tag. "That's just a little taste of what's in store for you at the Houston petting zoo. I'm Rebecca Fieldstone, KHOT 5 news."

The red light flickers off, and I collapse on the bench.

Eleven

CADE

STONE HAS THE best tits in the state of Texas, but she didn't intend to bare one to the city of Houston, population roughly two million. KHOT is the biggest affiliate here, so if only ten percent of viewers are watching (vastly underestimating) then two hundred thousand people just saw what happened.

Sure, it's funny—if I hadn't had my head between those glorious orbs two nights ago, and I didn't know what a predicament she's in. My lips flatten. Is it irrational to be pissed off and jealous at viewers seeing her tits? YES.

I'm not on air yet, but I watch from the side as the news unfolds after the live feed from Stone. From the anchor desk, Matt's lips are twitching as he struggles to keep from laughing. He covers it—unsuccessfully—by adjusting the papers in front of him and clearing his throat. "That Rebecca . . . always monkeying around."

Lori's smile is overly bright. "Sorry folks. Not exactly the kind of petting zoo you might have been expecting."

It's Matt turn to speak. "And now here's KHOT's Cade Hill to keep us *abreast* of what's up this weekend in sports . . ."

Matt gives me a look, as if expecting me to play along, but I ignore him and get down to business. "The headline this weekend is the big rivalry between Texas and Texas A&M. The teams haven't played in six years—since Texas A&M joined the SEC—and you know I'll be watching." I hold up my pinkie and index finger for the Longhorns. "My blood runs orange for Texas." I wrap up the weekend rundown as video footage rolls of the top teams in college football. I finish with the World Series playoffs, and Matt and Lorie take it back after I'm done.

A bit later, I head to the break room to grab something to eat before the ten o'clock broadcast. I pass by Marv's office and glance over. With dissatisfaction plowing his brow, he's glaring at a replay of the previous broadcast—specifically Stone. I knock on his open door and pop my head in. "Everything good, Marv?"

He starts, as if lost in his own thoughts, and spears me with a look. "Stone just bared her rack to our viewers—but trust me, it's nothing *I* can't handle. I've been doing this a lot longer than you, Hill."

Ah there it is . . . the ol' *you waltzed in here and got a job you didn't deserve* routine. I nod, tucking my hands into my pockets. I want to antagonize him, and it has little to do with the animosity he harbors for me and a lot to do with how he's been treating Stone.

"Should have given her the Smith story." I pivot away before he can comment.

In the break room, several reporters are at a table enjoying takeout from Wang's, a Chinese place down the street.

I walk to the back of the room to the ultramodern kitchen, complete with stainless steel appliances, a granite island, and the best pots and pans on the market. The station films cooking segments for the weekend show there, but during the week, we use it.

I open the fridge and pull out the ingredients for a BBQ chicken quinoa salad. Trent bounces in the break room wearing a lanyard pegging him as a visitor. He'd called earlier and wanted to have dinner together.

He strides over to me wearing his skinny jeans, Converse, and his favorite *The Lion King* shirt from when the stage production had come to Houston and he'd snagged a bit part. His blue eyes are twinkling as he takes a seat on one of the stools at the island and scoops up a handful of almonds I'd set out to snack on.

"What's up, bro? Haven't heard from you since the Pussycat." He leans in conspiratorially. "Did you go home with that hot little reporter? She was *all* over you on the dance floor." He sings the *bow-chicka-bow-wow* song.

I wasn't telling him shit. "Keep your voice down. I don't want people gossiping about us."

He shrugs. "Do you care?"

I scowl. I love Trent, but sometimes he can be obtuse. "Of course, I care. I don't want to make any waves for Stone—or me."

He thinks about it. "Fine then. I'll keep my mouth shut. Carry on with your sautéing of the chicken. I'm hungry."

I dish out the salad in two bowls, creating layers of quinoa, shredded BBQ chicken, leftover grilled corn, and black beans.

Trent dives in, talking between chews. "Have I told you lately how glad I am you love to cook healthy shit for me?"

"It's not shit. It's protein, vegetables, and spices."

He waves me off. "You know what I mean. You make my gluten-free diet amazing. I'm feeling good, no numbness in the joints or IBS—I was an old man before they figured out my allergy. Love you, bro." He pops a bite of avocado in his mouth.

"Just a recipe from my NFL days." I'm not a fancy cook, but I know how to cook healthy.

Trent is guzzling down the salad just as Stone walks in the door. She looks like a pissed off porcupine, ready to pop off a spear if anyone says a word. Her hair is a jumbled mess as if she's put it up and taken it down and few times.

And she's still wearing that damn shirt the monkey busted open.

The entire break room turns to take her in. It's like slo-mo.

Brace yourself, Stone, I mentally send her way, but of course, she isn't a mind reader.

No one has spoken and it's eerily quiet as she halts at the Wang table and runs her eyes over them. She raises her arms, her hands doing the come on gesture. "I know you're dying. Let's hear the smart ass remarks."

"Quite the booby trap you landed in, Becks," calls someone from the back.

"Hey Becks, you're my new breast friend," another one says on a snicker.

"That's one lucky monkey," someone else murmurs.

Savannah's nose is turned up as if she smells bad fish. She stares at Stone. "Did you plan to expose yourself like that?"

Stone throws back her shoulders and glares at the reporter. "Seriously? You think I *told* the monkey to paw me in front of millions?" Her frustration is palpable as she heaves out a long sigh. "No is the answer, in case that wasn't clear to you, Savannah."

"All I'm saying is it was very convenient that your shirt just happened to have a missing button—"

"It. Was. An. Accident," Stone enunciates.

"You don't have to get huffy," Savannah retorts. "It's just we all know you really wanted the Smith case."

Stone's eyes turn to slits. "Who is *we*?"

"Ah, no one. I just meant—"

Stone cuts her off. "Whatever. Speaking of segments, how did the Smith one go? Oh, that's right, I already saw. You stood there in the humid Houston weather and got nada. No verdict yet. You win some, you lose some."

Savannah's face tightens.

"Tell you what, Savannah, next time you can take the monkeys and llamas, and I'll do the courthouse beat." Stone is crossing her arms, her shirt is barely hanging on. One quick glance tells me that every guy at the table has his peepers glued to that straining paper clip.

I'm about to go over there—

"Feeling protective?" Trent asks me. I guess he's reading my face. I nod.

"What's going on?" he asks, his eyes bouncing between me and the table.

I quickly run down what happened on the segment.

His eyebrows are sky high. "Oh, damn. I missed it. I guess they won't reshow it?"

"No, they will not," I say dryly.

His eyes light up. "Doesn't matter. That shit will go viral. I bet it's already on YouTube."

Before I can reply, Marv marches in, his face still red. I wonder how many viewers have called in to complain. "Rebecca!"

She flinches as she turns to face him.

"My office. Now."

Her shoulders wilt and her face falls.

My hands clench.

If he fires her, I will beat the fuck—

"Can I have more chicken?" Trent's voice brings me back.

"Yeah, yeah," I say absently, my eyes on the door as Stone walks out and into the hall. I hear the clicking of her heels as she takes slow steps toward Marv's office.

I can only imagine what's going on in there . . .

Fifteen minutes later she's back in the break room and heading to the box of chocolate donuts we have delivered nightly. The defeated look on her face is killing me.

"Stone, over here," I call. "There's a fan here to see you," I say, nudging my head at Trent who's waving.

"Holla, girlfriend! Come give old Trent a hug! I miss my Pussycat friend." He stands and opens his arms wide. "Plus, I hear you might need one."

Stone comes our way, her face cool. "Hey, Trent." She gives him a quick hug and takes the barstool next to him.

She looks at me.

I look at her.

"Nothing to say?" she asks me. "Aren't you going to make a joke?"

"Haven't you had enough?"

She sighs. "Just say whatever you want to say and get it over with."

I shrug. "Fine. You make the news worth watching. How's that?"

Surprise crosses her face. "Dammit, why do you always say the nicest stuff when you're such an—"

"An incredibly handsome and talented man?"

"He really is," Trent says, chewing. "He made me this salad."

She perks up as she checks out Trent's dish. I quickly mix up another salad and slide it over to where she sits. She stares down at it in bemusement and takes a bite, bliss flitting across her face.

"It's really not fair that you can cook, too," she mutters, taking another big bite.

I laugh and Trent stares at Stone and me as if he's just figuring something out.

A few minutes later they are bonding over the *The Lion King* while I check my phone for any updates in sports. I'm glad they like each other—although I don't know why that's important.

"Are you over Mufasa's death—because I'm not," Stone says as she sips from a Diet Coke she'd pulled from the fridge.

"Right! I mean, I get you need to see Simba grow into his own person—especially when he kills Scar—but Mufasa? TEARS. Breaks my heart every time."

"Me too," she agrees. "So what Disney character is your fav, Cade?"

She's asking me?

I look up from my phone. "I don't watch those movies."

"He's the big sports jock," Trent comments. "Although I recall a few times when he might have indulged in a *Gossip Girl* marathon with me."

"Don't forget *Love Actually*," I say. "You made me go to the theatre with you."

"I suggest you start with *The Little Mermaid*," Stone says to me.

"Why?" I ask.

She shrugs. "I love it. So should everyone else."

"Is there sex in it?"

She fiddles with her drink. "No, silly. He's very handsome—Prince Eric—he even has a cute dog."

"I like cats."

"Really?"

"Yep. I even have one."

"Shut the fuck up."

I cock an eyebrow. "So ladylike."

"Ladies don't show their tits on TV." She gets that defeated look again, and I want her to stop—so I pick at her.

"Is the mermaid a blonde?"

"Redhead."

"Nevermind. Never going to watch it."

She flicks interested eyes over me. "Only blondes for the Killer?"

"All day, everyday."

"Figures. I saw your ex. You like them skinny too?"

"Don't go there, Stone. You won't like my answer. Or maybe you will." My voice is silky.

Trent is watching us with a rapturous expression. "You two are so . . . frisky. I like it. All I need is some popcorn. We def need a Disney marathon. Cade's place, after work. Wanna call Chas?"

"Shut up, Trent," I say.

He laughs.

But Stone isn't done. She's staring at me with an odd light in her eye—as if she enjoys our little run-ins. She eases back on her stool and considers me. "*The Little Mermaid* is about a girl who gives up what she holds most dear—her family and her singing voice—for the man she loves."

I smirk. "And how does that work out for her? Doesn't she get ostracized by her family?"

Stone gasps. "You have seen it!"

"I will neither confirm nor deny."

"Some say it's sexist in how it portrays women, but I don't agree," Trent says, stirring the drama pot—and never one to be left out.

"Why is it sexist?" Now I'm interested.

Stone is perturbed. "The movie is not sexist!"

Trent shrugs. "Beats me."

Stone is shaking her head. "Ariel is empowered and brave and daring—"

"Nice rack?" I interrupt, my gaze hot as it traces the curve of her body. I picture her in a coconut bra. Shit. *That's sexist.* But I can't help it. I fucking want Stone so bad I have a hard-on at work talking about a goddamn mermaid movie.

She ignores me. " . . . for example, Eric *is* the damsel in distress when Ariel rescues him from drowning—"

"That's enough for me. I'd do her. I like a girl who fights for her man." Now I'm just pushing her buttons.

Stone looks flustered. "You can't appreciate it if you haven't actually seen it."

"Then show me." I don't know what I'm talking about now.

"Like I said . . . movie marathon at Cade's tonight," Trent chimes in.

We speak at the same time.

"Shut up," Stone says.

"Give it a rest," I say.

We look at each other and burst out laughing. Something . . . small . . . seems settled between us. I don't know what it is. Maybe she's forgiven me for getting her assigned to the petting zoo debacle or maybe we're just having fun. Whatever. I go with it and grab her another Diet Coke when I see she's empty and looking around. She takes it and smiles. "Wish this was gin and tonic."

I grin. "If it was, this night would end very differently."

She giggles.

The conversation moves from Disney to current events and before I know it, I look up and the entire place is deserted except for the three of us.

Then Trent leaves—and we're completely alone in the quiet room.

We chat for a few minutes longer about inane stuff. It's just regular, mundane conversation—but so fucking comfortable. Before long, I'm sitting next to her on the barstool and our faces are close.

She gives me a thoughtful look. "I had these assumptions about you, but you're so different. You cook. You volunteer to help kids. You have a cat." She bites her lip. "I like it."

The air in the room thickens.

She swallows. "What are you thinking right now?"

I shutter my face. "You really want to know, Stone?"

She nods.

I lean across the island until we're nose-to-nose.

"I want to fuck you again," I say softly.

A small gasp of air comes from her parted lips. "What?"

My lids are heavy as I gaze at her. "We have an hour before I have to be at my desk. We can go to my office right now and shut the door. I'll strip you out of that tight-as-fuck skirt, take your underwear off with my teeth, toss you on my desk, and eat your pussy until you forget your own name. Then, I'll fuck you so hard and good that I'll have to cover your mouth when you scream. And when I'm done, you'll suck your cream off my cock like it's candy."

Her eyes glaze over as she clutches the side of the island. Her chest is rising rapidly.

I smile. "Or we can just finish our drinks here, head on to wherever we're going, and forget I ever said a goddamn word."

Twelve

REBECCA

*W*ITH EVERY WORD from Cade's lips, my scalp grows tighter, and I can't seem to breathe properly. He's watching me, waiting, and I slip off my stool, putting my face right at his chest.

"Cade . . ." His name is a burning wish on my tongue.

He stands, and his scent of warm fires and citrus is all around me, flooding my brain with every memory of our night together. I'm vibrating with need. If he actually did rip my panties off with his teeth, he'd see they're already wet . . .

"Are you with me?" His large hand cups my jaw, and he touches my bottom lip, lightly pulling it with the pad of his thumb.

My mouth falls open, and I can see my breath coming fast. "I-I . . ." I can't seem to form a sentence.

"I want to kiss you." His voice is low, husky.

My lips are heavy with need, and I can't meet his eyes. If I do, I'll forget everything. I'll forget all about anchor positions and good decisions and the future. *Oh, God, I want that kiss so much.*

"Look at me."

My eyes flicker up, and when our gazes clash, it's all over. His mouth covers mine, hard and fast, pushing my lips apart. A little noise escapes my throat, and just as fast, I'm kissing him back, chasing his mouth, hungry for everything him.

My hands are on his face. My fingers scratch through his beard, moving into the sides of his hair, threading in his soft, dark waves. He groans, and it's a shock of sheer pleasure to my core.

Cade Hill is the most amazing kisser. He pulls my top lip between his teeth for a gentle bite before that delicious tongue sweeps inside again to curl with mine. I'm on my tiptoes, holding him, my body burning as I strain into his chest.

His large hands squeeze my arms, pressing my softness against his hard. They move from my shoulder blades down to my narrow waist, farther down to cup my ass. "You feel so good," he murmurs, pulling me flush against him.

I can feel his length straining in his pants, and my knees are liquid.

"Oh, God," I gasp as his mouth moves into my hair, hot breath sending chills skating down my body.

I can't resist. I slide my hand to the front of his pants and rub it up and down over that amazing muscle. I remember riding him. I remember him stretching me, filling me, blowing my mind.

He releases a low groan, and it seems to get bigger.

"We need to go to my office. Now." His hand is on my breast, cupping and squeezing it through the thin fabric. "I want these perfect tits in my mouth. I've wanted them for three days . . . even more since I saw them at six o'clock."

"I had no idea . . ." I try to speak, and he kisses me again. Tongues collide, and I grab his shoulders, holding on through the electric swirl of sexy Cade Hill. Tipping my chin up, I moan as he kisses my neck, that luscious beard scuffing my skin. "You fell asleep on me last time." It's a breathless tease.

"Trust me, it will not happen again."

I start to laugh—it's more of a purr—when I hear a voice that throws ice water all over everything. Marv is speaking loudly and he's headed our way fast.

"Shit," I hiss, pushing out of Cade's arms and turning fast to where our leftover plates sit on the counter. Scooping everything up, I run to the sink and crank up the hot water full blast.

"You don't have to—" Cade starts, and I look over my shoulder at his rumpled shirt, his sexy waves all mussed from where I'd just run my fingers through it.

"Smooth your hair," I say, and he reaches up to comply.

Come on . . . come on . . . Finally the steam starts to rise, and I lean forward, hoping to mask the flush on my cheeks and the bright red scuffmarks I know cover my neck.

"Yes, I talked to her about it," Marv says. "It was clearly an accident. I appreciate that. It's just bad timing on top of . . . I'll call you back."

He's in the room, and I keep my back turned, quickly opening the dishwasher to load it. "Cade," he says. "Savannah said you were back here. You still here, Becks?"

"It's my fault," Cade jumps in. "We were . . . discussing the Deadrick story and possible ideas for coverage. I guess I lost track of time."

"Don't spend too much time on that." Marv's voice is dismissive, and his lecture this afternoon in his office echoes in my mind. *Viewer complaints . . . Indecency during the family hour . . . One more screw-up and you're out.*

I have a hard time breathing through the tightness in my chest. What happened at the zoo today was clearly an accident, and my contract is still in effect—breakable only by gross misconduct or negligence on my part, which will never happen. He can't fire me. Still, he can put me on the bench, give me all the shit stories, and take me out of the running for an anchor's seat, effectively sinking my chances of ever doing anything more than being a reporter, the lowest of the low, one step above being a camera guy.

"You forget, I choose the stories I spend time on." A definite edge is in Cade's voice, and I sneak a glance in their direction.

Both men's brows are lowered, and the muscle in Cade's perfectly square jaw ripples back and forth. I have got to get out of here.

"Either way, we need you in the newsroom. Vicky wants to do a quick rundown of the ten o'clock show. We're shuffling stories around in view of this afternoon's . . . mishap."

"I'll be there in a few minutes," Cade answers. "I'd like to finish up what I'm doing here."

Flipping the door closed on the dishwasher, I scamper to where I left my purse and jacket. "It's okay. I've got to get home."

"Probably for the best," Marv says. "Goodnight, Rebecca."

"Wait—" Cade is moving in my direction, and his tone twists my stomach.

"Goodnight!" I say brightly, not looking back. I'm moving so fast, it's just short of running, and I don't even stop as I pass through the newsroom, not even for Vicky calling out to me. I only wave. "Chat tomorrow!"

I'm out the door, snatching off my heels and full-out sprinting to my Prius. I can't take a chance Cade might follow me. It's a matter of survival, of holding onto my plans. Marv appeared at just the right time to keep me from making another huge mistake. Getting mixed up with my coworker, getting my heart smashed into a million pieces by the Killer, on top of everything else that has happened, it would be the third strike.

I am not going out.

Not without a fight.

"AND THE HITS just keep on coming!" Chas holds a martini glass in one hand, and with the other she does a large swoop straight over her head.

I'm curled on the couch in the fetal position with a pillow tight over my head. "You have absolutely no idea," I moan.

"Cheer up, buttercup! Your breast made prime time! If I were Lady Diana Ross, Miss Mahogany herself, I would give you a tit-check like she did Lil Kim at the VMAs."

"Don't talk about it. I never want to see another petting zoo as long as I live. Or a monkey."

"Then you'd better stay off the Internet for the duration. You've already racked up three million hits on Youtube, and it's only been four hours. You're hotter than that little girl who sang like a tree frog."

"Stop looking at it!"

"I wish I could, but it's like one of those car wrecks, or a drive-by shooting—a drive-by boobing."

Slowly pushing up on the couch, I smooth my hair. "It's one of the hazards of doing live coverage . . . like being a reporter in a war zone. Sometimes bombs go off. I was simply doing my job, and the wildlife got out of control."

"Mm-hm." Chas takes another sip. "I keep telling you no children, no animals. These are very basic rules of show business."

"It seemed like a fun idea!" Leaning forward, I rub my hands over my face. "How was I to know Pixie was an octopus? A hairy, brown, pink-bow-wearing date rapist."

"She's a mon-key!" My roommate drags out the syllables. "Didn't you hear about that woman in New York whose pet monkey went nuts and nearly ate her face off? You took your *life* in your *hands* holding that thing."

"Good lord, Chas!" Frowning, I look up at her. She's wrapped in a hot-pink satin robe and on her head is a cream-colored turban.

"Oh, sweetie, really with that frown. Think of your forehead."

Lifting my eyebrows, I shake it off. Just then our enormous flatscreen TV returns from commercial, and Cade Hill fills the frame in all his sexy, dark-brown, blue-eyed deliciousness. I fall onto my side again, hugging the faux-mink pillow against the ache in my stomach. "Pixie's not the half of my problem," I whimper.

"I'm doomed."

"Shew! That is one sexy sportscaster. That's gotta be great for ratings." Chas fans a hand in front of her face. "Tell me what's got you so doomed."

It's no use covering this up. Besides, if anybody can help me out of this bed I keep trying to fall into, my roommate tops the list. "I can't keep my fucking hands off him."

"Him . . ." Cade's dark eyes move to the side then a huge, white smile splits her cheeks. "HIM! Oh, yes, you know that's right."

"No! It's not right! Marv almost caught me climbing him like a tree this evening."

She's bouncing in place, laughing. "Once you get a taste, there's no going back."

That makes me sit up fast. "Stop bouncing—I have to go back! I have to stop this. It's the perfect ammunition Marv is looking for to kill my shot at the anchor chair."

"Why would he do that? You're the most experienced reporter up there."

"He wants to give it to Savannah Winston."

"Savannah Winston!" Eyes, mouth, Chas's whole face is an *O*. "That little blonde airhead? You know I heard her say *loof-leaf* instead of loose-leaf paper during a back-to-school story?"

In spite of it all, I snort. "You did not."

"I did!" Chas shouts, but I'm skeptical.

"You're just making that up, or she got tongue-tied. Nobody says *loof*-leaf."

"Well, she did call the poor citizens of Ghana *Gonorrheans* on a live broadcast."

"She did not!" I'm laughing harder now. "That was a lady from your church talking about a mission trip."

"Oh, that's right," my roommate nods. "Shirley Faye never was the brightest bulb in the makeup mirror. Still, she's better than that little girl pretending to be a newswoman."

This time, I lean over, placing my head on Chas's shoulder. "Thanks."

"Your boob was totally ready for prime time, by the way. No wonder that sexy sportsman wants to buy *everything* you're selling."

Taking a deep breath, I do a little growl through my exhale. "How did my life get so fucked up, Chas? I used to have it all together. This is all James's fault. He threw me off my game."

We sit in silence watching Cade on mute. I'm mesmerized by his full lips moving like pink pillows in a sexy sea of brown beard. I remember scratching my fingernails up his cheeks, and every tiny hair on my body rises at the memory of his kisses.

"Ugh!" I groan, scrubbing my hands over my eyes. "I've got to get him out of my head."

"James?" Chas is rightfully disgusted.

"No! Cade."

She kicks out her feet and leans forward, scooping up her silver MacBook Air. "Here's what we're going to do." Her long, brown fingers fly over the keys, and I watch the screen as it flickers to life with pictures of couples smiling into each other's faces, embracing, doing everything but skipping.

"What is this?"

"Let's get started!" Chas says in her best game show announcer voice. "Tell me a little about what you're looking for in a man."

"What. The fuck."

"Rebecca Fieldstone." My drag bestie turns those enormous doe eyes on me. "The best way to get over a man is to get under a new one. We're going to shake your mind loose from James and Cade."

Pushing off the sofa, I start to leave the room. "I am NOT going out with some weirdo you find on the Internet."

Chas grabs my wrist, stopping me. "That is a very medieval attitude. Don't you know that most people who meet on Hookup4Luv. com wind up married?"

"I do not want to get married!"

"Sit down."

She gives me a gentle tug, and I plop on the sofa beside my satin-clad roomie to see what in the world is about to happen.

"Do you want children?"

"No."

"Ever?"

"One day . . . just not today!" Not until I've landed that anchor spot.

"What are your political views?"

"Seriously?"

"Very liberal . . ."

"I don't want to go out with anyone crazy political."

"Nonconformist?"

"That'll pull up every patchouli-wearing hippie—"

"Ultraconservative."

My eyes narrow, and I watch as my roomie chooses *middle of the road*. "They don't have journalism on here as a career option. I'll choose creative-slash-performance. That nip slip definitely qualifies."

"My eyes can't narrow any more."

"Thank heavens for that or you'd definitely need a nip-tuck."

I watch, mesmerized as she continues entering information about hair color, body type, activities I like and don't like, until we finally get to the part where possible matches pop up. A screen of headshots appears, and my stomach sinks.

"I don't like the looks of any of them."

"We have to go deeper." Chas is on a mission, but I'm completely skeptical. "Ah, yes. Here we go. What about this? Phil is five-ten to six foot, non-religious. He loves television and is a fan of several series . . ." She nods and raises an eyebrow. "A TV fan is a big plus. Oh, look. He's pointing to a whiteboard. He does presentations. He reminds me of that Dwight Schrute fellow on *The Office*."

"Gross! Dwight is not hot."

"Did I say Dwight? I meant Jim, when he was doing his Dwight impersonation."

"That was not a good look for Jim. I don't like that look."

"Stop being difficult."

I don't like any of this. As much as I want to be open, I can't help comparing Whiteboard Phil to Cade's deep dimples, wavy dark hair, the beard, the abs . . ."I don't know, Chassy. I'm not feeling it."

My roommate shifts to face me. "You're done with James?"

"Yes." I can't answer that question fast enough.

"You can't go out with Cade?"

My chin drops, and I don't answer that question so fast. My fingers twist together, and I feel this weight pulling down from the center of my chest. It hurts. "It's more like dating him would give Marv another reason to demote me."

"So you need a transitional man."

My nose wrinkles, and I look up at her. "What?"

"A rebound guy. You don't want Cade to be your rebound guy once you finally get over yourself and go out with him, do you? You want it to last, don't you?"

"Of course . . . not?" I'm confused by the question, although, somehow I'm not convinced stringing poor Phil along is the correct answer either.

"Then I'm giving Phil the swipe right, and you'll have dinner with him this weekend."

"Wait!" It's too late. My roommate's long fingers have already clicked on the screen, bringing up the *Contact Made!* message. "Chas! Why did you do that?"

"Cool your tits. It's just dinner. You don't have to sleep with him." More eyebrow waggling. "Unless you want to."

"I don't!" I only want to sleep with one man in this entire city, and as much as I don't want to believe it, it's very possible I'm just a rebound for him as well. I don't even know when Cade broke up with his ex-fiancée. Maybe Chas is right.

"It's late, cupcake!" Chas bends down to kiss my temple. "Hit

the feathers or you'll look like Bette Davis tomorrow, the Baby
Jane years."

"Thanks." My voice contains absolutely zero sincerity, but it
doesn't matter. My roommate flounces to her room, and I'm sitting
looking at the picture of Whiteboard Phil.

Poor Phil, with his mustard shirt and glasses, pointing so ear-
nestly at his presentation. He doesn't deserve this.

A sudden buzz on my phone makes me jump, and I scoop it up
to see a text. *You ran out so fast. We never had a chance to talk.*

It's Cade, and the flood of joy and heat surging through my chest
takes my breath away. My fingers tremble as I text back.

Sorry. Reality set in at the sound of Marv's voice.

Fucking Marv, he texts.

I want to smile, but instead I press my lips together. My eyes
heat, my entire body is heavy, but I know what I have to do.

It was for the best, I text. *We can't do that again.*

Several minutes pass. My phone is silent, and I don't even see
the three little bouncing dots, meaning he's writing a reply. The
knot in my throat twists tighter.

He finally responds. *What are you saying?*

I take a deep breath and let it out slowly. I'm being pretty pre-
sumptive, but at the same time, it's who I am. I don't do casual
hookups, and if I'm just another notch on Killer's bedpost . . .

We can't see each other right now. It will only complicate things.

My bottom lip goes between my teeth, and I blink several times.
I think about Chas's warnings. I think about what I want, and I think
about rebound guys. I think about wanting it to last . . . If there
even is an *it* for me to worry about protecting.

I need a little space. Time to think, I add.

Again, silence. No dots. Nothing. I wait for several seconds longer, until I finally decide that's it. Killer isn't about waiting. It hurts like a kick to the stomach, but I push on my legs to stand, walking slowly to the bathroom where I'll brush my teeth, wash my face, do the ritual, prepare for bed . . .

I'm halfway there when my phone buzzes in my hand, making me jump.

I lift it, and two words glow in the darkness.

I'll wait.

Thirteen

CADE

I WAKE UP at eight on Saturday for my usual weekend jog through the park. I keep my eyes open for Stone in case she decides to come for a run. The early October air is crisp and the leaves are just starting to turn a golden hue. I'm thankful for the reprieve from the humidity, but disappointed there's no curvy blonde with a smart mouth in the vicinity.

I stop running near a lake and bend over to catch my breath. I replay what happened between us in the kitchen. I can't let it get that far next time.

So why am I pulling out my phone and calling her?

I lean against a stone bridge in the park and wait for her to answer.

"Whoever this is . . . you've reached hell. Go away." Her voice is husky and scratchy from sleep.

"Wake up, Stone."

I hear a sharp intake of air and scrambling around as if she's sitting up in bed.

She clears her throat. "Cade? What? Why?"

I grunt. "You're a mess in the morning."

"I-I didn't sleep well last night."

"Ah. Couldn't stop thinking about Pixie?"

"That and other things." She pauses and I wonder if *I'm* the reason she didn't sleep. "I dreamed I was on a planet ruled by crazy smart monkeys—"

"*Planet of the Apes?*"

"Yeah. I hate monkeys now."

I grin for no apparent reason.

"And get this . . . apparently someone posted the Pixie footage to my mom's Facebook page. I'm the laughing stock of my entire family."

I hear the anxiety in her tone. "You can't control what happened. It's done. Just move on and be better today. Show the world how talented you are. I believe in you, Stone."

There's a pause. "Can you call me every morning for a pep talk?" She laughs softly. "So what's up?"

I exhale. "I need you. Today."

"Oh?" Her voice is slightly breathless.

"Yeah." Then I explain to her what I have in mind, and once she agrees to meet me, I'm flying, my mind jumping with how to work this in her favor.

Professionally. That's all. Nothing else.

Because she'd asked for space, and I'd said I'd give it to her. Besides, I'm not a fan of rejection. Been there and done that with Maggie Grace.

We make our plans and by ten, I'm showered and in the Escalade on my way to Deadrick High School.

I park my car and jog over to the field where about several players are either running short plays or stretching. It's recovery day since the Wildcats played the night before. I'd missed it because of work, but Hart had sent me the video early this morning and I'd skimmed through it quickly before my jog.

Hart waves me over to where he's surrounded by the first string offense as they work on a quarterback sneak. He's a Goliath of a man with a slightly crooked nose from too many hits. He's got the biggest heart of anyone I know, which explains why he settled in Houston after retirement to teach in the poorest district he could find. His wife Marquetta is from the area.

He calls out a break and the guys run in all directions.

"Great game last night," I tell him. "Twenty-four to ten and you beat the best team in the district. I smell state championship."

"Don't jinx it, Killer. We're close, so close." He grimaces. "These kids need something good. Cheetah's mom was arrested last week on a drug charge. I don't know how the kid keeps his shit together."

"He's got you."

Hart shrugs.

He's telling me about the game just as Cheetah jogs over. A lanky Hispanic quarterback, he's grinning the entire way and already talking before he reaches us.

"Did you see me throw it in for sixty yards? Did you see the Hail Mary at the end? Dude. It. Was. Sick." He bounces around me and we bump fists. "I swear, man, it was that tight way you showed me how to throw the ball. Worked. Fu-freaking worked." His eyes go behind me. "You brought the news with you! Damn, I mean dang, this shiz is real."

Hart watches as Kevin and Stone walk over from the parking lot. Kevin's toting the camera and Stone is in front of him, notebook in hand. She waves at us and I grin. Marv can suck it. The school needs the attention, which might result in funding for other things besides athletics. This *is* a kick ass story, and it doesn't hurt to get some film in until I decide what to do with it.

Wearing an orange skirt and a tight matching sweater and heels, she makes her way over to us. Judging by how quiet the field is, I get the feeling I'm not the only one appreciating the swish of her hips. Her honey-colored hair is down and swinging around her shoulders.

Seeing her here, my chest automatically expands.

"Is that Rebecca Fieldstone?" Cheetah asks, his eyes wide. "Did you see her tit when that—"

I elbow him hard. "Don't bring up the monkey."

He nods. "You like her, huh?"

"I do," I say almost absently as she comes to a halt in front of us.

"Cade," she says and smiles. "Thank you for inviting us to come down." She focuses on Hart, her eyes sweeping over his broad expanse. "You must be Coach Williams. Cade has nothing but great things to say about you."

"Glad to have you. Maybe we can create some excitement for the school." He inclines his burly head.

Earlier, I'd called him on the way over to prep him for KHOT doing some field reporting to keep for a later story. He'd been enthusiastically on board.

The other players are back from their break and gathering around us as Hart makes the introductions.

While Cheetah and I head down the field to practice passing, Stone and Kevin set up an interview spot near the sidelines with the ramshackle stadium in the background. I hear the melody of her voice as she talks to Hart. Laughter spills from their direction as she interviews some of the kids. She directs Kevin on angles and they bounce ideas off each other. She's good at what she does in a genuine way that's often missing in real news. She's relatable—obviously. Plus, she's fucking sexy—

Stop it right there. Nip it.

I'm working with Cheetah on his passing game when the duo make their way over to us. Stone's eyes are transfixed as I take a few steps back and toss the football down the field. Cheetah mimics me, trying to perfect his pass. Kevin films for about ten minutes as we work. Still . . . Stone doesn't take her gaze off me.

I wrap up with Cheetah and walk over to them. Kevin is fiddling with the camera and headed to the van.

"Finally alone," she murmurs. "Thank you for this. It's going to be a great story."

I nod. "You're welcome. You're a natural. The kids love you."

She nods and shifts, fidgeting, her eyes searching mine as if waiting for me to say something, but I don't.

My phone pings from my shorts, and I pull it out.

Personal crisis. Come over after practice for lunch? It's not my cancer so don't worry. It's about a girl.

What the hell? My brow furrows. *Personal crisis? A girl?*

I'm intrigued.

"Who's that?" Stone asks, her tone inquisitive.

I glance up. Damn, she's pretty. "No one."

Her eyes narrow. "Is it your ex?"

"Jealous?" I can't stop my grin.

"No."

"Liar."

She pouts and my grin widens into a chuckle. "Don't worry, gorgeous. It's my mom."

"I'm not worried about your ex! Please." Concern flits across her face. "Everything okay with your mom?"

I nod. "I think so. She wants me to come over."

She stares up at me and clears her throat. "Well, thank you for today. It meant a lot just to get me out of the house and back in the swing of things. You're right. I can't let anything stop me from doing what I love. If you want, after you see your mom, maybe we can have coffee somewhere—just to talk about the story . . ."

"The last time we said we were going to have coffee, we ended up in your bed," I say quietly.

She blushes.

I get another ping.

My mom has sent another text, and it's a picture of a gorgeous brunette. I study it, confused as hell.

What is going on with Mom?

I need to go.

I glance back up to Stone and she's watching me, a pensive look on her face.

"Stone? You good?"

She nods.

"Rain check on the coffee? I need to check on Mom. I'll see you Monday at the station?"

Another nod.

"You got plans tonight?" I ask. My hands clench at the thought of her seeing someone, but that's utterly ridiculous. Jealousy is for losers.

She blows out a breath. "No. I'll probably just go home, eat some tacos, and hit the sack early."

I almost say that I'll call her later—or stop by—but my brain is determined to keep her at a distance. *Give her space.*

I nod and walk away, saying my goodbyes to the kids and jogging to my SUV.

Half an hour later, I'm sitting outside on my mom's patio in the prestigious River Oaks neighborhood.

Petite and soft-spoken with a husky drawl, she's the single reason I still speak to my father. She still sees good in him, even though she left him a year after the Trent debacle.

She pours me a glass of tea and brings it over to me. I give her new hair that's just coming back in an affectionate rub.

"You don't have to wait on me," I tell her and she waves me off.

"Don't be silly. I made you rush over here."

She positions a plate in front of me with a huge turkey and cheese sandwich with a side of her famous fried green tomatoes.

I arch my brow as she takes the seat across from me. "You're buttering me up for something. It can't be too pressing or you would have told me already."

She takes a sip of her tea. "You're right. I need a favor."

"Hmm, so this is more than just planting a clematis outside your kitchen window?"

She squishes up her face as if dreading what's going to come out of her mouth. "I need you to go to dinner tonight with a friend's daughter."

I squint at her. "A blind date? Mom . . ." My voice is full of dread.

The girl in the photo.

"I know, I know, you hate them. But I *really* owe this girl's mom—we were suitemates in college and I may have accidentally stolen one of her boyfriends. It broke her heart, and she's never let me forget it. She called this morning telling me about her daughter who's just moved to Houston. Apparently, she's very lonely and not used to the big city."

She keeps talking, her voice in a rush as if the faster she talks the quicker she can convince me. "She's the sweetest thing—

"Great personality?"

Mom half-snorts. "Stop. She's beautiful. You saw the picture I sent?"

I'd halfway looked at it. I sigh my displeasure. "The game's tonight and I really want to watch it."

She smiles. "Please. You and I both know you can DVR that. Come on. I promise I won't ask you to go out with anyone else—although it sure would be nice to have some grandkids soon. You're so dang picky, Cade, and you're not getting any younger."

"I'm thirty!"

She grins and shrugs. "Also, Maggie Grace called. She seemed so . . . contrite about what happened between you two. Maybe you two could try again?"

I settle back in the chair. "I'm not calling Maggie Grace."

She nods. "Well, if that ship has sailed, why not try with someone else?"

Stone?

No. I can't.

But . . .

It *is* Saturday night, and what else did I have to do? *What could the harm be?* Get in, get out, and then watch the game in bed. Alone.

In retrospect, my life is pretty fucking lame.

I glance at Mom and exhale. "I'll do the blind date, but don't do it again. I refuse to be your Get Out Of Jail Free Card just because I'm hot and single." I wiggle my brows at her.

She claps her hands, a glint of excitement in her eyes. "I'm so excited! You never know, you just might meet your match tonight!"

By the time I leave, I have the digits to a girl named Sissy from Oklahoma in my phone and I'm meeting her at Paulette's, a fancy French bistro. I try to get myself stoked.

You just might meet your match.

Right. I'm pretty sure that's already happened.

I'M PLEASANTLY SURPRISED when I walk in and find Sissy at the bar. She's pretty with long brown hair and big eyes. Wearing a short green dress with a plunging neckline, she stands as I approach and throws her arms around me.

As far as blind dates go, I've hit the fucking lottery. I can do this.

"Nice to meet you. I hear our moms are dear friends," I say.

She flutters long lashes and gushes. "Thank goodness. I don't know the first thing about Houston and meeting *you* is such a treat. I'm a huge college football fan—went to OU."

Then she sings the fight song.

"I'm Sooner born and Sooner bred and when I die, I'll be Sooner dead! Rah Oklahoma! Rah Oklahoma! OU! Boomer Sooner! Boomer Sooner . . ."

I wince. It's not that I don't like enthusiasm, but I'm a Longhorn and the Sooners are our number two rival behind the Aggies. Also, she's a bit shrill.

The maître d' finally escorts us to our seats near the back of the restaurant. I pull out her chair, and she smiles up at me. "I love this place. It's so romantic—like marriage proposal romantic." She sighs.

My entire body draws up. "Uh, yeah. If you say so."

We settle in with the menus while she talks about growing up in a large family with four brothers. She's the youngest and spends her free time knitting hats and blankets for her local orphanage. Nice.

Our waiter arrives, a young man who sweeps appreciative eyes over Sissy. I request a Jameson on the rocks.

"And for you, miss?"

Sissy sends him a blinding smile. "What do you recommend?"

He grins, clearly liking her attention. "We have an excellent lemon martini. Our customers rave about it."

"Sold! I'll have it—make it a double please with sugar on the rim. Also, I'd *love* a shot of Silver Patron. Cade, you interested in celebrating with me? It's not often I get away from work to go on a real date."

"I'll celebrate with my Jameson."

Shots make me think of Stone. I focus back on Sissy.

I turn back to her as the waiter scurries off. "So what brings you to Houston?"

"I'm a worm poop girl." She giggles.

"Oh?"

"Well, the scientific term is *vermiculturist*."

"Fascinating." I keep my face impassive.

Our drinks arrive and she throws back the tequila and then starts with the martini. "It's okay. Most people have never heard of it, but I thought maybe you'd done your research on me like I did you."

My stalker radar is up and tuned in.

"I Googled you." She wiggles her fingers at me. "Number One Bachelor in the city according to the *Houston Herald*. And now that I've met you in person, I agree." Her gaze drifts over my face. "Any interest in settling down soon?"

I cough. "No." I take a big drink of whiskey. "So . . . tell me about the worms."

"Lemme get another shot first." She waves at the waiter and points at her empty shot glass. She clears her throat as if settling in for a long talk. "A vermiculturist is someone who manages worms to convert waste products, such as uneaten food, grass clippings, and spoiled fruit and vegetables into healthy, nutrient-rich soil and organic fertilizer." She smiles prettily. "I know that sounds all scientific, but basically, worm poop is gold. Plus, it's on trend. Everyone's eating organic. Farmers love it. Moms love it."

She chews on a breadstick, but all I see are worms in my head.

I search for a topic change, but she's still talking.

" . . . and Red Wigglers, the big fat ones are unparalleled as soil excavators. They spend their lives ingesting, grinding, digesting, and excreting soil—"

"Mind blowing," I say, interrupting her as the waiter drops off her shot. "What else are you interested in?"

It's like she doesn't hear me.

"Here look at this." She shoves her phone in my face and shows me a picture. It's a blurry image of a reddish brown blob.

"What am I looking at?"

"That's Wally! He was my first worm—dead now. Their life span is only a few months." A tear shimmers in her eyes.

What the fuck.

"Do you need to compose yourself?" Like in the restroom—far away from me.

She shakes her head and smiles. "No, it's fine. It's just . . . he started the company and now we're the most successful worm farmers in the Southwest. We owe him everything." She munches on another breadstick. "People get squeamish about worms, but to me, they're like people who sacrifice themselves for the greater good."

"Uh-huh. How's the knitting going—for the orphanage? Do you make hats or blankets?"

But it's too late. She's in full-on worm mode.

" . . . slime is what we call their secretions, which is nitrogen, an important plant food . . ."

I think about the game. I consider dashing to the restroom to check the score.

"... best thing to feed them is kitchen scraps. Amazing, right?"

"Totally," I murmur.

Where the hell is the waiter? I'm waving at him.

"... worms will love you if you blend their food in a mixer." She pauses. "I'm not boring you, am I?"

"No."

I'm saved by the waiter who's returned. He runs down the specials. "Would you like to start with an appetizer?"

I turn to Sissy, and I can't resist the words I say. "Escargot sound good?"

Sissy sputters—but at least she's quiet.

I forget about my date and everything else when I see Stone walking into Paulette's—with some dark-haired dude.

My hands clench around the menu and my nose flares in distaste. *Who the fuck is he?*

I can't think straight, and I don't remember what Sissy or the waiter say. All I see is Stone and her companion being led through the dining area and given a table several feet away from us. I watch them talk for several minutes as my date continues lecturing about poop. Sissy let's out a laugh, and Stone's eyes meet mine.

The entire room disappears.

Fourteen

REBECCA

YOU KNOW THAT pain in your chest when your heart literally stops beating? It's exactly how I feel this evening when my eyes land on Cade's. He's here, in Paulette's, with another woman, another completely different woman, who is also completely gorgeous. I'm pissed and angry and hurt, and I really want the ground to open and for him to fall right down the crack and burst into flames.

But let me back up to earlier today . . .

After spending the most amazing time with him this morning, watching him work with inner-city kids, coaching them and encouraging them, I'd fallen for Cade in a completely new way. He's not just sweet to his family, he and his football buddy Hart are really dedicated to helping these kids break the cycle of poverty and disenfranchisement surrounding them. They're heroes.

Kevin has so much amazing footage, and I have so many great notes. I could barely take my eyes off Cade the entire morning, and not just because he's so fucking hot in his tee, throwing passes, muscles flexing, Mr. Big swinging low in those long shorts, taunting me with dirty promises of mind-blowing orgasms.

He really cares, and it's so refreshing and so sexy. At one point, he'd caught my eye and given me a wink. It was my signature move, and it made me laugh. It made my entire body warm, and I'd returned to my apartment with rainbow clouds floating around my head and dreams of white picket fences and little dark-haired boys playing with their daddy.

It's ridiculous, I know, but I'm pretty sure I ovulated more than once this morning.

"Girl, you need to get in here and get ready." Chas is at the door waiting. "Your date is tonight at eight."

"Tonight!" I shriek, all dreams of having Cade's babies gone. "What have you done?"

"Apparently, clicking *make contact* means Wonder Hookup Powers Activate!" She's leading me to my bedroom and tearing through the hangers in my closet. "Look at all these wire hangers. Mommie Dearest would be apoplectic."

"I'm having second thoughts about Phil—"

"No!" Chas looks over her shoulder at me, eyes wide. "You can't blow him off or he'll leave a bad review and you'll be ostracized."

Now I'm pissed. "You go out with him!" I sit on my bed, slamming my hands beside me.

My roommate turns and levels her gaze on me. "Now you know good and well Whiteboard Phil would stroke out if all this fabulousness met him at the door. He might anyway. You are the *tit*-tular queen of Houston."

"Not. Funny." It's just short of a growl, and Chas's shoulders drop.

She crosses the room to sit beside me on the bed. "I confess, I might have accidentally accelerated this one." Reaching up, she slides my hair behind my shoulder. "I'm not familiar with this site. All my hookups are on Grindr, and it's very clear what's happening and when."

"We just have to call him and let him know we had a technological glitch. We didn't understand how the program operated."

Chas's face brightens, and she gives me a dazzling smile. "Does this mean you're going to start dating that sexy sportscaster? It will be so nice having him around the place."

That weight pulls through my chest again, and my chin drops. In spite of my revelation this morning, none of my reasons for maintaining distance have changed.

"No," I say quietly.

"Then I don't understand. Why would you crush poor Whiteboard Phil's dreams if you're just going to sit at home and date no one?"

Here we go. "I'm not crushing his dreams. He doesn't even know me."

My roommate's eyes narrow. "Have you seen Whiteboard Phil? Trust me, Rebecca Fieldstone will be the highlight *of his life.*" She rolls out *life* as if it's the Lipsync for Your Life round of *Drag Race*.

"It will not," I grumble.

All I get is The Look.

"Stop it, Chassy. I'm not going out with Phil. It's just mean."

My roommate's voice changes to patient instruction. "Buttercup, you don't understand the point of dating apps. You get twelve new possible dates *a day*. It's all about getting out there, enjoying life, embracing the possibilities!"

"Using all the colors in the crayon box?"

"That's it!" Chas claps. "Now get in there and get gorgeous!"

With a sigh, I go to the closet.

THE NICE THING about Hookup4Luv is I'm meeting Whiteboard Phil at the restaurant. Paulette's is actually a classy French bistro, which is a check mark in the good column for Phil. The only problem is I don't see him anywhere.

"Do you have a reservation?" The perky, black-clad hostess looks up at me with a smile, and her face instantly changes. "Have we met before?"

Shit shit shit! I'm sure she recognizes me from that stupid YouTube clip of Pixie dragging my boob out, but she hasn't put two and two together yet.

Moving us right along. I slide my hand down the front of my red silk dress and clear my throat. "I'm meeting someone named Phil Byars? Is he here yet?"

She's studying me, searching for who I am, but just as fast a man swirls up from behind me, grasping my wrist and lifting it, pressing our palms together, fingers spread in a strange *V.*

"Rebecca Fieldstone?" His voice is swift and direct, like he's telling me rather than asking.

"Wha—"

"Rebecca Fieldstone!" the little hostess practically shouts.

My face snaps to hers, and I cut her off with one word: "No."

"NuqneH!" The man coughs . . . sneezes?

"Gesundheit," I say.

He's still gripping my wrist, pressing our palms together, so I give mine a pull. He releases me, and ice blue eyes sear into mine. "I am Phil Byars."

"You are?"

He's clean-shaven and wearing slacks and a long-sleeved shirt. With his dark hair tied up in a man-bun, I see tattoos rising out of his collar all around his neckline.

"You look . . . different."

He smiles, revealing straight white teeth. "I use a fake profile picture."

"I don't understand."

He sweeps an arm toward the dining area, and I notice more tattoos peeking out from his wristbands. "Let's have drinks."

"B-but . . ." I look quickly from the smirking hostess to Not Whiteboard Phil.

"Right this way." The girl grabs two menus and takes off into

THE LAST *Guy*   125

the restaurant.

My stomach is squirmy, and I feel trapped. New Phil isn't bad looking—he looks like the lead singer of a metal band or that magician guy in Vegas. But why did he sneeze on me? Was that a hex?

We're led to a table in the middle of the somewhat crowded restaurant. I notice Phil's ass isn't too bad in his black jeans. He's too skinny, and when he turns to face me, our eyes are level. He isn't very tall.

"Here you go, *Miss Fieldstone!*" The hostess emphasizes my name, and I give her the death glare.

My date studies me curiously as we sit. "Do you know her?"

Is it possible he's the last man on Earth who hasn't seen my boob on live TV? "I . . . uh . . . I work for KHOT News."

"Ah . . ." He lifts his chin. "The enemy of the people."

"I'm sorry?"

I'm interrupted by our waiter. "Welcome to Paulette's! What can I start you off with?"

I answer fast. "Martini, double, and keep 'em coming."

"Of course, Miss Fieldstone." My eyes cut up, and he gives me a signature wink. My face flames hot. "And for you, sir?"

"Corona."

"Of course. Your bread and water will be right out."

Phil leans back in his chair, and his fingers form a steeple in front of his mouth, chunky silver rings on most of them. I decide to take this bull by the horns. I'm a reporter after all.

"So you have a fake profile picture. What's that about? Witness protection program?"

"Nothing so elaborate." He turns serious, scooting forward, dark brow clutched. "I grew tired of the superficiality, of women only responding to my picture. They only wanted the exterior, this mortal shell."

"Okay . . ." I'm still on the fence about calling an Uber. If he tries to blackball me, I'll claim deception. I thought I was dating

Dwight Schrute, not Criss Angel. "But it takes time to get to know someone, right?"

His eyes move up and down my body. "What if I were only interested in you for your height, your directness, your sturdy build?"

Did he just call me *sturdy*? I lean back as the server puts my drink in front of me. As soon as it's down, I take a huge gulp of the pine tree-flavored beverage.

"Would you like to order?" the man asks, and I look to Phil.

"Give us a minute," my date says, and I nod.

"I'll have one more of these while we're thinking."

The waiter nods and disappears, and I stare at my date a moment, waiting for the martini to hit me. Once more Phil holds up his hand in that weird salute. His first two fingers are stuck together and his ring finger and pinkie finger are stuck together, with a deep V in the middle.

"Is that the universal sign for spread your legs?" I snort a little laugh. It's possible my martini is kicking in now.

His dark brow furrows. "It's the *Star Trek* salute. It means 'Live long and prosper.'"

"Oh," I nod, taking another sip, holding up my hand. "Shama lama lakum."

"Most people don't know the Star Trek franchise is based on a whole universe of novels by Gene Roddenbury. He wrote galactic civilizations, complete with customs, languages, fashions . . ."

"So you're a Trekkie." It's not really a question, more an acknowledgment that Fate hates me—as if I didn't already know this.

Loud female laughter echoes from the other side of the room, and I automatically glance in that direction. When I see the source, I almost drop my drink. I almost forget my own name. Right here, in the middle of Paulette's, Cade Hill is sitting across the table from Miss Universe Brazil or something. She's long and lean with silky brown hair and smooth, caramel skin. She's a freakin supermodel, and Cade had said he was spending time with his mother. *Liar!*

Quickly, I regain my footing and focus on Phil. I'll be damned if Cade Hill thinks I'm going to sit here and brood over him while he's over there having a ball with some brunette Giselle Bündchen. Criss Angel and I are about to have ten times as much fun.

"I've been a Trekkie most of my life," he continues, and I study him thinking. I suppose some . . . very special girl would find this appealing. I simply have to channel her.

"Qapla!" he says loudly, and I jump back.

"Kerplah?" I'm pretty sure that's the sound my boob made when it fell out on camera.

He grins. "It's the Klingon word for success."

I cut my eyes up, putting on my best sex-kitten face. "Is Klingon the only foreign language you know?"

"I can speak a bit of Romulan."

Of course, he can. "Is that what you said in the foyer?" I try to imitate the snorty-cough sound he made, and he chuckles.

Good. I want him to laugh. I want him to laugh and laugh like I'm the greatest date in all of Houston—because who says I'm not?

He does the noise again. "NuqneH! Is the traditional Klingon greeting."

Heaven help me. I've got to steer us to a topic I can follow. "Do you play any instruments?"

"No, although, I am learning to play the theremin."

I sneak a glance and see Cade smiling that ridiculous, deep-dimpled smile, and Wonder Woman leans back and laughs as if he just said the funniest thing in the world. My nose wrinkles.

"I've never heard of that." Another martini magically appears before me, and I scoop it up, taking a long drink. "What's a theremin?"

"It's an early electronic musical instrument controlled without physical contact."

I give up. *Of all the things* . . . Who would have known Hard Rock Phil is even more of a geek than Whiteboard Phil? *Dig deeper, Rebecca.*

"Okay . . ." I look around, avoiding Cade's table. "So Klingons are the little guys with the weird ears and the pointy teeth?"

Phil's eyes light, and I get a huge smile. "Those are Ferengis! You are familiar with *Star Trek*!"

"I think so . . . but I mix those guys up with the Orcs."

His enthusiasm dims only slightly. "They're actually part of the Tolkien mythology."

"That's *Game of Thrones*?" I take another, longer sip.

"*Game of Thrones* is George R.R. Martin." Phil shakes his head. "*Lord of the Rings* is J. R. R. Tolkien."

"So many *Rs*. Are they related?"

"Not that I'm aware . . ." Phil clears his throat and forges on. "As far as fantasy humanoids go, Orcs are possibly the most sophisticated, with their base of operations in the Misty Mountains, Morder and Isengard . . ."

Holy space balls. I look around and catch Cade's eyes staring right at us. It's like a lightening strike to my core, and I snap back to Phil.

"Oh, my goodness!" I say loudly, reaching across to cover his hand with mine. "That's so funny!"

He pulls back, confused. "Sauron and Saruman are actually the worst villains in the entire trilogy."

"Their names are *sour*!" I smile bigger, giving his hand a slow, affectionate stroke.

"Yes, I suppose that's true . . ." He takes a slow sip of his beer and watches me as if *I'm* the one saying a bunch of crazy shit.

I'm about to ask about Klingon villains when I feel the heat of bodies near the table. I look up to see Cade and his Amazonian princess standing right beside us. The look in Cade's eyes could laser-decapitate Phil the Fantasy Nerd.

"Hello, Stone, funny seeing you here." A definite edge is in his voice, and it pisses me off. He's got a lot of nerve.

"I was just thinking the same thing," I say, meeting his tone and raising it. "I thought you were visiting your mother."

"You know him, too?" Phil's eyebrows rise.

"We work together," Cade and I answer simultaneously.

"You're Rebecca Fieldstone!" The impossibly beautiful woman at Cade's side says, and I brace myself for a boob comment. She shakes my hand. "I'm Sissy. I just loved the report you did last year on the fossilized remains of the ichthyosaur they found in Del Rio! It was a huge part of the reason I wanted to move here."

"Is that so . . ." My eyes drift to Cade's.

"Sissy is a vermiculturist," he says in a superior tone, as if everybody knows what the hell that is.

"Ah!" my date interjects. "You study the conversion of waste and dead tissue into organic material by earthworms. Very specialized work!"

"That's right!" Sissy moves closer to Phil.

Cade pulls my attention right back to him. "I thought you were eating tacos and going to bed early."

Again, my face flames red. I never should have told him that.

"You like tacos?" Phil cries. "I know the best place for tacos in all of Houston!"

"What?"

He's up and digging in his jeans, and I'm looking from my half-finished martini to him as he takes Cade's hand and pumps it. "I'm Phil Byars."

"Cade Hill."

Phil puts a wad of twenties on the table and grins at me. "Let's split."

"What about dinner?" I'm confused.

"Forget all this superficiality. If you love tacos, you're having tacos."

"I want to go!" Sissy takes another step closer to my date.

"Didn't you just eat?"

"There's always room for a taco," she laughs, and I can't decide if I like this girl or if I want to punch her for being a size zero and saying something like that.

"Sure, we can join you," Cade's voice is still irritated, and it fans my own irritation.

"We don't want to spoil your evening." I slug the rest of my martini and go to Phil's side, putting my hand in the crook of his arm.

"I don't mind!" Sissy looks expectantly at Phil. "So you know about vermiculture?"

"Only a little." My date steps forward, out of my grasp.

Wonder Woman saunters off with Fantasy Phil, and I'm left following them at Cade's side. The tension vibrating between us is like heat on my skin.

We pause as Cade tosses a few hundred-dollar bills on his table. I take in small appetizer plates and several shot glasses and raise an eyebrow at him. "Doing shots with all the girls?"

His lips tighten. "Only you, Stone. Only you."

I half-snort as we pass quickly through the foyer and out into the cool night. It's actually a perfect night, not too cold, no wind, and a sky full of stars.

Phil looks around and calls to us. "We can walk from here. It's two blocks up and to the left."

I fumble through my memory. The only thing in that direction is White Oak Park. "It's in the park?"

"Trust me," Phil says, returning to his conversation with Sissy.

Cade and I follow, and the tightness in my shoulders is almost unbearable. After the amazing day we had today, I can't believe he just flat-out lied to me about going to his mother's. Five more steps, and I can't take it anymore.

"You said you were going to your mother's." My voice is way poutier than I'd intended, but I don't care. I am a woman wronged.

"You wanted space." His voice is simmering with anger. He looks at me and then glares at Phil's back. "Is that what space looks like to you?"

As a matter of fact . . . I consider my ridiculous conversation with Phil. I think of my recurring dream of the handsome man who blasts off to Mars shortly after giving me the greatest O of my life. Looking ahead, I see Phil and Sissy have stopped at a silver food truck right at the entrance to the park. Of course, Mr. Mortal Shell would take us to a food truck. Still, they're laughing and talking like old friends.

My chest sinks, and I realize everything is wrong.

"I hate space," I say softly.

Cade steps in front of me and puts both hands on my shoulders, stopping me. "What do you really want, Stone?"

I blink up, our eyes meet, and I can't deny the heat flooding my core. I think I know what I want . . . I know for sure what I *don't* want.

Giving up the fight, I confess. "I want you."

His anger melts into a smile. "Let's get rid of these guys."

"But we're on dates." My gaze flickers to the couple now munching on Mexican and sitting on a park bench.

"I have an idea to fix that."

"Does it involve you and me alone?"

His eyes sweep over me, and I shiver at the lick of fire that moves up my spine. "Yes."

Fifteen

CADE

MY IDEA IS simple: I pretend like I've gotten a call from the station about an incident at a college football game and they want me to come in. I inform Sissy—who doesn't seem all that interested.

She glances from her taco to Phil. "Do you mind if I hang out here with these guys?"

Yes, sweet baby Jesus. "Absolutely not. Enjoy yourself." I shoot a quick look to Stone. "Good to see you tonight, Stone. I'll see you back at the office on Monday."

The next second she pretends to get a text from Chas who suddenly needs a ride to the ER because she isn't feeling well.

"Poor Chas," Stone says with a hand over her heart. "She's too weak to drive. I should go."

Phil stands. "Do you want me to go with you?"

Stone at first looks horrified then quickly recovers. "Oh, no. She's projectile vomiting, and she'd die if a stranger saw her that way. You stay and enjoy chatting with Sissy." Her eyes brush over the pretty brunette.

She pretends to start to call an Uber.

"Don't do that," I say. "Your place is on the way to the station. Let me drop you off . . ."

"Oh, that would be wonderful. You're so nice, Cade." Her eyes flutter up at me, and I bite back a grin.

Sissy watches us suspiciously. "How convenient that you can ride together," she murmurs.

"Isn't it?" Stone says brightly.

"Maj ram," Phil says with a little bow.

We're forgotten as Sissy turns to him. "That's *goodnight* in Klingon!"

I'm pretty sure I see stars in Phil's eyes. "You're right!"

"Right," I say shaking his hand.

We say our goodbyes and hustle to my Escalade in valet parking at the restaurant. The tension is thick, and my fists are tight on the steering wheel as I drive as fast as traffic will allow. I don't care if Phil is weird or Sissy talks too fucking much about worms—all I can focus on is an image of Stone in my apartment, spread out and naked.

My parking job is sloppy, and I take her arm as I escort her to the elevator. The doors slide open, and thank God it's empty.

She wraps her hand around my bicep. "You're shaking."

I repeatedly push the button for the penthouse. "I want you so bad I can't breathe."

"I can't breathe either," she whispers.

My eyes find hers, and all at once, her back is against the metal wall. I run my lips up her exposed throat and suck on her soft skin, groaning at the taste of her. "You taste like everything good, Stone."

She sinks into me, her tits hitting my chest.

I fuse my mouth with hers and take what I want. Hard. A small part of me is still angry about Phil even though I have no right to be. We kiss like we're starving, our lips clinging, our hands roaming.

She cups my ass as I kiss across her neck, nibbling on her collarbone.

I need more.

Unzipping the back of her dress, I push it down just past her shoulders until I see creamy bare skin.

"You're fucking beautiful," I say as I tilt her face up and kiss her again.

She hisses in pleasure as I wrap her leg around my hip and press the steel pipe in my pants against her core. "You feel that Stone? That's all you."

"The elevator . . ." she says between kisses. "What if someone sees us?"

"I don't give a fuck."

I kiss her breasts, tugging them out of her red lace bra but leaving it on. My mouth zeros in on one nipple while my fingers tweak the other. Her breasts are calling my name, and I suck them, needing as much of her in my mouth as I can fit.

She moans as I pull her dress up from the hem and slip a finger inside her underwear. She's soaking wet, and it ratchets up my need. *Fuck.*

"I want to eat you. Now." I sink to my knees and yank her red panties to her ankles.

Trembling, she kicks them across the elevator and lifts a leg up to the metal bar that runs along the wall. "Now it is." Her voice is breathless.

I love how wild she is.

Thank fuck I have a slow ass elevator.

She's already swiveling her hips before I even touch her, shuddering and then groaning when my tongue snakes out to find her clit.

"Cade," she cries.

Need. Desire. Lust. It all bangs in my head . . . in my cock.

"Please," she moans as I tease her, my nose tracing along her legs, her thighs, and then back to her pussy.

"Look at me," I rasp out.

Her hooded eyes flutter open, her irises dilated. Her mouth is red and swollen from my kisses and I get a shiver of satisfaction.

She's mine.

"Don't ever fucking see Phil again."

She inhales sharply at the order.

"Stone?" I rub my index finger over her clit, teasing her with little brushes. "Do you understand?"

She nods and bites her lips. "Yes."

"Good." With languid thrusts, I play her with two fingers. "You want more?" I ask.

"Please." Her voice is guttural. "Your mouth."

I grunt, my caresses faster as I try to beat the elevator, dipping inside her and then out. "Have you ever felt this kind of heat before?"

"No," she moans, her chest rising rapidly.

That's exactly what I needed to hear. My mouth takes her wetness again, inhaling her scent as my tongue dances across her pink skin.

She stifles her voice with her fist and comes undone, her muscles vibrating around my fingers.

I watch her come, stroking her through the sensations, getting a thrill at how her eyes gloss over. I'm king of the fucking world.

Slightly dazed, she rests against the wall.

Ping. We've arrived at my floor. I tuck her back in her clothes, zip her dress up, grab her underwear, and escort her off the elevator to my door. I'm barely coherent.

"I-I can't believe we did that," she whispers. "Aren't there cameras in there?"

"I'll take care of it," I say as we enter the apartment.

I shut the door behind me, turn her around and kiss her again, the taste of her still on my tongue. I can't get enough.

I sweep her up in my arms and carry her to my king-sized bed.

While she sits on the bed, I quickly whip my jacket and shirt off, tossing them on the chair in the corner.

She licks her lips. "Are we really going to do this? I-I don't want to be hurt. I've had some shitty stuff happen . . ."

"We both have." I unzip my pants and my hard cock pops out

as my slacks pool on the ground. I toe my socks off and kick my clothes away. "Are you having second thoughts?" My jaw clenches with control. I don't want her to see how the thought of not having her kills me. I want this to be her decision.

She swallows, her gaze molten as it sweeps over my shoulders, down to my chest and then to my legs.

I smirk and turn around so she can see my ass. I pose and flex.

She lets out a contented sigh. "I want to bite it."

"What's stopping you?" I turn back and walk toward her, stopping at the edge of the bed. She leans forward and takes me in her mouth as I groan and clutch her head, guiding her how I like it.

She sucks, sliding her tongue over my shaft from base to tip. Her fingers wrap around my length as she devours me.

"*Fucckkk.*"

Her mouth explores me, and I am losing control.

"Stone," I growl.

"You want me to stop?" she murmurs.

"I'll kill you if you do."

She laughs softly around my cock.

Pleasure—and something else—settles deep inside me. "What are you doing to me, woman?"

"What I want to do every time I see you at work."

I tilt her face up and slide my thumb across her lips. The moment is serious. Intense. "This will change things for us. I don't know how it will end."

She nods, her eyes heavy with desire. "I just want you," she says.

We make quick work of getting her dress off, and we're both naked.

She moans for me to hurry, but I take my time, positioning her under me so I can do what I want. I gently pin her arms on either side of her and kiss her languidly, exploring and mapping her skin . . . the column of her throat, the bend in her elbow, the freckle on her chest. Her skin feels as hot as mine.

She whimpers and pushes her pelvis up to rub against my hips. "I'm ready for you to fuck me."

I laugh and kiss her on the lips. "Beg me," I say and then lean down and take one of her tits in my mouth and suck.

"Cade, *please* . . ." Her fingers claw at me, pulling me down and crushing our bodies together.

Fuck me. I can't wait any longer to get my cock inside her.

I get up to grab a condom. We'd been pretty careless last time, and I have no intention of pulling out tonight. I rip it open, slide it on, and go back to her.

"I'm clean," I tell her. "I know what the gossip magazines say about me, but I'm selective about who I fuck."

"Am I just a fuck?" she asks.

Her hair is everywhere, and I lean over and tuck it behind her ear. "Never."

My fingers slip inside her again, sliding, curling over the bundle of nerves in her G-spot. I suck her clit—fuck I can't get enough. I grab her hip to pull her closer.

Need claws at me as my cock pushes inside her. She's so wet it's as smooth as silk.

I flip her over like a ragdoll, raise her hips, and slide inside her on a groan. I grunt and toss my head back, maneuvering to get deeper. More of her.

But something's missing.

"No," I growl and flip her back over. "I want to see your face."

"Whatever you want," she whispers.

I bury my face in her neck and fuck her hard. I twist my hips for a new position, deeper, grinding, and she writhes underneath me.

"More," she begs, grabbing my shoulders.

Our sex is hot, fast, and furious, my strokes scooting us up to the headboard. She calls out and clings to me, milking my cock with her orgasm.

I go over right after, vibrating as I roar my release. I arch my back, grabbing her hands and riding it out, my cock tightening and expanding.

Collapsing down, I pull her up to the pillows and settle her in front of me with her back to my chest. "Stone," I stop and swallow, my voice thick. "That was . . . fucking amazing."

"Yeah."

Her stomach rumbles.

I rise up and brush a hand down to cup her shoulder. "We never had dinner."

She turns to face me, her expression soft. "I have Door Dash. How do you feel about Doritos Locos Tacos?"

I kiss her nose. "I'm in, babe."

All the way in.

Sixteen

REBECCA

CADE'S DRESS SHIRT is the only thing covering my naked body, which is covered in the scent of his expensive body wash. I'd taken a quick shower while he waited for our delivery, and now we're sitting facing each other with two beers, a pile of orange and white Taco Bell wrappers, and hot sauce packets scattered between us.

"I like the nacho cheese best."

"I bet I could whip up a healthier version of this," Cade says, examining the vivid red-orange shell. An unexpected surge of happiness filters through my stomach at his words. I watch as he takes a bite and groans, nodding. "Mm—maybe later."

We both sit back crunching and grinning. I allow my eyes to run down the black silk robe he's wearing. It's open to reveal the lines in his stomach, and my body hums thinking how I was just all over that. Naked.

My mind is absolutely blissed out, and I'm taking a sip of Modelo when, "Oh!" A fluffy white head peeks out from behind the black leather sofa. "Cade! It's your kitty!" I put my beer down and jump up.

"Killer, meet the famous Rebecca Fieldstone. Stone for short." His rich voice follows me as I tiptoe around the glass coffee table toward the tiny white furball.

Cutting my eyes back at him, I almost sigh audibly from the sight of that gorgeous man draped in black silk and surrounded by tacos. I'm pretty sure I've died and gone to heaven.

A little mew pulls me back to Earth. "Killer? You call this pretty kitty *Killer*?"

"Don't be fooled. She's like that bunny from Monty Python." The tease in his voice does all kinds of crazy things to my insides.

"Is that so?" I kneel down to stroke her soft, white head. "Then I'd better get the Holy Hand Grenade."

"Of Antioch."

That makes me laugh, and I scratch the side of Killer's cheek. She studies me with huge blue eyes then pushes forward against my hand, rubbing along my forearm. "You are a surprise a minute, Cade Hill."

"I could say the same to you."

His voice is low and rich, and my stomach flutters so hard, I know I won't be eating any more tacos tonight. I stand, shaking my head.

"What?" he asks.

Racking my brain, I try to think of something to say besides, *Let me have all your babies!* My red-tipped toes sink into the plush black rug covering the dark wood floors of his apartment, and I look around his ultimate bachelor pad as his cute white cat trots behind me.

"This is a beautiful place." I stop in front of the enormous flat-screen TV hanging above a gas fireplace. Orange flames flicker, and it's inviting and homey.

"My mom hired the decorator."

"Your mom . . ." I nod, turning my back to the black television and narrowing my eyes in pretend annoyance. "You never said why you weren't with your mom tonight."

He leans back, and that robe falls open a little more, revealing one side of the V of muscle disappearing into his boxer briefs. "You never said why you were with Phil."

A challenge. "I asked first," I say.

"You know, you're very sexy standing there in only my dress shirt." He's grinning, and the appreciative smile on his lips is like hot liquid in my veins.

His eyes cut away, and he exhales, sitting forward to collect our paper wrappers and stuff them into the white bag.

"I can help with that." I step forward and kneel in front of him, placing our uneaten tacos on the glass coffee table beside our beers.

"My mom asked me to take Sissy out," he says, not lifting his eyes. "She's a friend of the family, just moved to Houston. Doesn't know anybody."

I sit back on my feet and look up at him. "Chas thought I should date some random guy so I'd have a rebound . . . that wasn't you."

Cade's gaze is level, not smiling. "Were you planning to sleep with him?"

"No!" I whisper-shout. "I didn't even want to go out with him, really. We were just looking at this silly dating site, and Chas clicked something that apparently meant 'Let's date right now!' and then she said I had to go or I'd be blackballed and he didn't even look like his picture and then he started talking like a Klingon and—"

Cade's warm hands cup my cheeks, and he pulls me in for a rough kiss. Full lips capture mine, pushing them apart and allowing his tongue to curl inside, wiping my brain. A little noise comes from my throat, and if my body was on fire before, it's molten-hot lava now. Holding his shoulders, I scoot onto his lap in a straddle. My eyes are closed against the heat blazing in my brain, and I swear to God I ignite when his large hands grip my ass.

"Oh, Cade," I gasp as his mouth moves to my ear.

"I want to be inside you again. Right now."

"Yes . . ."

The man is strong as Hercules. His hands go under my butt, holding my body against his torso as he stands in one fluid movement. My arms are around his shoulders, my mouth on his cheek, his ear, his neck, kissing, touching my tongue to his salty skin, giving him a tiny bite as he carries me to his bedroom.

"Fuck, Stone." The way he growls my name when we fall back onto his enormous bed nearly gives me an orgasm right then and there.

I'm on my back in the gray, soft-as-silk sheets, and I watch with heavy eyes as he quickly discards those boxer briefs, freeing that huge muscle with which I'm obsessed. Condom quickly on, he grips the bottom of his dress shirt I'm wearing and rips it open, causing my breasts to bounce out.

"Oh!" I sigh at the sensation.

Cade's eyes are navy with hunger, and he's on me in a lunge, sliding inside so fast, I let out another loud moan of pleasure. *God, this never gets old.* Large hands are on the sides of my breasts, pushing them together as he devours me, pulling my nipples between his lips and teasing them with his teeth. I'm squirming and flying when he grips my ass again and flips us, positioning me on top.

"Do that thing with your hips." His voice is thick. "That hula thing."

Warm satisfaction floods my lower pelvis. The only thing hotter than looking at this amazing man is hearing that tone in his voice, knowing I'm driving him wild. I sit back and for the first time in a long time, I feel sexy. It's the most amazing feeling. The raw need in his eyes sends currents of pleasure rushing up my thighs straight to my core, and I rotate my hips in a circular motion.

"Yes," he groans, thrusting up with his hips.

"That feels so good," I gasp, throwing my hair back. I am a wild sex goddess.

He grips my ass, his hips still thrusting, and I only get in two more twists before I'm breaking apart, crying out loud, and riding his rigid cock like there's no tomorrow. Another loud groan from him, and I feel Cade break apart, holding me steady as he pulses deep inside, filling that condom.

I collapse forward onto his chest, and our lips meet in a sensual, after-glowey kiss. I hold his face as my hair falls around us, and our lips touch again and again. His hands are on my waist, and I'm so deeply contented. We come down together, kissing, bonding, meshing in every way. Sliding a hand between us to hold the condom, he pulls out. It's quickly disposed of, and we're together again. He puts my back to his chest and holds me firmly around the waist. It's the most amazing spooning position I've been in since . . . well, since he spent the night in my apartment.

"Sleep now," he says, kissing the top of my shoulder. "I've got you."

A smile curls my lips as I close my eyes, drifting away in a fizzy haze of bliss, two strong arms my only anchor to this world.

THE LOW DRONE of voices pulls me from my pink cloud of happiness. I blink several times, trying to place the sound. It's so familiar . . .

"Another Houstonian was attacked last night by what police are now calling the GreenStreet Grabber . . . or Grabbers." I sit up in bed, holding the sheet under my arms. It's Matt on the enormous TV hanging on the opposite wall, and he's reading KHOT's Sunday recap of the news. "It's as yet unclear if the muggings are the work of one person or a gang of thieves."

Cade enters the room carrying a dark wooden tray. "I brought you coffee. How do you take it?"

"One sugar, two creams," I say, melting back against the smoky suede headboard as I watch him. The black robe is draped over his shoulders again, a newspaper is tucked under his arm, and he is so damn yummy.

"Matt is working seven days a week . . ." He passes me a steam-ing mug. "They've got to fill that weekend anchor position soon."

My chest rises at the thought. "It's what I've been working toward."

"I know."

Matt is still talking, and Cade scoots into the bed beside me. I barely feel the movement, and I realize he must have one of those memory foam mattresses. With that and his strong arms around me most of the time, it's no wonder I slept so well.

"Another mugging." He drops the paper between us, and I glance up to see the muscle in his jaw tighten. "An elderly woman this time. They sneaked up behind her and pushed her down. Sprained her ankle and stole her purse. Assholes."

"Oh my God!" I set my coffee aside and pick up the paper, looking from the front page up to the footage of the gray-haired granny with bloody scuffmarks on her knees and palms. "Do they have any leads on who's doing it?"

"None." Cade is clearly pissed. "No fingerprints. No evidence. These guys move fast, and they hit when nobody's around."

My eyes scan the story. "Parking garage, early evening, after rush hour. It's like something out of a movie. Classic mugger behavior."

I can't help feeling a little sick reading the story. The GreenStreet shopping area is one of Houston's newer developments and not too far from my apartment.

"You need to be sure you're with Kevin or Chas . . . or me . . . if you're going out anywhere after dark."

His protectiveness is adorable, and I lean my head against my hand. "I'll be careful." While this rash of robberies is troubling, I don't want to focus on that right now. "Should we go out for brunch or something?"

He turns to face me as well. "Do you think that's a good idea?"

That answer is completely unexpected. "I thought that was

my line."

"Well, you're the famous Rebecca Fieldstone." He reaches out and wraps the end of my hair around his finger. "We're bound to draw attention."

"Don't remind me!"

"Only one thing is as hot as your right breast . . ." I groan, covering my face with my hand, but he continues, "your left breast."

I start to laugh, playfully shoving his shoulder. "Stupid wardrobe malfunction."

"I wanted to punch every person who saw you in the face. I guess I'm selfish. I want to be the only one seeing your body." He smiles, and those irresistible dimples appear.

A flush creeps up my neck. "Are you saying you're holding me hostage?"

"I wish." It makes me laugh more, but his smile dims. "I was just thinking about how much you want that anchor spot . . . and how much of a dick Marv can be. I don't want to be the reason you don't get everything you want."

The meeting in Marv's office after the Planetary Princess story fills my mind. I remember Cade being there while Marv said those things about my appearance, and all my feelings from last night of being a sex goddess disappear.

My chin drops. "I'm not sure how I got on his bad side. Marv used to be very supportive and encouraging . . ." Until Savannah showed up.

"Hey," Cade's voice is soft, and he lifts my chin. "I'm happy to say fuck him. I want everybody to see you on my arm." I confess, hearing Cade Hill say these words makes it a little better. "I just don't want to put you in an awkward situation."

"You want to order in again?"

"Nope." He hops out of bed. "We can walk down to the park. It's a pretty day, and they have a little farmer's market there. I'll buy you breakfast, and if anyone sees us, we can say we're working on our story."

I smile, but I feel squirmy inside. "I guess that's how it has to be for now, sneaking around and lying."

"We're not sneaking, and we're definitely not lying." I watch as he steps into a pair of faded jeans that hug his ass absolutely perfectly. "We are working on our story."

He gives me a little wink, and for a moment, I'm not sure how to take that. Is it possible Cade Hill is actually serious about me? He pulls a navy tee over his head and steps into the bathroom. I hear the sound of brushing teeth, and I hop out of bed, skipping to the living room where I retrieve my panties and my dress . . . It's red silk. Clearly, a dinner outfit, not brunch. I'm frowning at my reflection when he returns to the bedroom.

"What's wrong?"

"This dress." I lift the sides. "It's too fancy for a farmer's market. I've clearly spent the night with you."

"What's wrong with that?"

"Walk of shame much?"

He shakes his head and goes to his dresser, opening drawers. "You could wear one of my shirts. I don't know about the bottoms . . ."

"One wardrobe malfunction is enough for me, thanks."

"What if you put my dress shirt over it and here . . ." He pulls a new white shirt over my arms and twists the ends into a knot at my waist. "Now you look even more fuckable."

"Cade!"

"Is that a bad thing?"

"Come on." I catch his arm, and we make our way to the first floor and out into the brilliant sunshine.

It's another perfect fall day, with low humidity and a light breeze. Cade pulls my hand into the crook of his arm, and I'm pretty certain we look nothing like coworkers meeting for brunch. We look like a couple out for a stroll after the most amazing night of fucking in the history of ever. The park is a brilliant blend of autumn colors along with purple and gold Halloween decorations. Tables are arranged under large white tents, and we stop at one where a lady is working with several of her kids, whipping up the most delicious-smelling breakfast foods.

Cade stops and orders us both huevos rancheros wrapped in soft tacos with coffee, and we carry them to a nearby bench to eat.

"Did you grow up here in Houston?" I ask around a bite of breakfast.

He nods, swallowing quickly. "Born here, went to private school here . . . I went to college in Austin, but my first real move was to Atlanta to play for the Falcons." I'm nodding, devouring the luscious Tex-Mex as I listen. "You?"

"I was actually born in Galveston." His eyebrows rise at this revelation. "My parents loved being near the coast, but they wanted more crystal-blue waters. It's why they moved to Key West as soon as I left for college."

He shakes his head. "My family is not like that. Mom claims she cried every day I lived in Atlanta."

"That's really sweet." I have the sudden desire to meet his mom, but I keep it to myself. "And Trent?"

His brow lowers, and he takes a sip of coffee. "He didn't cry . . . as far as I know. Still, he's part of the reason I came back."

I remember the things Cade has told me about his dad. I remember his anger. "Was your dad also glad you came back?"

"Yeah, but for completely different reasons."

We've ventured into unhappy territory again, and I want to steer us back to the light. Cade's eyebrows quirk, and I can tell he's with me on changing the subject. "What else, besides that cute little nose, made you pick TV news, Stone? Over law?"

I grin at him. "Hmm . . ." I look around at the people strolling by, holding hands, walking dogs, carrying children. "I like getting outside, meeting people, talking to leaders in the community . . . or even just regular people making a difference."

"That'll change if you become an anchor."

"It's true," I nod. "But as an anchor, I can be more involved in story selection, and I can still get out and do interviews occasionally."

Cade stands and takes our breakfast trash, tossing it in the can before coming back to hold out his hand to me. I take it and we follow the walking path around the small park. I'm preoccupied with another reason for why I love my job, one I've only ever told Nancy.

"You look like there's more," he says.

"Well . . ."

Cade steps in front of me, stopping our progress and looking straight into my eyes. "What is it?"

My chin drops, and I let out a little laugh. "It's silly."

"Now you have to tell me."

Shaking my head, I look up at him. "You know that nervous feeling . . . that flutter in the stomach . . . like right before you pick up a newborn baby for the first time?"

"Yes." He answers so fast, I laugh more.

"It's the feeling I get when I'm right there, on the edge, capturing a great story for everyone to see. Like when I interviewed Petal, or . . ." I stop myself before I say *or like the first time I saw you.*

"Or?"

Shaking my head, I say instead, "It's the most amazing thing. It's exciting and electric, and I love to share it."

Without a word or a moment's hesitation, he steps forward and kisses me, warm lips on mine, no tongue, all feeling—*that* feeling. The one I never want to lose.

Seventeen

CADE

I'M IN A fantastic mood when I drop Stone off at her apartment around five and head to my next destination, the River Oaks Theatre, a cinematic Houston landmark. I'm meeting Mom and Trent for our Sunday date. Last week we'd hit a local art gallery where one of Mom's friends had a photography exhibit. It's a new place each week, usually Trent's choice.

I walk in the majestic entrance of the smallish theatre. Built in the thirties, the interior's been refurbished but still has the original Art Deco feel with black marble sculptures, triangular-shaped lighting fixtures, and modern lounging areas with clean lines and straight edges. Grinning, I take it in. I know this "artsy" stuff because Trent tells me.

My mood plummets as I get a gander at who's here. My father is standing next to my mom at the concession stand.

I'm going to need a stiff drink with my movie.

Trent waves and strides over, seeming fairly cool for a guy who hasn't seen Dad since Mom's birthday party about three months ago. Sure we get together as a family periodically, but only for holidays and funerals. Even then, the tension between Dad and Trent is thick.

"What the hell is he doing here?" I hiss.

"I invited him," Trent murmurs.

I rear back. "Why?"

He lifts his hands up and shrugs. "He called me last week—and the week before. I didn't answer because I never answer my phone unless you've texted me first. But get this . . . yesterday he sent me a text: *Please call me. I need to talk to you.*"

"Dad texted?" My voice is incredulous.

He nods. "Yep. I thought about it and called him. He just wanted to say that *he'd been thinking about me and could we get together.*" He pauses. "He also wished me happy birthday. Is it possible he's dying and hasn't told us?"

I shake my head. "He just had a physical for the company's insurance."

"Maybe he's trying to get Mom back," Trent replies.

Narrowing my eyes, I sweep them over my father who's currently purchasing a combo for my mom and smiling down at her. No matter their differences—mostly dealing with Trent—I never doubted he loves her. I'd seen the pure joy on his face the day she'd told him she was in remission. He'd dated periodically in the years they'd been divorced. So had she. But neither of them had formed long-term attachments.

Still . . . I'm suspicious.

Tonight my dad has left the suit and tie at home for khaki slacks and a maroon V-neck sweater. At sixty, his hair is snow-white and thick, combed back in a slick style he's worn for as long as I can remember. Still broad-shouldered with a tapered waistline, he's aged with class.

It's his stubborn heart that pisses me off.

"What's his game?" I say.

"Regrets about the past?"

I scratch at the scruff on my jaw. "But why would *you* invite him?"

He thinks about it, a serious expression flitting across his normally carefree visage. "He's my dad. I still love him."

He takes a sip from the Diet Coke he's holding. "Part of me feels sorry for him. He's ignorant—and is it stupid that I still crave his approval? Me. A twenty-six-year-old man." He shakes his head as if bemused.

Trent loves hard and forgives quickly. Impulsively, I give him a shoulder squeeze. "I just don't want you to be hurt by him again."

I'd been there to pick up the pieces when he'd moved out of the house, and I never wanted to see him go through that again.

They turn and make their way toward us, and Mom rushes up to me with a big smile, glowing. I nod at my father then hug her. She smells like lemon shampoo and I ruffle her hair.

"I swear it gets longer every day."

"You just saw me yesterday!" She laughs and fingers the small gray curls on her head.

Classy and elegant as usual, she looks radiant in a black flowy dress that fits the theatre style. A white beaded cardigan is thrown over her shoulders, and I smile; she never goes anywhere without a sweater.

"So . . . how was the date with Sissy?" she asks, looking up at me.

"You mean the worm farmer, a detail you conveniently forgot to tell me?"

She laughs. "I didn't think it mattered what she did. Isn't she beautiful?"

"She left me for a Vulcan."

Trent snorts. "Dude. I'm confused. Why are you going out with this Sissy when you have the hots for Rebecca Fieldstone, monkey wrangler extraordinaire?"

Mom perks up. "The girl on the news? Her video is everywhere!" A gleam grows in her eyes. "I like her. She does that little wink at the end of her broadcasts and her outfits are so stylish. I bet you'd make pretty babies."

Babies? FUCK.

"I do *not* have the hots for her. She's a professional career woman—"

"Who wants to get in your pants." Trent smirks as he tosses an arm around Mom's shoulders and whispers conspiratorially. "When I had dinner with them at the station, they could barely keep their eyes off each other. Not that I blame him. If I were straight,"—he shoots a look at Dad—"I'd be all over that. We must invite her next Sunday. I suggest dinner at Raven. The lighting there is *perfect* for falling in love, plus the piano player is delish. I predict a marriage proposal by the spring."

Mom claps. "You always have the best ideas. Let's do it. Text her and invite her for next week. Oh, better yet, see what she's doing tonight!" She wiggles her eyebrows at me.

"Yes! Invite her!" Trent pipes in. "And ask Chas too!"

My jaw tightens. "I'm not texting Stone." She's probably resting from our wild night of sexcapades, not to mention I don't want her at the center of my family's machinations to get us together.

"Who's this girl?" Dad asks, and we all turn to look at him as he stands a few feet behind Mom, fidgeting as he holds a cardboard tray with a tub of popcorn and two beers.

He's the outsider and knows it.

"Rebecca Fieldstone," Mom says. "She's the reporter who flashed her boob to all of Houston—but Cade's being all secretive about her."

I groan. "There are no secrets . . ." I stop. It's no use explaining Stone to them. It would only make things worse.

"Friction in the workplace?" she exclaims. "Sounds exciting."

I exhale. "Mom. Don't get any ideas. Stone and I—it's complicated. She's trying to get an anchor spot."

Trent's eyes are dancing. "You like her. Admit it. Call her."

I glare at him. "We aren't in third grade, Trent. Plus, it's too late to call."

"You're probably right," Mom says. "Anything this last minute is a booty call."

Trent laughs, and I just shake my head, steering the conversation to Deadrick and the football team.

"You think they might win a championship?" Dad asks a bit loudly as he inserts himself in the conversation. He looks uncomfortable as hell. *Good.* It's going to take more than one movie date to make me change my mind about letting him in our circle.

"Undefeated so far," I say. "I just wish I could do more for them. Those kids need everything: better security, laptops in class like the more affluent schools." I think back to Marv's comment about fundraising. "They need money."

"I can help with that," he says.

I arch my brow. Hill Global is worth billions, but the only charities the board supports are renowned research hospitals in Houston. I can't see them jumping to help a forgotten school—not enough publicity involved.

Mom ushers him farther into the little group we've unintentionally formed. "What are you thinking, Baron?"

He pauses a moment, and I think I see a bead of sweat on his brow. "Well . . . we need to branch out with tax breaks and helping a local school seems advantageous, especially if my sons are involved." His gaze flickers to Trent, and he clears his throat. "In fact, I think—and this is just off the top of my head—Trent would be a great help with getting a charity gala together for your school. He's creative . . . that type of thing . . ." his voice dwindles and he fidgets, an unsure expression crossing his face—almost as if he's surprised by his own words.

We stare at him, and it's quiet except for the bustle of moviegoers as they brush past us.

Trent's the first to speak. "Would I get paid?"

Dad straightens. "Of course. You'd be in charge of the event, organizing it, being the liaison between the company and the school."

Sounds like a completely made-up position.

"What's your fucking game?" I ask.

There. I say what I've been thinking since I walked in.

He just blinks at me.

Mom pops me on the arm. "Be nice and stop saying the *F* word."

Trent focuses on Dad. "You know I'm still gay, right? And no matter what you do for us—*or me*—I'll still be gay."

He stares at his feet for a few ticks and then looks up. "I'm okay with that."

Am I in the right universe? *What is up with my dad?*

Regrets?

Mom?

Terminal illness?

I don't know.

An announcement lets us know the movies are about to start. Dad glances around nervously, his eyes bouncing off the various posters. "So, um, which show are we seeing?"

I follow his gaze and check out the lineup of films. There are only three screens in the entire place—and it's Gay Pride Month at the theatre.

Trent smiles brightly. "It's either *Brokeback Mountain*, *Philadelphia*, or *Transamerica*. I'm open. I love them all."

"I wish I knew how to quit you," I quote from *Brokeback Mountain*.

Trent grabs his chest. "Be still my heart. I love Jake Gyllenhall."

"Yes! I pick that one!" Mom takes Dad by the arm and steers him toward the screening area. "You'll love it." She pats his hand. "Probably. It has cowboys."

Trent and I fall in line behind them.

"This is so fucking weird," I say to Trent, watching them enter the darkened theatre and head for seats in the middle.

"I'm bringing a date next time. I wanna see how he handles that," is his reply as we take our seats next to Mom.

I watch the promo for the coming attractions and my mind drifts to Stone . . . and babies . . . and surprisingly I don't have a panic attack. I think about my dad and wonder if it's possible for him to change.

Life is strange and unpredictable.

Who the fuck knows what tomorrow will bring?

IT'S TEN O'CLOCK Monday morning, and I'm on fire to see Stone. I dreamed about her hula dancing on my cock and woke up with a raging hard-on. It's time for our monthly meeting with the board, and as I'm headed to the lobby elevator, Marv enters from the opposite entrance. He hoofs it to wait beside me in front of the shiny silver doors.

"Morning," I murmur, looking down at him. He's at least a foot shorter than me, and I enjoy the shit out of it.

"Cade." He nods with a spaced-out expression, seeming lost in thought.

Once the passengers exit, we slip inside the elevator. I push the button just as I hear Stone's voice.

"Hold it, please! I'm coming!"

I'd heard those words a few times this weekend. I grin and hit the hold button.

She shows up at the entrance and her eyes crash into mine. She's fucking gorgeous in three-inch heels, a tight red skirt and a soft cream sweater that hugs those luscious curves. I want to eat her up. She dips her chin, a blush rising up her cheeks. I love that she's got a shy streak in her.

Her eyes scoot to my companion and she flinches. "Oh! Marv! I didn't see you there. Good morning! How was your weekend? Mine was great. Awesome! So, so awesome!" She throws her hands up in exclamation.

I grin.

He scowls.

She backs away.

"Are you getting on or what, Rebecca?" he asks in an exasperated tone.

I put my hand out to hold the door open. "Well?"

She shakes her head. "No, no, that's okay. I-I forgot something in the car. Bye!"

And she's gone, practically running away from the elevator.

I sigh, my mind dancing back to our elevator interlude this weekend.

"What are you smiling at?" Marv asks as the door swishes shut.

"Just a beautiful day, Marv."

He grunts. "I have nothing to smile about. I'm still getting complaint emails about Rebecca and that damn monkey. She needs to be in production."

I stiffen, anger bubbling up. "If anything, it may have garnered us more viewers—like those eighteen to twenty-five-year-old males you're so worried about. Plus, it was an accident."

He harrumphs. "Nothing with her is an accident. She probably planned it—"

I cut him off. "She didn't, and you know that. You're being obtuse and frankly unprofessional. I don't wish to discuss Stone with you." My tone is haughty and domineering, and I don't give a fuck.

"Wish or not, I'm telling you now. I have the final say in who gets that anchor job, and it won't be her." A smug expression is on his thin face.

"Who then?" I ask as a muscle ticks in my jaw.

He shrugs and brushes lint off his navy sport coat. "Savannah. She's young and malleable . . . damn perfect."

"So you've decided for sure?" My tone is angry. I can't help it.

He shoots me a steely look. "Didn't think you cared about my department, Cade? Change of heart? You can help me present it to the board."

My mouth tightens. "I'm not helping you present anything. Savannah doesn't have the brains to lead the news. She can't even find Russia on the map."

His gaze hardens. "That's for the board to decide, based on my recommendation." The elevator door swishes open and we exit. He sends me a side-eye. "Trust me, Savannah is going to send our ratings sky high."

My hands clench and I resist the urge to shove him up against the wall.

I think about what he just said, what he's about to recommend to the board, and my stomach drops. This is going to crush Stone.

Eighteen

REBECCA

KEVIN'S LOUD SLURP fills the van, and I'm too excited to care if he gets diabetes. We're headed to another live event, this time covering the mayor's speech and press conference on the GreenStreet Grabber—or Grabbers, depending on if there's more than one. It's my golden shot at serious reporter redemption, and I couldn't be happier.

Vicky came through for me, giving me a sly thumbs-up when I arrived in the newsroom wearing my red pencil skirt and a cream short-sleeved sweater. No wardrobe malfunctions today!

Marv's acting way grumpier than normal, and I just *know* he'd planned to give this assignment to Savannah. Vicky cut him off at the pass, saying she needed someone who could think on her feet, and Savannah doesn't have the gravity for a story like this.

Of course, gravity has not been my friend lately. Still, I got the gig, and I won't even be bothered by Marv's parting jab about keeping my clothes on. *Bastard.*

The mention of taking my clothes off sends my mind straight to Cade. I'd spent an hour last night filling Chassy in on all the details about the disastrous Hookup4Luv date—which I guess turned out to be a dream come true for Fantasy Phil . . . and me. Anyway, after we'd squealed and lay on the couch discussing all the details, the pros and cons of dating a co-worker, I'd floated to my room to sleep.

A text from Cade was waiting on my phone: *Sleep well, beautiful. I'll be looking for a chance to get you alone tomorrow.*

It sent a charge straight to my hoo-hoo and made me giggle like a teenager before I slipped beneath the sheets to drift away on fantasies of tomorrow.

We'd almost had our chance, but Marv had cock-blocked us in the elevator. I'd looked as dumb as Savannah trying to back out of that near-mess. I'm sure the elevator would have burst into flames if I'd ridden up beside Cade.

I'd chosen this sweater because it hugs my curves in all the right places. I could see the appreciation in Cade's eyes, and I could just imagine his large hands starting at the hem of my red skirt, sliding lightly up the sensitive skin of my thighs to my—

"Why is your face all red?" Kevin's obnoxious voice pops my daydream like a soap bubble.

"It's hot in here. Is it hot in here to you?" I reach forward and press the button to turn off the heater in the van.

"It's fifty degrees outside!"

"You're drinking a slushie. It's hot in the sun."

Pressing my hands to my face, I banish the flush from daydreaming about my sexy lover.

My *luvah* . . .

Stop it, Rebecca. I have to be professional. This is my last shot at proving I'm the most worthy reporter for that anchor seat. Examining the printout, I study the plan for the mayor's speech. Every news station will have a team at the event, even cable. These muggings have the entire downtown area on alert, and of course, the business community is up in arms.

"They're setting up the podium in the central courtyard near

Forever 21," I read aloud. "Mayor Newson will speak for approximately fifteen minutes then do a brief Q&A."

I'm scanning my questions, which cover increased police presence, business hours, tourism, when I glance up to see we're right in front of the elaborately designed parking garage.

"Get some B-roll of the garage," I say, sliding out of the seat. "I think the last attack happened on the second level."

"On it." Kevin takes off with his small Avid camera, and I've got my makeup bag on the passenger's seat. No mistakes this time.

Earlier, the crisp fall weather had helped my hair and makeup, but as the afternoon progresses, the heat and humidity continue to rise. We might have started the day in the fifties, but we'll finish closer to eighty.

"Why hello, Rebecca." Brad Simpson from KLIV, our competing station, sidles up to me. "Great work on that petting zoo story last week. Although, it seems they edited later broadcasts of your . . . eye-popping report."

"Shut up, Brad," I snip, which only makes him laugh.

"You and I should go out for drinks sometime."

I can't help it. I have to pause and glare at him. "Has anyone ever told you subtlety is not your strong suit?"

"I noticed Matt's doing every news show these days. Thought I might toss my hat in the ring for that weekend spot."

Ice filters down my spine. Marv would love another guy on staff. "Sick of being at the number two station in town?" I cover, hoping he doesn't notice the color rushing from my cheeks.

He only grins. "I'm serious about those drinks. I'll call you later."

"Don't waste your minutes," I mutter, turning away, more determined than ever.

"My plan is unlimited," he quips.

I'm sure it is. My heart's beating faster, but this time, it's not the excited nerves I love. This time, it's straight-up fear. I've got to nail this.

One last check in the mirror, and I step back, closing the door and smoothing my hands over my sweater and down my skirt. I couldn't look any more put-together, and my recent efforts at exercising and eating right—Saturday night excluded, although all that wild sex had to burn some calories—seem to be working.

Kevin's back, setting up the antenna and the monitor box for the live feed. I make my way through the mob of reporters to a reserved spot near the front. I catch Mayor Newson's eye, and I don't miss his attempts to stifle a grin. Everybody has seen my boob. I have to own it, and put it behind me. With a lift of my chin, I get ready to process what this politician has to say.

"Ready when you are, Becks," Vicky says in my earpiece. "I've managed to snag you first question."

"You're a rock star," I say under my breath to my producer back at the station.

It's a similar setup as at the zoo. We'll break in on scheduled programming to cover the mayor's speech live. Kevin is on my left and to the front in the bank of cameras, and he'll zoom in on me for my questions.

"What show are we breaking?" I ask her.

"We'll cut in at the end of *Jeopardy*."

"They're going to love that . . ."

And we're live. I'm listening closely to the mayor's speech for any answers to my planned questions. Fifteen minutes passes fast, and I'm praying for no surprises.

"Start with the increase in police force," Vicky says in my ear. I've sent her a copy of my questions, and I know she's jotting notes to use in voiceover for the anchors to read in later broadcasts.

"I'll now answer questions," Newson says. "Miss Fieldstone."

"Thank you," I speak loudly and clearly. "What are the plans for increasing police patrols until these muggers are caught?"

He proceeds to answer, and I won't have another chance for at least two more questions. Kevin's recording, but I'm momentarily distracted by a kid in a gray hoodie lurking at the edge of the press pool.

"Vicky," I say softly once the mayor moves to the next reporter. "What would make the grabber happiest right now?"

Seconds pass, and I listen with one ear to Brad asking if businesses are planning to reduce their evening hours. *Scratch that one off my list.*

"What would make the grabber happiest?" Vicky repeats my question aloud. "I guess the notoriety, the media coverage."

The girl from cable is asking her question, and I know it's my turn to jump in next. Still, I can't take my eyes off the tall, skinny kid with his hands shoved deep in his pockets. An inappropriate smirk is on his face, and that little tickle is in my stomach.

"You're up," Vicky says. "Go with tourism numbers."

My hand shoots up, and Newson acknowledges me. "Have we seen any decrease in the number of tourists visiting downtown Houston as a result of these burglaries?"

Newson launches into his "the sky is not falling" prepared answer, but again, I'm only half listening.

"Vicky," I say softly. "How much money have these guys, or this guy stolen from any one victim?"

"Not much," she says, as if she's catching on to what I'm saying. "I think the most they got was fifty dollars from the little granny Saturday night."

The mayor is saying his final words, and everyone's on their feet. My eyes are on Skinny, who's glancing toward the parking garage and back to our group.

"He's not doing it for the money," I say. "We're going to be here a bit longer."

"Rebecca!" Vicky shouts. "I need you to do the tag."

"Trust me, Vicks. Pitch it to Matt!"

The reporters move toward their respective photographers, but I signal Kevin to come with me. He frowns. Still, we've worked together long enough that he makes his way around the perimeter of bodies. I'm slowly drifting toward the parking garage, keeping my guy in sight.

"What's happening, Becks?" Vicky is still in my ear, and I decide to just say it.

"I think he's here. I don't know for sure, but I've spotted a suspicious kid keeping his eye on everything. He's headed toward the parking garage now."

"No way, Rebecca! It's too dangerous."

Her voice is loud, and I know the anchors can hear her as well as I can. She's in all our ears during the shows.

"What's going on?" Cade's deep voice in my ear surprises me.

"Cade!" I whisper. "What are you doing?"

"What are you doing?" His stern tone sends a simmer through my stomach.

"I've got him, Cade, I just know it."

"Do not follow that guy, Stone. Do you hear me?"

"Settle down. Kevin's with me."

"Stone!"

I pull the earpiece out of my ear and stick it in my pocket just as I spot my doughy partner emerging from the bodies near the entrance to the garage. Our target has already disappeared into the stairwell. My chest is tight, but that flutter is in my stomach. I know we're onto something big.

"What's happening?" Kevin meets me, and I motion to the metal door.

"A kid in a gray hoodie and jeans just went through that door. I want to follow him."

Kevin's face scrunches. "A kid in a hoodie? Why?"

"I can't explain it, but I have a feeling. What if the grabber lives in the parking garage? What if he's in there right now, waiting for his next victim?"

"Why would he live in a stairwell?"

"I don't know! Desperate people do crazy things. Maybe he's homeless."

Waiting in the courtyard, I try to think of the best plan of action. I don't want to scare him off. I want to do what he does—wait until everyone is gone and bust him before he hurts another old lady.

"These are petty thefts, only enough to last a few days. He's unarmed in the police reports . . ."

"Who's to say he hasn't armed himself? Maybe he's working up to really hurting someone."

"Don't be a coward, Kevin."

The parking garage is shadowy and smells like gasoline and urine. The LED sign at the entrance says the first and second levels are full, most likely thanks to the press conference. Mondays are typically slow shopping days.

"Is there another way up to the third level?" I whisper, walking toward the back of the garage. "We need to find a place to hide and wait."

"Hide? I've got to get back to the station so I can prep this for ten."

"Vicky can prep it for ten," I snap, hoping I'm not giving Marv the third strike he needs to fire me.

My heels click on the concrete, and I'm walking fast. Kevin is huffing and puffing beside me. I look down at my watch. It's six forty, and the news has wrapped. It's also around the time our grabber loves to strike.

Holding the slam-bar, I ease the metal door open and glance up the concrete stairs. "Empty," I whisper. "Be quiet."

A knot is in my throat. I swallow it away. My chest is tight, but I carefully go up the block of stairs. My palms are sweaty. I'm literally shaking when Kevin's phone goes off, and I swear to God I jump out of my skin.

"Shut that thing off!" I hiss.

"Hello?" Kevin is on the line with someone. "Yeah . . . Yeah, we're still here. Sorry, I had my earpiece off for a bit. Uh, yeah, I don't think she's going to wait . . ."

"Who is it?" I cut my eyes at him. My breath is coming fast, and all I can think is we're losing time.

"Marv. He's been trying to reach us. He says Cade left a few minutes ago to come down here. Maybe we should wait?"

I don't have time to wait. My big story could be over before it even starts. I walk faster and we're halfway between the second and third level when I hear a scream.

Shit! I was right!

"Kevin! MOVE!" I shout, running up the remaining steps and bursting through the metal door.

Nineteen

CADE

I FINISH THE sports report and toss my earpiece on the anchor desk. Stone's ignoring me. A tingle of worry zips up my spine as I picture her being a detective, lurking around darkened parking garages. My gut's been churning since the moment she said she saw a suspicious character at the scene and now she's gone off halfcocked?

All for a fucking news story.

My eyes land on Marv. I blame him for this shit. She wants to impress him for the weekend anchor position—that someone else is going to get.

"What's going on?" Marv asks as I stalk from the set and gather my things. "Is she following someone at the press conference? Does she think it's the mugger?" He's practically rubbing his hands together in glee as I give him a death glare.

"She could be in danger," I snap.

He taps his headpiece. "Rebecca? You there?" When he doesn't get a response, he shrugs. "No reply, but she's probably fine. I'll keep trying."

Fuck fine!

I want to be sure and the only way to do that is to get myself down there.

Once I get to my car, I drive like a man possessed, my tires squealing on the pavement as I run two red lights.

I park on the curb next to the garage, assessing the scene. The mayor is shaking hands with local businessmen and most of the reporters have gone except for one station. I search the crowd for Stone and when I don't see her, I jog to the garage. I've just opened the steel door to climb the stairs when I hear a scream.

Taking the steps three at a time, I listen, trying to pinpoint where the yelling is coming from. The sounds get louder as I reach the third floor. I burst out of the metal door, my chest heaving from the sprint, but it's nothing compared to the way I feel seeing Stone tangled up with a young man with stringy hair and dingy jeans.

He's wearing a ripped gray hoodie, and an older lady with white hair is crying as she huddles in a corner next to a concrete beam. Kevin hovers behind Stone, playing defense to keep the guy blocked between two cars while balancing his small Avid camera on his shoulder, recording everything.

My first instinct is to yell her name and tell her to get away, but I don't. First, there's no time, and second, I don't think she'd listen.

"Call the cops! Now!" I bark at the lady as I rush toward Stone who's currently grabbing at a black bag the guy is clutching close to his chest. It must belong to the old lady.

"Give . . . it . . . back!" Stone yanks on the purse as she and the mugger do a back and forth. The straps break and the contents of the bag go flying.

I've reached them and once the young guy takes stock of me, he freezes. *Yeah, that's right. I'm here to kick your goddamn ass.*

With a grunt, he shoves a fiery Stone to the ground and takes off running.

I briefly make sure she's fine and dart after him. "Stay here," I yell in her direction as I fly by.

The young man scuttles away, careening and bumping into vehicles as he heads to the EXIT sign over the stairwell. I gain on him, noticing a slight hitch in his gait.

Maybe it will slow him down. *He can't outrun me*, I tell myself. Even with my knee injury, I'm still badass—but my Tom Ford slacks and loafers are slowing me down.

His hand slips on the metal bar and it's just enough time for me to reach out and snatch the hood on the back of his shirt. I jerk him backwards. A strangled noised comes from his throat as the fabric holds him in place. His hand slips off the door as he simultaneously flips around and launches himself at me. We go to the ground, and he jabs his fist toward my stomach and groin, which is about all he can reach.

I avoid the punches and hurtle to my feet.

Panting, he doesn't miss a beat, coming up with me and flinging himself in my direction.

He's wiry and thin, but quicker than I'd anticipated.

A flurry of footsteps and raised voices penetrate my brain, and I presume it's Stone, making me all the more determined to finish this off.

His face twists when I grab his right arm to hold him still. "It's over," I bite out. "Give it up."

He grunts, a fine sheen of sweat on his face when his left fist comes out of nowhere and connects with my chest. *Oomph.* It's a weak shot, but it takes my breath. I dodge the next one, itching to pound into him but restraining myself. If he had a weapon, I'd go for it, but he doesn't appear to.

Stone shows up in my peripheral and that panicked feeling sets in again.

If anything had happened to her . . .

"Get out of here and call the damn cops!" I bark.

She stares at me, eyes wide as she clutches the purse to her chest. *It's okay*, I want to tell her. *I'm going to take care of this.*

But just then his fist connects with my jaw and my head snaps back.

He's landed a punch.

Sonofamotherfuckingbitch.

Enough.

I'd been playing before.

I turn, grab him by both hands, and twist them behind his back until he screams out in pain. Using my knees on his backside, I maneuver him to the ground as I clench his wrists. He whimpers and wiggles his legs, but gets nowhere. With my chest heaving, I sit on him.

Hell, it's all I can do until the cops get here.

"Are you okay?" I ask Stone. My eyes rake over her, doing a mental check, looking for injuries. If she has so much as has a scratch on her . . . I'm going to pummel him.

She swallows, her throat working. "I'm fine. Kevin called the cops."

For the first time, I notice Kevin is next to her, camera still in his hand.

I glare at him. *Idiot.*

But Stone's ready. She shoots a look at Kevin, gets in the frame, and starts talking. Her blonde hair is a mess, but damn if her shirt isn't secure and her skirt straight.

She's talking about the incident as the mugger twists under me. I tighten my grip and keep my focus on him. Thankfully, the door from the stairwell bursts open and a parade of cops spills out and runs our way.

" . . . my cameraman Kevin and I caught the suspect, who we can only assume to be the GreenStreet Grabber, in another attempt to attack an elderly woman." She gets a serious look on her face, leveling her eyes at the camera, a determined glint there. "It was during the mayor's press conference when I noticed a suspicious character headed toward the parking garage, the same location as the last three attacks, and while it was unclear if this man was the Grabber, it was clear something was amiss. We kept our eyes on him." She is conveniently omitting the dangerous stalking vigilante stunt. "We heard screams and saw him accosting an elderly woman. We intervened on her behalf, and I managed to retrieve her purse from him before he ran." She holds up the tattered bag like a trophy. "Our very own sportscaster Cade Hill chased him down. Thank goodness, he's a former NFL superstar and athlete."

Her eyes bounce to the police as they swarm, telling her and Kevin to step back. "As you can see, law enforcement is on the scene. We'll have all the latest at ten. I'm Rebecca Fieldstone with KHOT 5, the station that goes *beyond* reporting to keep you safe."

I stand as the cops sweep in and take the suspect from me, putting him in cuffs. He glares at me and mutters curses as the men separate us.

Grimacing, I step back and let them do their job. One of the cops pulls Stone, Kevin, and me to the side while another escorts the older lady to a quiet corner.

My shirt is ripped at the collar from the scuffle, my pants have a tear on the left side and I've lost a shoe. My adrenaline is ramped up so tight I'm ready to snap. With a clenched jaw, I send a narrowed gaze at Stone. When I get her alone, I don't know if I'm going to yell until my voice is raw or fuck her silly. Or both.

A FEW HOURS later, we're sitting at a rowdy sports bar near the station. Earlier, we'd finished our interview with the police and had headed to the news station to piece together the footage Kevin shot along with some B-roll from earlier in the day for the ten o'clock news.

Stone is next to me on a stool, Kevin has gone to the bathroom—he's still shell-shocked—and Trent's on the other side of me buying drinks for the whole place. Apparently Dad has officially hired him as the liaison for the school, and he's feeling gifty.

I stare at Stone, my gaze heavy-lidded, as she tosses back another shot of Fireball my brother has pushed at her. She's giddy with leftover excitement.

"Another round for the famous heroes here," Trent calls to the bartender as he gestures toward Stone and me. "They saved lives today, people!"

"Here, here," some of the crowd murmurs, having already heard the story from Stone.

Glasses clink as we do another toast and Stone grins at me over the rim of her cinnamon-flavored gasoline. "I'm glad you're not mad at me anymore."

I cock an eyebrow. "You're going to make it up to me later."

The thing is I had been pissed at her for taking on the mugger, but once I got her alone in the stairwell, all I'd wanted to do was put my mark on her—like a caveman.

So I had.

I'd taken her fucking pouty mouth with punishing kisses that had receded and turned soft when she moaned and pressed closer. I have no defenses when it comes to her—and I don't even understand it.

She blushes and settles her hand on the bar. Being stealthy, I rest my hand alongside hers so that we're touching but just barely. Still, it's enough to make every hair on my body, every cell in my body, every muscle I have stand at attention.

The heat from her hand is miniscule but enough to make me hyperaware that my need for her is growing. The attraction between us is thick, and I want her more than I've ever wanted any female in my life.

Kevin wobbles back from the restroom and stands behind Stone. I move my hand that's happy near Stone and use it to rub the back of my neck. I wonder how much longer I can pretend we're not together.

Does it really matter now that Marv's going to move her to production?

And that thought ramps me up.

80346890123456789013456789023467890

I hadn't told Stone about Marv's decision.

How can I?

As if she senses a change in my emotions, she stops talking to Kevin, her eyes drifting to me.

I look at Trent to avoid them.

"Dude. You look like something your cat killed and dragged home," Trent says, pointing at my torn shirt and pants.

"You be a hero next time," I counter.

"I like this look on you," Stone says. She adjusts the collar of my shirt, her fingers conveniently brushing at the sliver of bare chest that's visible. Her greedy gaze is all over me, and Neanderthal that I am, I puff out my chest even more. She leans in to brush at a speck of dirt I'd missed earlier at the station, and I catch her sweet scent.

Kevin claps me on the shoulder and Stone eases back.

"Thank you, man. If you hadn't shown up . . . I don't know what would have happened."

He's thanked me at least a hundred times.

"No problem. Next time, though, save the criminals for the police. Got it?" My eyes land on Stone when I utter those last words.

Her lips twitch at my comment.

There'll be no telling this woman what to do. Ever. And I know it.

I hear the music of KHOT and yell over the crowd for the barman to turn up the TV. He does and we watch as Matt and Lorie do the lead story. Of course it's the footage Kevin shot.

Trent blows a piercing whistle. "Pay attention, everybody! My brother and Stone are on the news!"

The place gets quiet as the screen shows me sitting on the mugger. Stone gets a resounding cheer when she shows the purse she saved.

"Go, Rebecca!" someone in the crowd calls and she glows.

Later, Trent and Kevin are in an animated discussion over their favorite Slurpee flavor, so I lean over to Stone. "Do you have any fucking idea how gorgeous you are up there on that big screen?"

She bites her lip. "It was crazy, wasn't it? At least I kept my shirt on."

I laugh. "My mom would say you're crazier than a sack full of rattlesnakes."

"I'm not a snake!" She giggles.

"How about a sack full of kittens?"

She smiles sheepishly. "That's better. Makes me think of Killer. She'd never hurt me."

Killer makes *me* think of my penthouse, and I'm picturing Stone spread out on my bed like a naked feast.

Her expression goes serious as she cups my cheek and levels me with those emerald eyes. She inhales a deep breath. "Truly, Cade, I *am* sorry for worrying you." Emotion fills her gaze, and she blinks. "Thank you for tonight. You very well may have gotten me that anchor job."

The anchor job.

I close my eyes. *Fuck.*

Forget that. Focus on *her.*

So, in front of everyone at the bar, I lean in and take her lips. Her mouth is soft and clings to mine as our tongues tangle together.

I pull back, and she's breathing hard.

Kevin is staring at us with wide eyes and Trent is snorting.

I tug her up from her seat, slap a few hundreds on the bar (just in case Trent needs help paying the tab), and without a word to anyone else, we leave.

Prickly, stubborn Rebecca Fieldstone is mine tonight.

Because I don't know about tomorrow . . .

Twenty

REBECCA

"YES! OH, CADE—OH, *YES!*" It's happening. The most amazing *O* of my entire life is rocking my body and soul right now. My mind is erased. I'm soaring through the universe as Cade Hill pounds into me from the foot of the bed.

He's the most amazing, the most beautiful, the sexiest thing I've ever seen, and I'm on my third orgasm of the night as his massive hammer claims my body forever.

I'm on my back, my ankles on his shoulders, and he's leaning forward, both hands on each side of my head. A bead of sweat traces down his temple, and his hair swings in messy, sweat-tipped waves around his face. His eyes squeeze shut, and he reaches up to grip my calf as if for balance.

"Fuck, Stone . . ." A low swear groans from his chest as he pulses deep inside me. He holds tight, his dark brow creased, and I'm in the stars, pinned to this bed, by this gorgeous man now lowering to his forearms above me and capturing my lips in a gentle, worshipful kiss. My lips follow his, in a lazy, completely sated response.

"Adrenaline sex is amazing," I sigh, and he laughs.

"Don't get any ideas."

"Hmm . . . I have lots of ideas."

His nose is in my neck, and he's kissing my collarbone. His beard scuffs my sensitive skin, and it's absolutely divine. It's too divine . . . A shock of panic hits my chest, and my body stiffens as a memory shoots to the forefront of my brain . . .

"Cade?" Even I hear the tremor in my voice.

His head pops up. "What's wrong?"

I look down at his chin, reaching up to run my fingers through his silky hair before I say it out loud.

"You haven't . . . applied for any top secret government programs, have you?"

Confusion is in his eyes. "Top secret government programs?"

"Anything with NASA?"

He draws back more and his eyes run all over my face and up to my forehead. "Did you get hit in the head tonight? In the struggle?"

"No, I was just wondering."

"I've never done any work with NASA, and I haven't applied for any government jobs."

Relief bubbles in my stomach, and I laugh—blissed-out, happy laughter. "Good. Don't ever do that, okay?"

His brow furrows, but that amazing dimple appears in his cheek. "Crazy Stone."

I touch a red-tipped finger to that little indention in his cheek, and I have another thought about tonight. "Thank you."

"For that mind-blowing orgasm? You're welcome."

"No, Mr. Cocky . . ."

"That's Mr. Cock to you."

"Oh my God," I roll my eyes, pushing against his shoulder. "Forget I said anything."

He laughs more, pulling out and reaching between us to dispose of the condom. I move up into the pillows and wrap the blankets around my naked body, waiting for him to join me. Both our heads are on the long, king-sized pillows, but we're in the middle of his enormous bed, facing each other with amazed smiles. Being Cade's girlfriend—secret girlfriend—is even better than I imagined.

"Okay, seriously," he says in that deep, rich voice I love as he reaches out to smooth a lock of hair away from my cheek—another thing I love. "Why are you thanking me again?"

"I was thinking about this evening . . . earlier in the parking garage."

His dark brows pull together, but he's still smiling. "I don't understand."

"Thanks for not charging in and taking over when everything went down. Thanks for letting it be my story."

"It was your story."

"Yes, but you know what I mean." I look down, thinking about his instinct to protect me. "I've worked so hard, and I . . . I don't know. I guess I just wanted you to know I appreciate you support-ing me and not treating me like . . ." I don't even want to say it out loud. *Like Marv.*

I'd been studying the sprinkling of dark hair across the lines in his chest as I said it, but now I look up to his beautiful blue eyes. His expression has changed. He blinks away quickly, but I saw the hesitation . . . concern? I'm not sure what it was.

"What's wrong?" I ask, reaching out to place my palm against his skin.

He doesn't meet my eyes. Instead he reaches for my waist, turning me so my back is pressed against his chest.

"Let's sleep now. We'll talk tomorrow."

"Are you tired?"

"It's hard work being a hero, chasing down bad guys, keeping you safe while making it look like I'm not even there."

I exhale a little laugh and lace my fingers with his around my waist.

"Just know it means a lot to me," I say quietly. "More than you probably know."

His voice is serious again, low and quiet. "I know."

MY EYES POP open with the dawn. Cade is still sleeping, making noises somewhere between loud breathing and snoring, and I wrinkle my nose with a smile. I never thought I'd find snoring adorable, but somehow when he does it . . .

Taking a deep breath, I slide out of his enormous bed and pick up my clothes. I have to get home so I can shower and change before we both have to be at work. I wish we could go for a jog together. I wish I could shower with his delicious-smelling body wash. I want to be covered in the scent of warm woods and citrus and Cade all day, reminding me of last night . . . reminding me of heroes . . . reminding me of amazing, real boyfriends who aren't dreams . . .

Chas is sitting at the table when I walk into our apartment, carrying my shoes. Her legs are crossed, and she looks like a classic 1950s housewife—full makeup, pink silk robe, pink turban, and a cup of coffee. Our oversized television is blasting the KHOT morning show, and it's right in the middle of my hero story.

"Girl!" Chassy jumps up from the table and runs to hug me at the door. My face barely reaches her chest in her feathered, high-heeled slippers. "You are the talk of the *town*, Rebecca Fieldstone of KHOT News, keeping us safe from hoodie bandits!"

"Did you see it!?" My voice is a little loud as all the excitement from last night comes rushing back.

"Ew, girl, don't shout. I had a performance last night."

"Sorry!" I hop over to the couch and sit on my feet on the cushions, grabbing the remote to rewind it to the beginning of my story.

Footage floods the screen of me holding the lady's purse, of the cops rushing in, of Cade with his knee on that creep's back, with my voice-over on top. " . . . *while it was unclear if this man was the Grabber, it was clear something was amiss. We kept our eyes on him . . .*"

"I love that part," I say, hitting pause. "Hear how I did the parallel between the two *clears*? I just said that, right on the spot."

"You're a regular Christiane Amanpour."

"Don't make fun."

"I'm not!" Chassy's eyes go round, and she places a large brown hand on her chest. "That story was as thrilling and important as anything happening in Iraq. Maybe more, because I was seriously considering never going to GreenStreet mall again."

"Yes!" I hop onto my knees. "That's it. We helped catch this guy, and in doing that, we saved local business, tourism . . ."

"You're a hero!"

Taking a deep breath, I rock back onto my butt. "I just know I'll get that anchor spot now."

Chas pats my leg. "You know you've got my vote."

My phone vibrates, and I lift it as she takes the remote from me.

Hate waking up and finding you gone. It's Cade, and his words send tingles all through me.

Sorry. Had to get ready for work. I don't even try to hide the enormous smile breaking across my cheeks.

Can't wait to see you again, he texts.

Me too.

"Mmm, and apparently you've got sexy Mr. NFL's vote, too! Yeah, baby, look at that ass!"

I look up at the screen and see Cade talking to the cops in the background of the news report, his perfectly tight backside on glorious display. "I missed that last night."

Large brown eyes sweep up and down my body "Don't even try lying, Miss Walk of Shame. You got all up *on* that ass last night!"

"Oh," I laugh, shaking my head. "I mean, I didn't see it on the news last night. The TV in the bar was too small."

"That's a shame." My roommate turns away, and I watch a moment, thinking about how awesome life can be when it finally stops sucking all the time. "So you're sleeping with him."

It's not a question, and I can't keep the smile from returning. I'm so damn happy. "He is so hot, Chassy. Last night . . . it happened."

"Great big *O*?"

"Enormous *O*. Huge. Unbelievable *O*. Or *O*s . . ."

"Don't tell me . . ." I watch as my six-foot-two roommate rises from the couch and retrieves her coffee. "This morning he got the call. NASA is sending him to Mars for three years."

"No!" I jump up and run to the coffee machine, opening it and dropping in a pod before positioning a mug under the spout and hitting the button. "He has zero interest in space. I haven't even had that dream since we started seeing each other."

"So what do you think it means?"

"I don't know," I answer honestly. "I'm no longer a commitment-phobe?" I wait for the machine to stop gurgling and take my cup away.

"Are you ready to settle down? Quit your job? Start having babies?"

My eyebrows shoot up, and I take a sip. "That anchor spot has been the only thing on my mind for months . . ." Another sip, and I know that isn't entirely true. "Besides Cade's ass."

"Yeah, girl!" Chas laughs, and we both giggle into our mugs.

LIVE with Kelly and Ryan flashes across the screen, and I jump off the couch. "I've got to get ready for work!" Coffee mug deposited in the sink, I scamper into my room to grab my clothes before heading to the bathroom for a shower. "I did think about having his babies after that Saturday at Deadrick," I say as I pass Chas on the couch. "I don't know. Should I be thinking about having babies now? I'm only twenty-eight. Do you ever think about having children?"

"Children bring head lice into the house," Chas says.

"Among other things!" I call back, thinking of cute little chubby dark-haired babes and warm fuzzies . . .

I'm showered, dressed, made up, and giving my roommate air-kisses less than twenty minutes later. We say goodbye, and I leave her in the apartment, curled up on the couch watching *Mother, May I Sleep with Danger.*

"It's a classic!" she cries in response to my snorts on the way out.

Nerves flutter in my stomach when I get to the studio, and not just because I'll be seeing Cade again after the most amazing night of my life. It's very possible everything I've been working for is about to happen. Right before I open the door leading to the newsroom, I take a moment to inhale and exhale three times slowly.

"This is it, Becks," I whisper as I glance up, saying a little prayer of thanks for yesterday.

Making my way quickly down the hall, I hear the noise of voices. They sound happy, like a celebration is happening.

I am not prepared for what I see next.

A colorful balloon bouquet is tied to the back of a chair, and an enormous sheet cake with *Congratulations* in rainbow on a field of white frosting sits in the center of the room. It's almost ten, so for a few brief moments, the entire news department is in the room. The morning show crew is headed home after arriving at two AM, and the rest of us, who will stay until after the six o'clock broadcast are arriving to pick up our assignments.

Vicky spots me, and she crosses the room quickly to where I'm standing with a half-smile on my face. My mind scrolls through all the possibilities: the mugger story was a huge success, Marv had to make a decision about the new anchor this week . . .

"Is this for me?" I ask her.

"Becks . . ." Vicky's voice is urgent, making me more confused than ever. "I talked to Marv first thing this morning about giving you a raise, possibly rewriting your contract to include an executive news position—"

"Rebecca!" Marv calls to me over the noise of voices.

That flutter of excitement is in my stomach. *This is it!*

I start to go to where he's standing, but Vicky's hand is on my arm, holding me back. Confusion lines my brow, and I notice Cade is standing beside Marv, and his face is tight with what looks like anger.

That's when I finally notice Savannah. She's walking toward the cake with a gloaty expression on her face and a sparkly card in her hand.

"I was just thanking Cade for supporting my decision in the board meeting yesterday."

"I don't understand." My voice is breathless.

I'm speaking more to Vicky than to Marv, and Cade is moving around the bodies making his way toward me. It's like he's moving in slow motion. It's like the entire newsroom goes into slow motion and drifts away from where I'm standing. I'm left alone in a narrow tunnel of humiliation and broken dreams.

"What's happening?"

Marv's voice is the only loud thing. "Please join us in congratulating Savannah Winston, KHOT's newest weekend anchor!"

Applause hits me straight in the gut like a medicine ball, knocking all the wind out of my body. My legs go weak, and I grasp for anything to hold me up.

Vicky still has my arm, but I pull it away. "Savannah?" It's a whispery shriek. *Cade supported this? He knew? All this time, he knew?*

He's still making his way toward me, but it's too late.

Panic jabs at my wrecked insides and I want to crawl under one of the tables.

My heart beats so fast I can hear it in my ears, my throat, my mouth.

It's over. Everything is over. Cade, my dreams, my plans, my future at KHOT . . .

I only have one choice left.

I have to get out of here.

Twenty-One

CADE

MARV IS A giant dick.

With his squirrely face preening, he announces Savannah scored the anchor job, and someone produces a bottle of champagne. He beams in satisfaction as he pops the cork and raises a glass, doing an off-the-cuff toast about what a perfect fit she is for the weekend position.

I focus in on Stone, wishing I was closer to her, but I can't get through the crowd. *Fuck!* This isn't how I'd wanted her to find out.

She appears frozen as she surveys the room with wide eyes. Her gaze careens from Savannah to Marv to Vicky and then me. She rubs her neck with a hand that trembles, the motion calling attention to the pulse beating rapidly in her throat.

Get to her, Cade.

She takes a step back and darts out the break room door.

"Stone!" I call but she doesn't acknowledge me, her legs eating up the distance between us as she stalks down the hall, headed in the direction of her cubicle.

I push past the reporters at the door and jog to catch up with her.

"Stone, wait a minute—"

"Get away from me." She never stops her stride, and her voice is low and shaky.

She cuts the corner and enters her space, her gaze everywhere but on me as she picks around at the items on her desk. She mutters under her breath as she shuffles papers aimlessly then picks up a scraggly-looking cactus plant and clutches it. About a foot tall, it's green and spikey with branches that resemble arms.

"What are you doing?" I ask.

She ignores me as she jerks up her blazer and tosses it over her arm. Her gaze scans the rest of the desk, deciding what to take with her.

"Are you quitting?" My voice is incredulous. I won't stand for it.

"How astute of you." Her voice is cold, her face a shuttered mask as she teeters on her heels for a moment then reaches up to the shelf above her computer to jerk down pictures she'd pinned to a bulletin board.

There's one of her and Kevin outside the courthouse during the Giovanni trial last year, one of her and Vicky smiling at an office party, and one of her and the other reporters accepting an award at the Broadcast News Association convention in New York last year—all of them had been taken before I'd arrived at the station. It hammers home the fact that Stone has worked at this station longer than my own NFL career. She can't just toss it away.

I pinch the bridge of my nose. "Look, don't let Marv win. This Savannah thing, it came out of nowhere for a lot of people. Marv is way too determined to put her in your spot. It's weird as fuck, and I promise I'll get to the bottom of it—"

"Don't bother," she snaps. With the cactus in one hand, she shoves the photos in her bag, pivots back around, and brushes past me to get back out in the hall.

There are a few stragglers from the break room wandering around, holding plates of cake and wearing smiles. Kevin looks as if he is going to say something when he sees Stone but stops when I shake my head at him.

This isn't the time, buddy.

They give her a wide berth as she powers through them, heading for the door.

I grab her elbow and flashing green eyes fly up and meet mine. "Don't touch me, Cade Hill. Don't you even dare—not after what you did."

My mouth flattens. "You can't believe what he said in there. I had absolutely nothing to do with Savannah getting the anchor job."

"It doesn't matter. My time at KHOT is over. No one wants me here." Her breath catches, and her chest rises and falls rapidly.

Without giving her a chance to say no, I take her arm again and steer her in the direction of the sports den. "You aren't storming out of here without talking to me."

She struggles to get her arm back, but with her hands full she's having a hard time. I take advantage of it and usher her into my office where I shut the double doors and turn to face her.

Stiff as a board, she stares at me, anger flitting across her face.

I swallow and heave out an exhale.

God, I wish I'd told her.

"I should have told you," I say softly as I approach.

Her gaze is hard as flint as she straightens her back even more. "Why don't you tell me now? Tell me how you *helped* Marv choose Savannah and how you *knew* the entire time and didn't say a damn word to me about it. I told you how much I wanted that job. I told you everything!" She dips her head. "God. I was so fucking gullible. Just when I thought you were . . ." Her voice stops and trails off.

My chest freezes. "What?"

She shakes her head furiously. "Nothing. It's not important." Her posture goes limp, as if all her bones have dissolved away, leaving only her skin. "Not anymore."

My heart beats double time. "I had nothing to do with Savannah."

"But you were there at the board meeting."

"I'm on your side, Stone." My hands clench, remembering the hurried meeting on Monday. Marv had gone in with a tight plan, using the consultants' logic and then the viewers' complaints about Stone's monkey pawing episode. I'd asked him for the proof of the complaints, because I doubted they were as widespread as he'd claimed, but it had fallen on deaf ears. I'd brought up how Savannah was too immature to handle the pressure, and obviously I'd chimed in about her apparent lack of knowledge when it came to basic geography. But, he'd been adamant about Savannah being the new, young fresh face of Houston, and nothing I said had helped.

"I was against it, but Marv managed to push it through. He had sound reasoning and on paper, Savannah has everything—"

"She's been here less than a year and has somehow managed to take everything!" Her face crumbles and she looks away from me.

"You deserve that job over anyone else," I say gently.

"Words, just words, Cade. Tell me this: did you know last night—when we were fucking—that I was going to come in here and get blindsided?"

I bury my hands in my hair. "I'm sorry. I didn't think he would announce it so soon. I didn't want to hurt you."

"And you didn't think today would hurt?" She grimaces, the cactus wobbles, and I'm waiting for it to crash to the floor. She manages to secure it.

Her face is red as she glares at me. "I fell right into your lap, knowing it was dangerous to get involved with a co-worker, but in the end, it didn't even matter. Because it wasn't *you* that screwed me up, it was *me*, believing for half a second that Marv and you and Vicky would look at me and my record. It was me believing that I deserved that job, but obviously my brain isn't pea-sized enough. I'm not young enough . . ." She sucks in a shuddering breath and looks blindly around the room. "I hate this place."

"Marv made a mistake. Let me—"

She slices into the air with her hand. "You are not going to do anything. Whatever we had"—she motions between the two of us—"is over and done. I trusted you."

I deserve that, but her words cut like a sharp knife.

"Don't go," I say and take a step toward her.

She scrambles away from me, her hands somehow awkwardly finding the doorknob and flinging it open.

I follow, trying to give her space but also wanting to stop her from walking away from me. Because it feels final. I keep pace behind her as she whips through the den and back out into the hall where she bumps into Savannah holding a balloon bouquet.

"Isn't this the best news ever?" Savannah beams with pride as she thrusts the bouquet under Stone's nose. "It's a dream come true—my own show!"

Stone stares at her, blinking rapidly, and it kills me to see her face is turning blotchy. Her gaze is frantic as she searches for an escape and tries to move around Savannah.

Savannah's eyes are like slits as she rakes them over Stone, taking in her plant and her overstuffed purse. "On your way out the door for good, Rebecca?" Her tone is saccharine sweet, and my anger ratchets higher.

A resounding pop fills the silence as one of the balloons careens into Stone's cactus. I'm not sure if Stone poked it at the balloon or if it was unintentional, but it causes everyone to stop and stare.

"How rude!" Savannah is saying as I approach.

"Shut up," I snap right back.

She huffs and glares at both of us.

Stone just stands there, and I think I see tears pooling in her gaze. "Goodbye, Cade." Her voice is small and thin, and it breaks my goddamn heart.

Before I can say anything else, the door is shut.

She's gone.

TRENT ADJUSTS HIS bowtie for another picture in front of the backdrop the photographer has set up. It's Saturday evening, and we're inside the Areosol Warfare Gallery, a sleek place with cement floors and graffiti-covered walls. It's hip, urban, and cool as hell. Just inside is roughly three hundred attendees—all here to support Deadrick and the surrounding schools. Of course Trent had managed to organize everything in just three weeks. His official title is Director of Better Education in Houston at Hill Global. The job is more stable than the acting gigs he manages to get every now and then, and Dad giving him a swanky office is the icing on the cake.

"He did a great job," a voice says. I turn to see my father in his black tux, looking trim and dapper.

Mom is with him, dressed in a blue evening gown. Her eyes glow as she looks from Trent and then back to us.

"I love having my whole family together," she murmurs.

I arch a brow, but I get what she's saying. We aren't a normal family by any means. I guess we never will be, but then who the fuck is? Dad isn't suddenly going to be fine with Trent's lifestyle, but at least he's learning to deal with it. Acceptance. That's all a person needs.

Trent's brought a friend with him, a slender dark-haired guy named Ramon, and I watch as Dad makes his way over to them. I strain to hear the introductions and distinctly hear the word *special friend* from Trent's mouth. Dad takes his hand and shakes it. Fucking progress. I lift a toast to an imaginary being in the air. Apparently with age does come wisdom.

"Too bad Rebecca isn't here with you," my mom says quietly as she hooks her arm through mine. "Will I ever get to meet her?"

I let out a long breath, my chest squeezing at the sound of her name. Mom knows the story of how Stone had walked out on KHOT—and me.

Yeah. When Stone had said she was done . . . she was fucking done.

"You okay?" Mom asks.

I nod, focusing on keeping my face shuttered. "Fine."

But I miss her.

More than miss her.

My penthouse isn't the same without her in my bed.

I find myself looking for her face wherever I go.

At Deadrick. At the office. In the grocery store.

"Why don't you call her?" Mom is facing me now. "She seems so delightful and sweet."

"I *have* called her. She won't answer." I slug back my whiskey and place it on a waiter's tray. A man can only take so many unanswered phone calls and texts before he gives up.

Mom sighs, her brow furrowing as she pats my arm. "Well, I am sorry for it. You just haven't been yourself lately . . ."

I smirk at her, trying to lighten the mood. "Forget about Stone. She's moved on and so will I."

"Want me to call up Sissy?" She giggles.

"Hell no." I laugh and it feels good—because I haven't for a while. These past few weeks of being frozen out by Stone have gotten under my skin more than I'd realized.

She nods her head toward the entrance where a group of people wearing media passes have walked in. "KHOT is here."

I follow her eyes and wave at Matt, Kevin, and one of the beat reporters who Marv decided would follow up with the Deadrick story.

Seeing them here without Stone reinforces the fact that she isn't part of our circle anymore. She won't be showing up tonight.

Sighing heavily, I wave them over and introduce them to my family.

For the next few minutes, as the gala attendees continue to enter, I stand next to Coach Hart, Cheetah, and a few more of the players as Matt asks questions about the school, the football program, and how they know me.

"How much money has Better Education in Houston raised tonight, Cade?" Matt holds the mic in my face, and I shoot my usual cocky smile at the camera. "Hill Global has collected over three hundred thousand tonight, and I suspect it will be even more after the evening is over."

Matt nods. "So how excited are you tonight about your speaker? Didn't you guys face off a time or two?"

I grin. "True, true, Eli Manning is speaking tonight about the importance of giving back. He's also interested in forming an NFL organization that gets pro players involved with school districts in their hometowns. We're delighted to have him. Lucky for us, he's a family friend."

A platinum blonde in a red dress appears in front of me, crashing the interview. "Cade! Darling! This event is simply amazing." Clutching my arm, Maggie Grace sweeps her gaze over to Matt and smiles at the camera. "Isn't he the most generous person ever?"

Matt jumps in with the microphone. "Indeed. And who are you, miss?"

She glows and bats her eyelashes at the camera. "I'm Maggie Grace, his fiancée."

Then she throws her arms around my neck and kisses me.

Twenty-Two

REBECCA

THE NOVEMBER SUN blasts in my face and there isn't a cloud in the sky. A steady breeze blows the side of my hair into my eyes and mouth.

"Should we wait for better weather?" I position myself in front of a used Kia Sorrento with a giant red bow across the windshield. Two enormous balloon bouquets are tied to the side mirrors.

Tommy Thompson, Houston's Used Car King, is beside me. He's dressed in a cornflower blue polyester suit, and a bead of sweat rolls down his neck as he squints up at the clear sky. "Can't get much better than this!"

I smooth a hand down my flower-print pencil skirt. "Don't you think the light is a bit . . . harsh? And the wind . . ." Another blast flutters my white silk shirt and sends more hair sticking to my lip gloss. I do a little laugh. "It's like being in Dallas!"

"It's damn fine Texas weather. Best weather in the world." His grin is enormous. "Don't you worry, Miss Fieldstone. Just say those lines, and it'll be great."

I can't believe I've been reduced to making amateur used-car commercials with this guy. In fairness, Tommy is paying me more

THE LAST *Guy* 191

money than I ever made as a reporter. The red light goes on, and I start to move. Naturally the wind sends the balloons flying in a colorful spiral right at my face.

"Safety isn't just my priority, it's also the priority of Tommy Thompson Pre-Owned Vehicles—oh!" I bounce off Tommy, who's standing with his feet spread and both hands on his hips like it's a barn raising. "Excuse me," I mutter.

"CUT!" Terence, Tommy's neighbor or brother-in-law or cousin or I forget what, shouts like he's Martin Scorsese. "Back to the top."

"Gotta keep those eyes open, Miss Fieldstone!" Tommy's voice is like my grandpa's, and he lifts a meaty paw like he might pinch my cheek.

I swear to God, if he touches my face . . .

Taking a step toward the car, I bat a shiny gold balloon away from my head. "Maybe I should move toward the car? Hold my hand out like this?" I do a sweeping *Price is Right* motion toward the vehicle.

"I like it!" Terence calls from behind the camera. He's a skinny guy shaped like a Coke bottle. "Let's shoot it!"

I barely have time to get to my starting point before the red light switches on. Naturally, the wind kicks up to full-blast as soon as I start to walk.

"Safety isn't just my priority, it's also the priority of—shit!" The tornado of balloons twists around my arm, tangling in my bracelet. They're around my waist. One bounces off my nose.

"CUT!" Terence yells, skinny shoulders falling. "Can't use that!"

"Now, Miss Fieldstone, we'd like to run this during family hours," Tommy laughs.

At least he has a good attitude. I'm ready to throw in the towel.

"Right . . ." I manage to untangle myself from the balloon ribbons. "How about I just stand beside you?"

"Great idea! We can act like we're having a regular ol' conversation."

"That'll give them something to watch." I'm fighting to keep the sarcasm out of my voice.

"I know!" Terence's skinny head pops out from behind the camera. His bushy brows are clenched. "Rebecca, how about you loosen your top button? You know . . . make it more interesting for the boys at home?"

"NO," I snap.

Tommy lets out a loud laugh, I assume to gloss over his cousin's bone-headed suggestion. Terence is back behind the lens.

"From the top!" he yells, and I take my place at my stocky employer's side.

"I HATE DOING commercials!" My yell is muffled by the throw pillow. I can't even say *Thank God it's Friday*, because I have to be back out there tomorrow.

I'm lying on my stomach in our living room after a mind-numbing fifty takes, and Chas stalks from the kitchen holding a pitcher of pink liquid.

"You're making more money than you've made *in your life!*" She emphasizes the words as she nudges my legs. "Have a drink."

I sit up, pulling them under my butt and reaching for the flared martini glass. "But it's not what I love. It's not what I want to do."

"You're not speaking to what you love and what you want to do."

My stomach cramps, and the ever-looming tears try to cloud my vision. "Stop!" I hold up one hand. "Do not say his name."

Chas's eyebrows rise and she shakes her head before sipping her Cosmo. My mind trips back to the night after it all came crashing down. That horrible night after that horrible morning when I'd arrived to see Savannah celebrating her new job . . .

After breaking up with Cade, I'd gone home to my apartment and cried until my head felt like it was going to explode and my nose was a snotty mess. I'd finally fallen asleep from exhaustion, and when I woke, it was nearly eleven—the perfect time to go back to the studio and finish cleaning out my desk.

I'd been so shell-shocked by what had happened and crushed by Cade's involvement, I could barely see for fighting the tears. I was not going to cry in front of them. Now I had to make sure I didn't leave anything behind.

"I was hoping you'd come back." Vicky had met me in the hall. Of course, she'd still be at work. "I wanted to talk to you, and you aren't answering your phone."

"I turned it off." My body was numb, and I continued to my desk without even lifting my eyes. "I don't want to talk to anyone."

"I'm sorry, Becks." She followed me to the small area I'd managed to strip of most of my personal things earlier, in spite of my insides spiraling. "I had no idea the board would take Savannah seriously."

Something about her tone made me snap. "You didn't think the board would listen to Marv? You didn't think they'd go with whatever their news director recommended?" I hadn't meant to shout, but my emotions were all over the place. "Nobody even objected."

"You're right." She'd nodded and looked down. "I let you down."

"You never talked to Liz, did you?"

Her red head moved slowly back and forth. "We were so busy. The grabber story blew up, and then you were a hero. I didn't think—"

"You didn't think. It wasn't your job on the line, so you didn't care."

Her eyes snapped to mine. "You know that's not true. I've always cared what happens to my reporters."

"Your reporters." I surveyed my office space and decided I didn't want anything else from this place. "I thought we were friends."

I'd gone back to my apartment and spent the rest of the night sobbing in Chas's lap. "She was supposed to be my friend."

"Friends let you down." Chas had stroked my head and fed me more alcohol.

More sniffing, more stomach cramps. "And him . . . I *loved* him."

"I know, cupcake."

"No," shaking my head harder, "I *really* loved him. Not like James . . . Not like anybody else . . ." My chest squeezed, and more tears flooded my eyes. "He was . . ."

My roommate's voice is sad. "He was your Star-Lord."

Eventually I'd thrown up in the toilet, and cried myself to sleep on the cold bathroom floor. At some point Chas had gone to bed, and I'd woken up the next day covered in her fluffy pink robe, determined to move forward and not look back.

Three weeks later, it still hurts like hell.

"He betrayed me," I say softly. "Vicky betrayed me . . . I counted on all of them, and they didn't even fight for me."

Chas is thinking—I can tell by the way she sips her Cosmo, but she isn't saying what's on her mind. Instead she rises with a flourish and returns to our small kitchen.

"By the way, this came for you today." She picks up a white business-sized envelope and hands it to me.

"A letter?" I frown, ripping the linen envelope open and sliding out a single sheet of paper. "Who writes letters anymore?"

Across the top in gray ink surrounded by a sweeping circle in all caps are the words *NBC 4 New York* and the rainbow peacock.

"What is this?" I whisper, sitting up straighter and setting my glass aside.

My eyes fly down the sheet so fast, I'm barely reading the words.

"What is it?" Chas scoots closer to read with me. "NBC!"

"Brian Caldwell. He thanks me for my interest in working with their station . . . 'Vicky Grant has spoken very highly of your work ethic and your recent assistance in capturing a criminal preying on senior citizens in the Houston area . . .'" My eyes are huge, and I look up at my roommate. "He wants to schedule an interview! He says to call at my earliest convenience!"

Chas screams and jumps off the couch to do a boogie dance.

I'm trying to swallow the knot tightening my throat. Working for a network affiliate in New York is one step below working for the network. It's the chance of a lifetime.

My eyes go to the clock. It's almost ten. "It's too late to call him."

"Fuck you, Marv!" Chas is singing and pointing her long fingers toward the door.

"I have to call Nancy . . ."

"We have to celebrate!" Now my roommate is clapping. "Get dressed—we are going dancing!"

I think about the texts Vicky had sent me over the last few weeks, apologizing again, asking if I were okay. I'd ignored them all. "I have to call Vicky and thank her."

"You can do all that later. I'm calling for a car. Put on your party dress!"

Twenty minutes later, we're in Barbarella, a funky-fun downtown dance club with 1960s Space-Race-era décor. We're in the center of a smoke-filled, semi-crowded dance floor. Neon-purple lights flash all around us, and we reach for the stars, which are little white points of light scattered across the black ceiling. It looks just like the Milky Way, and with our arms up, we twist our hips to classic 90s house music. Chas is in a short sequined slip dress, a classic Julie Newmar flip wig, and sky-high stilettoes. I'd thrown on my red dress and heels, touched up my lipstick, and ran out the door behind her.

"It's Priscilla!" Chas cries, and we jump up and down, singing and dancing to "Finally" by CeCe Peniston. "I'm Queen of the Desert!"

The song mixes into Robin S's "Show Me Love," and Chas pulls my arm toward the bar. I make a pouty face. "I love this song!"

"Too much desert. I must have refreshment."

We're stopped on the way off the floor by one of Chas's fans wanting an autograph. I snort a laugh when she signs the guy's bicep then squeals about how *big* and *hard* it is. Selfies taken, we make our way to the crowded bar.

"Why aren't you performing tonight?" I ask as we wait for fresh Cosmos.

"I have the week off," she says, rocking her hips to the beat. "Maybe I'll go with you to New York. I haven't seen Nan in *ages!*"

My eyes drift up to the flat-screen television hanging behind the bar. The news is ending with a recap of scenes from the charity ball earlier this evening. I'd done my best to avoid all coverage and put the event out of my mind, since it's to benefit the same inner-city school where I'd started to fall in love with Cade. Eli Manning appears with other local celebrities, and my stubborn gaze searches every face looking for his. I see Coach Hart followed by Cheetah . . . and my heart stops when Cade appears on the screen.

Dark hair flops onto his brow, and his steel blue eyes laser from the television to burn a hole in my already decimated heart. The television is on mute, but I watch his full lips surrounded by that beard, his perfectly straight teeth as he smiles, waiting patiently as Matt asks him a question.

Tears burn my eyes as much as I fight them. It hurts so bad to see him standing there, looking healthy and amazing, like he doesn't have a care in the world. I can still hear his voice. He stopped calling me, but I still have one of his voicemails saved on my phone. Sometimes, when it's really bad, I'll press it to my ear and listen to the rich vibration of him speaking. Hot tears will stream down my face, and I'll cry myself to sleep . . .

Those are the bad nights, the nights when I wonder how much I truly care that he knew the entire time, every time I'd thanked him . . . when I'd told him everything, when I'd bared my deepest feelings, my hopes and dreams. He'd known it had been over for me the whole time. He hadn't even tried to warn me.

"Be My Lover" by La Bouche comes on, and I turn to find Chas. I want to dance—correction: I *need* to dance. Only, I don't turn fast enough to miss it. The last shot of the gala is that same blonde stick-insect prancing up to Cade and planting a kiss right on his face. *Maggie Grace* in a mixture of words including *fiancée* appears under her image, and my heart drops to my feet. I lift my martini glass and chug the rest of the pink liquid, ready to slam it on the bar when a deep voice freezes me in place.

"She's always looking for some way to be on camera."

Spinning around, I almost fall when I see Cade standing behind me staring up at the TV screen. He looks just as luscious as he had when Matt was interviewing him, except his black tie is gone. The top button of his white shirt is undone, and both hands are in his pants pockets.

"Cade . . ." My stomach clenches, and my voice is just above a whisper.

"I didn't expect to see you here. Trent wanted to celebrate." His blue eyes move around my face. "The gala was a big success."

A sharp pain shoots through my forehead, and I fight back the tears. I remind myself my life is better now. I don't need Cade Hill or his player ways and half-truths. I've just gotten the chance of a lifetime. I am not focusing on the past or betrayal or how much I want to bury my face in his chest and lose myself in the scent of warm fires and citrus and him.

I clear my throat. "I'm glad to hear it." I sound way calmer than I feel. "Deadrick is a worthy cause."

Cade waves at the bartender. "A Cosmopolitan and a Jameson."

"You don't have to buy—"

"So you're working with Tommy now?"

Shaking my head, I do a dismissive wave. "It's just a temporary thing. I-I actually got a letter from Brian Caldwell today. He's with the NBC affiliate in New York. They want to interview me."

Cade studies me a moment, and I can't figure out the expression on his face. It's some strange mixture of pride and anger. "You're going to work in Manhattan?"

"It's just an interview." He hands me my drink, and I nod. "Thanks. I don't know that anything will come of it. It'll probably be just an expensive trip, but at least I'll see Nancy." His brow furrows, and I continue, borderline babbling. "My old roommate. She moved up there to go to culinary school and hopefully get a job with the Food Network, although—"

"They'll offer you the job." He cuts me off, and it sounds almost like saying the words makes him angry. "They'd be fools not to."

I don't know how to answer that, and we fall quiet. House music fills the gap, *Be my lover* . . .

"So you're engaged now?" My stupid brain just has to know.

"No." He answers quickly. "I don't know why she . . . I'll get Vicky to correct it."

I look down, taking a slow sip of my drink. I don't want to dance anymore. I'm buzzed and sad and having him this close is killing me. I'm not sure how much longer I can keep talking to him this way.

"You look . . . really good," he says, and pain echoes in my chest with every heartbeat. "I always liked that dress."

"So do you." My voice breaks, and it's time to go. I have to get out of here before I lose my grip on control and completely humiliate myself by falling apart. "Well . . . good luck to you."

I turn and almost bounce off Trent and Chas prancing up arm in arm. "Rebecca Fieldstone!" Trent presses his hand against his chest. "Watch where you're going, girl! My safety is your priority!"

I force a smile as we air-kiss each other's cheeks. "Congratulations on the gala tonight." I squeeze his forearm. "I'm sorry I can't stay to celebrate."

"Houston! We have a problem!" Chas cups her mouth dramatically with one long hand. "What's up, buttercup? You're calling it a night?"

"I'm sorry." I step forward to air-kiss my roomie. "I think today's hitting me all at once. I'm suddenly exhausted."

"Do you need me to see you home?" My roommate's chin starts to lift in Cade's direction, and I see her trying to make history repeat itself.

I grip her arm, and my jaw tightens. "I'll be fine. I've already called an Uber."

"Bolt the door as soon as you get inside." Chas uses her exaggerated mom-voice.

"I will."

Trent and Chas are calling "Byeeee" in unison, and the heat of Cade is burning at my back. Without looking over my shoulder, I adopt a confident stride and make my way through the crowd and out the door.

Only a few steps more, and I can fall apart . . .

Twenty-Three

CADE

THE CLUB IS smoky and packed to the gills with writhing bodies, but the only thing I see is Stone's curvy backside as she walks away from me.

Her hair is down and long in the back, the sleek strands like a cascading waterfall. God, I sound lovesick. My fingers itch to pull her head back against my chest and put my mouth on her neck. She'd taste like coconuts and summer, and I inhale sharply at the rush of adrenaline flooding my veins.

I want her.

She doesn't want you.

"Go after her," Trent hisses in my ear and gives me a nudge toward the door. Of course, he and Chas had been texting tonight, hence the reason we'd ended up at the same bar.

"She's almost gone," he says to me. "It might be your last chance!"

I *want* to go after her. I *want* to follow her out and beg her to forgive me for not doing more to stop Marv and his stupid shenanigans.

But I can't.

My body tightens with tension. "No. She hasn't forgiven me." I force myself to shrug nonchalantly. "She's moving on anyway to New York." I clear my throat. "Which is great for her. Fucking great."

I slam my drink and signal the bartender to bring me another one.

I want to feel numb.

Chas, who's been shimmying to the music, takes a seat at the bar and pats the one next to her. "You look down, Star-Lord. Come here and talk to Mama Chas. I'm a good listener."

I manage a smirk. I don't acknowledge the Star-Lord comment but know it has something to do with Stone.

"Trying to psychoanalyze me?"

"Naturally, darling. My aunt LouVerne lived in Little Rock, but she was a New Orleans gypsy."

"That so?"

"She said I inherited her gift. Come on, sit your hot ass down and show me your hand. Let me tell you what it means."

I heave out a long breath, suck down the rest of my drink, and plop down. "Alright, lay on the bullshit."

"Right hand, please." She nudges her head at my hand, and I place it on the bar.

With a serious expression, she studies my palm, her long mocha fingers drifting and tracing over the intricate lines.

Trent is fascinated and hovers around us. "Do you read tarot cards too?"

"Sure, honey. I do it *all*," she says, without looking at him. "Fortune-telling, tea leaves, astrology, crystallomancy, feng shui—"

I pop an eyebrow. "You're part Chinese now?"

"I sense a hostile vibration," she says.

I roll my eyes, and Trent pops me on the arm. I chuckle, the alcohol kicking in. "Okay, okay. Just get it over with."

Chas points to a line at the top of my hand. "See this here? It's a long fate line, which means lots of happiness . . . although here you have an interruption."

"Is he going to die?" Trent gasps.

Chas's lips twitch. "Don't freak . . . he has a long life line, but sadness and heartbreak have plagued you recently. You made a mistake . . . a tiny one . . . and it hasn't been rectified. You must fix this or never have happiness again."

"Dude. That sucks," Trent says, giving me a sympathetic look. "You can't leave things unsettled. Think about Dad. I mean, we aren't perfect—never will be—but things are better."

I exhale. "Okay, what else?"

Chas peers at my hand, tracing the line near my thumb. "This is your love line."

I smirk. "I bet it's horrible."

She ignores me, intent on her reading. "You love deeply, but you've been hurt in the past." Her heavily lashed eyes flick up to mine.

My mouth tightens. "Hasn't everyone?"

"Maggie Grace, aka Lying Bitch," Trent exclaims. "She walked out on him when his knee was busted. Didn't even leave a goodbye note and then goes and tells everyone she's his fiancée. Crazy ass—"

"That's enough," I say.

Yes, she'd left me, and it had stung. But it was nothing compared to watching Stone march out of my office.

Chas nods, her voice low and serious. "Fear of being hurt and a mountain of pride are keeping you from getting what you want. There is someone you care for very deeply—*not your ex*—and you must tell her or nothing will ever be right again. If you want something, you must fight for it." Her knowing gaze sweeps over me. "You feel me?"

Even though my bullshit meter is going off, a tingle goes down my spine, and my heart thuds. I *am* a fucking fighter. Always have been. But when it comes to Stone, she'd walked away from me. So. Fucking. Easily. I have my pride, and if a shit ton of phone calls and texts aren't enough . . .

I jerk my hand away from Chas.

"*She* gave up, not me." Picking up my drink, I take a deep swallow. It burns going down, and I'm glad. I need it.

With my index finger at the bartender, I order another one. He quickly obliges.

Trent gives me a concerned look as he watches me suck it down. "Bro, you okay? I haven't seen you drink this much—"

I cut him off. "I'm fine. Bathroom break." I stand, weaving for half a second until he straightens me.

"Want me to go with?" he calls as I walk through the crowd to get to the back of the club. I raise my hand up and flip him off without even looking.

Making my way down the narrow hallway, I find the restroom, shoving open the door with my palms. *Thank fuck it's empty.* I grip the sink and peer at myself in the mirror. My face is ashen and there are bags under my eyes from lack of sleep. It isn't because of work or the gala or Trent.

Stone, fucking, Stone.

And right there, I allow myself to process what she'd said.

She's going to New York and going on to a hell of a lot bigger things than being in car commercials in Houston. She isn't just walking out of my office . . . she's walking to another part of the goddamn country.

A wave of nausea hits me, and my knuckles whiten as I hang on to the sink.

"Get yourself together," I mutter.

I'm going to be sick because I drank too much.

That's a lie—I'm sick because of Rebecca Fieldstone.

My chest tightens at the thought of her. I straighten my shoulders and roll my neck, needing to alleviate the pressure.

Suck it up, Killer. Move on.

Right.

That ship has sailed.

Trent pops into the room, his nose wrinkling. "Damn, this place reeks." He shudders. "I hate public restrooms. Can't use them."

"What do you want then?" I bark.

He smirks and takes my arm. "Simmer down, princess, I'm rescuing you and getting you out of this dump."

I let him lead me out. "Where we going?"

He pats my arm. "I'm taking you home and tucking you in."

"I don't want to go home."

"If you don't want to be alone, I'll sleep over."

I don't say it, but it's scary how he reads me.

We weave through the dancers, and I wonder how we must look, me the six, four bulky guy being lead around by the lean and much younger Trent.

I reach over to ruffle his hair and my words are a bit slurred. I focus on enunciating. "I might be drunk, so disregard anything I might say, but you're my favorite brother."

"You are definitely drunk, and I'm your only brother."

"Thank God."

He beams. "I love you, too."

Chas is on the dance floor and waves us air kisses as we pass her and head to the exit. "Come by the apartment," she calls. "I have a crystal ball . . ." The rest fades out as we exit and Trent calls us an Uber. The ride home is a nightmare, and I find myself staring out the window, fighting with my roiling stomach.

When I finally get inside my apartment and get into bed, I can't sleep, which is the whole reason I drank. The room spins, and I close my eyes, digging for solace. All I see is a spunky blonde.

Stone. She's got me tied up in a knot and the only way out is to—fuck, I don't see a way out.

THE REST OF the weekend passes excruciatingly slow. I wake up with a pounding headache and an uneasy stomach. Ditching my run, I spend Saturday morning in bed with Killer watching pregame football shows. More times than I care to admit, I find myself studying the lines on my hand. *I am a fighter,* I keep telling myself, but when the car commercial with Stone comes on, I turn it off. I don't even want to see her face.

If she's leaving . . . then that's the end of it.

By the afternoon, Trent calls about our Sunday get-together at the movies. I drag myself out of bed, shower, and head to meet my family at the local cinema to see *Guardians of the Galaxy 2.* Star-Lord . . . I'm not him. I'm right here on this planet wanting her.

That night, I toss and turn, my body wired and on edge. I finally sleep when I flick on the TV and the monotonic drone lulls me under.

By Monday, I'm still feeling dark though, mulling over the weekend as I dress in a Tom Ford suit and head to work. I arrive earlier than usual, and the lobby is empty except for a page dropping off some mail. I mumble out a greeting and stalk to the sports den. My grouchiness is heightened when I can't even find a pen that works on my desk. With a growl of frustration, I stomp to the supply closet.

It's the low throaty moan that gives me the first clue something isn't as it should be, and it's confirmed when I fling the door open. I don't know what I expect to see—maybe the cleaning lady had gotten locked inside overnight—but it sure isn't the sight of Savannah on her knees with Marv's skinny dick in her mouth.

With the backdrop of copy paper, toner, and boxes of pens, she's deep throating him and he's pumping between her lips, a blissed-out expression on his thin face. He eeks out his orgasm, and she swallows it down. I steel myself not to barf. They haven't even seen me yet.

I open the door wider and clear my throat. "Morning, party people!"

She chokes.

He screams like a girl.

His expression is part horror, part ecstasy.

I shake my head and say, "Well, well, well, this explains a lot."

Marv shoves a disoriented Savannah off him, and she falls down and screeches. Her shirt is off, and her tits flop around. Ignoring her calls of protest, he quickly zips his pants and tries to buckle them.

"This isn't what it looks like, Cade, not at all. What about you and Rebecca? I heard there was some heat there. You know the game."

I bark out a harsh laugh. "Fuck you, Marv. You don't know shit. Stone's my co-worker. *Savannah is your employee.* Big fucking difference."

I open the door a bit wider when I hear the familiar female voice that seems to be talking to someone on the phone.

Marv starts, his eyes darting past me into the hallway. "Let's just forget about this, okay? We don't need anymore disruptions at the station."

"Oh, I have to disagree." My smile is tight.

One part of me is pissed as hell, knowing I've just exposed the entire reason Savannah got the anchor job in the first place. The other side of me is fucking thrilled.

Blocking the exit in case he decides to run, I call over my shoulder. "Vicky? That you?"

"Yeah?" Her voice is questioning. I assume she's staring at my back and wondering why I won't turn around. "What's going on? You find a big hairy spider?"

I shrug. "You could say that."

Her steps increase. "Let me have a look. I might need to go get my flyswatter . . ." Her voice stops as she reaches me and gasps. With wide eyes, she sputters, obviously struggling to find words.

Marv flounders around, still trying to get his belt latched, and Savannah is scrambling to tuck her boobs in her bra. But it's too late. It's plain as day what's happening here.

Disbelief combined with a dawning realization settles on her face. "You and Savannah? *At work?*" Her voice rises, shock morphing into anger. "Do you have any idea what the board will say?"

I chuckle and look at Vicky. "Oh, I have a *really* good idea what the board will say, and I'm heading up there right now to hear it." I salute Marv and smirk. "Good riddance, Marv."

I turn and do a little dance as I head toward the elevators.

Twenty-Four

REBECCA

I'M CURLED UP on the couch with all our soft pillows around me when my phone starts buzzing and vibrating on the end table. It's so obnoxious, it's impossible to ignore, and I vaguely recall it's intentional so I won't miss important calls.

Pushing out of my cozy nest, I try to think who would be calling me at this hour. My mind skitters over the last few days. Chas and I went out Friday night . . . I'd seen Cade and proceeded to drink all the alcohol in Houston before crying myself to sleep . . . Saturday morning, I'd looked like death warmed over and sent a text to Tommy saying I had the stomach flu . . . I'd stayed curled up right here all day yesterday while Chas fed me tacos and made me watch *Co-ed Call Girl* with her (another classic!) . . .

This morning I'd gotten up determined to shake off the past and be the strong, independent woman I am. I'd spent the day dodging balloons and singing the praises of five-point safety inspections and certified used cars, before coming back here to collapse on the couch. Without even looking, I grab my phone.

"Hello?" I say, trying to hide the fact I just woke up.

"Are you asleep?" The rich male voice vibrates through the line, and every nerve in my body simmers to life.

"Cade," I stammer. "Why are you calling me?"

"Are you sick?" The touch of sternness in his voice has my panties hot.

With a sniff, I fight for control. "It depends on what you mean by sick. Am I sick of the hypocrisy? Am I sick of the double standard? Am I sick of doing my best and being treated like—"

"Are you going to Manhattan?"

"I haven't decided." I slide back down into my multitude of pillows, my phone at my cheek, wondering why I haven't called New York. Why am I hesitating? It's the chance of a lifetime . . .

"Look, Stone, I've been thinking about you for two days. The way Marv treated you was shitty, and it pissed me off. But running away isn't like you either. You're a fighter."

He's been thinking about me? I refuse to acknowledge the flutters in my stomach at the idea. "I would hardly characterize a job interview in Manhattan as *running away*."

"Do you have plans for dinner?"

My brow crinkles as I try to register what he's saying. "No . . ."

"I'll pick you up at seven. We'll discuss it over dinner—before I have to be back at the station for ten."

"I didn't say yes!"

"Seven."

The line goes dead, and I hold my phone in front of me a few seconds staring at the screen. It's six o'clock. *Holy shit, he'll be here in an hour!* I kick my way out of faux mink and satin coverlets. Glancing down, I realize I need to do a little personal grooming . . . all over actually. My hair's a rat's nest; I slept in my makeup. *Gross!* I wouldn't even date myself in this condition.

A little less than an hour later, I'm pulling up my zipper when a strong, insistent knock sounds on the door.

"You're early!" I shout, giving the clock a quick glance. It's only six fifty.

"I came here from . . . work." The last word is right in my face.

Cade fills my doorway. His dark-brown hair is slightly mussed, and his blue eyes are as intense as ever. My insides sizzle. Pulling the door open causes him to lean forward slightly, and as if from muscle memory, everything in me draws right to him.

Clearing my throat, I take a step away. "It's a good thing I'm ready, or you'd be waiting in the hall."

"Is that so?" A sly grin curves his lips. It's too much.

Turning on my heel, I step into the kitchen to retrieve my purse. "As a matter of fact, it is."

"Where's Chas?" He steps inside, looking around in the direction of our bedrooms and back to me.

Every single bit of this is triggering images of all the ways we touched and kissed and fucked all those weeks ago right here in this apartment, and I have to bite back a sigh.

"Chas is actually meeting with a retail executive about launching a makeup line."

"Wow!"

"I know . . . Are you ready?"

Cade pushes an elbow toward me. "Do you like the Flying Saucer?"

I do a little shrug. "It's one of Chas and my favorite places to eat when we need to catch up."

"Perfect. I'll buy you a beer."

WE STEP INTO the enormous wood and linoleum space. It's a former department store, and old china plates cover the walls between bicycles and gold paper star lanterns.

A waiter is right with us. "We'll each have a Stone IPA," Cade says, and I shake my head.

"It's what you always get, right?"

"I've never had it," I confess.

"What?" He narrows his eyes at me before returning to the

waitress. "And two Space Club sandwiches."

"Another first," I say.

"Stone." His voice is grave. "Don't tell me I have to start ordering for you."

It's quiet a beat, and I've reached my limit. "What's going on, Cade?"

A guy hurries up and places two pint glasses in front of us. We both take a moment to sip the bitter, slightly hoppy pilsner.

"That's good," Cade says, leaning back and running his palms down the tops of his thighs.

I nod in agreement then sit back as well, doing my best not to let my eyes follow those hands up his thighs to what I know is hidden in his slacks.

"Let's put our past aside for just a moment," he says, blue eyes assessing me. "Can you do that?"

I do a little frown and put on my professional mask. "Of course."

"I like to think we've always had something of a . . . healthy working relationship, wouldn't you say?"

"We're not on the same beat. You're sports. I'm hard news."

He pauses a moment, his perfect lips twitching. "Hard news?"

"Okay," I confess. "I drifted into features at the end there—"

"Marv sent you nothing but features, you mean." I don't miss the anger that enters his tone.

All of this is getting to be too much. First, we had the most glorious three weeks of my life followed by the most hellish three weeks. I'm on the cusp of leaving this nightmare, and he shows up out of the blue saying all these things.

"What's your point, Cade?"

"You're too good—and too smart and beautiful—to leave Houston. It's your home. It's where you've built your reputation. You belong here."

I shrug and lift my glass. "Life doesn't always go the way it should."

"Marv was screwing Savannah. It's why she got the anchor job instead of you. I told the board, and they fired him on the spot for sexual misconduct with a subordinate."

He catches me mid-sip, and I almost snort pilsner up my nose. "What!?" I slam the pint glass down on the polished wood table.

"It happened pretty fast today after I caught them in the supply closet. They made Vicky news director, and we both want you back . . . We want you beside me at the anchor desk."

"Beside you? But what about Lorie?"

"She asked to have the weekend position—she wants to be a stay-at-home mom."

For a few moments, I can only blink at him. My mouth is slightly open, and I don't even care.

"But . . . Wha . . ." Clearly, I'm having trouble speaking as well as thinking. "What about New York?"

The muscle in his jaw clenches attractively. "Do you want to go to New York?"

Quiet falls over the table. The waitress has put our sandwiches in front of us, but my throat is closed. I couldn't eat a thing if I tried. Cade slips his arm across the top of the table, reaching his hand to me.

"We hoped you might consider staying. KHOT is your family . . . We love you."

All the air leaves my lungs, and I can barely say the words. "We?" It's a whisper, and my eyes flicker up to his dark blue ones.

The air around us is tight. It crackles with electricity, and I slip off my stool. It's there in the way he says my name, but everything is crowding together in my mind—my goals, my dreams, my future . . . the chance of a lifetime.

"I have to go. I'm sorry."

"Stone . . ."

Shaking my head, I hurry to the door and out to the sidewalk. I have to think, and I can't with him right in front of me. I'm hastily pulling up the Uber app as I walk, not sure where I want to go . . . I don't want to go home. Where can I go to think?

Nearby attractions pop up, and I hit the bottom one without even reading the description. A car is less than a minute from me, and I pause at the corner.

The Waterwall is an enormous, curved fountain, sixty-four feet tall at the back of a quiet park in Uptown. Even at this time of night on a Monday, tourists and visitors mill around, looking up at the thousands of gallons of water roaring past in a constant, hypnotic force.

I stand in front of it as cascade upon cascade crashes onto the concrete steps, sending a faint, chlorine-scented mist into the atmosphere around us. Everything in my life is racing at me so fast like these columns of water. I feel out of control. I don't know the right choice.

Back at my apartment is a letter, an opportunity that would change everything.

Back at the restaurant—or I guess back at KHOT now—is something different, someone I never saw coming, someone who would change everything as well.

"Cade . . ." I whisper, thinking of the unspoken words hanging heavy between us.

He fought for me. He busted Marv and fought for me. Vicky helped him . . .

We love you . . .

"Rebecca Fieldstone!" The small voice jerks me from my confusion.

I turn to see a pint-sized princess, complete with aquamarine mermaid skirt and trident flouncing toward me.

"Petal?"

"I thought that was you." She holds out a small hand, and I shake it.

"You're Ariel." I study her costume and thinking of happier

times, quinoa salads.

"I was over there doing promo for Disney on Ice. It's part of my duties as Planetary Princess."

"Oh." We watch the fountain a moment before she turns back to me. "I've seen you on those car commercials. I thought you were a journalist."

Exhaling a laugh, I shake my head. "I did, too."

Her chubby face scrunches. "What's that supposed to mean?"

I look up at the falling water and think about it. "I worked really hard for something for a long, long time . . . It was my dream, and someone else got it. So I left."

"And now you're doing commercials? With the used car king?" The astonishment in her voice makes me defensive.

"I'm considering a move to New York . . . to be a reporter again." I think about the chance I thought had passed me by, and the last guy I ever expected to help me achieve it. "Or I could stay here and have my dream."

"Diane Sawyer is one of my role models. After she won America's Junior Miss in 1963, she went on to become the highest paid female anchor in television history."

"I know," I say, nodding.

"She said 'The dream is not the destination, but the journey.'"

The roar of water fills the pause, and I look up, thinking about all of it. The dream, the destination, the little mermaid . . . *We love you.* "I wanted to conquer the world."

"What good is that if you're alone?" Glancing down, my eyes meet clear blue ones, shining up at me from beneath a helmet of red hair topped with an iridescent tiara. "You remind me of Mrs. Sawyer. What are you going to do?"

Like a star burning in the night, the answer shines through the darkness. I bend down and give her a hug. "Thank you, Petal. I've got to go."

Turning, I tap the Uber app as I jog all the way to the entrance to the park. I'm breathless when the car meets me, and I'm pushing my feet against the floorboard, my hands gripping my knees the entire drive to the center of downtown.

Less than ten minutes later, I'm standing in the lobby of the luxury high-rise apartment building, pressing the button for the penthouse. Glancing up, I can see the security cameras trained on me. It's after eleven, so I'm pretty confident he's home.

Not a sound comes through the intercom, but the light flickers on above the shiny silver doors. My heart beats faster as the numbers slowly count down, as the elevator descends to the first floor and pauses with a ding. Another pause, a swift whoosh of air, and everything stops. My breath disappears.

Cade leans against the wall just inside. A smile curves his sexy lips, and he has one hand in his pocket.

"Hello, Stone," he says in that low, luscious rumble.

"Hi," I manage to answer.

"What are you doing here?" Steel blue eyes hold me captive.

"I-I wanted to say this in person."

"Did you think about my offer?"

"I did."

"And?"

"I'd be an idiot to say no," I say with a shrug.

"That's my girl." He reaches out, and I take two stumbling steps forward as he pulls me close against his firm torso. My palms are on his chest, his arm is tight around my waist, and everything around us seems to fade away. "Let's have a toast to the future."

To dreams coming true in the most out-of-this-world way, I think as our lips collide.

THREE HOURS LATER . . .

"YES! RIGHT THERE!" I cry, gripping the headboard, my breasts bouncing as my hair flies forward on my cheeks.

Cade reaches forward to pinch my tight nipple, rolling it in his fingers, and my insides clench. "Fuck," he groans.

He's behind me, his massive dick hammering so deep into my pussy, my back arches involuntarily. I'm holding on for dear life, bucking against him like I never want it to end. His hand moves to my clit, and I'm on the edge, a hairsbreadth from falling over into sweet, sweet bliss.

All at once, his fingers leave me and SMACK! he slaps my ass hard. I jump and gasp. The stinging mixed with the intense pleasure causes my insides to clench around has cock again.

"You love that." He growls and SMACK! he slaps my ass again. "How about this?" His thumb pads at the small pucker of my ass before slipping inside, and . . .

"Oh shit!" I wail as the orgasm rips through my body.

My elbows give out, and I collapse forward on the bed, boneless as the shudders ripple through me.

Cade grips my hipbones, jerking me up against his still-hard cock. He's driving deeper, chasing his own orgasm, and I'm moaning, trying to catch my breath. It's penetrating and punishing and so fucking sexy. His hardness stabs and withdraws from my clenching insides as they desperately try to hold onto him, milk his orgasm, when at last he breaks with a shout. It's deep and strong, and he holds me flush against his body.

I feel his dick pulsing as he fills the condom. I finally return to Earth, and I arch up, slowly rising to press my back against his chest and wrap my hands around his neck. I tilt my face, and our lips crash gently again and again. His hands cup my breasts and I sigh, slipping my tongue out to touch the salty dampness of his skin.

"That's what I call a touchdown," I purr.

His body vibrates as he chuckles, and his arm goes around my waist. "A touchdown in the last seconds of a tied game headed to overtime against our fiercest rival."

That makes me laugh, and he kisses my shoulder before giving it a little bite. Another pulse moves through my core. He groans in my ear, "Yes."

I sigh just before placing my teeth against his jaw and biting him back. He holds me tight against his chest as he slides us down onto the mattress. We're wrapped in dark navy sheets in his very masculine bedroom.

"Are you going to remember any of this tomorrow?" he says, kissing the back of my neck, right at the center of my shoulders.

A shiver passes through me, and I laugh, remembering the celebratory Fireball shots he poured for each of us. "I only did half a shot, and it was only because you made me."

"It was for old times' sake." His lips are at the top of my head, and I tighten my arm over his. "Fuck shots. I couldn't keep my hands off you."

My entire body heats, and I turn so I can face him. "I'll never forget a moment of this. Not as long as I live." Our eyes meet, and I can't hold back any more. "I love you, Cade Hill."

Warmth fills his blue gaze, and he leans forward, capturing my lips with his. My mouth opens, and his tongue finds mine, teasing gently, claiming definitively. Cade Hill is my man. He's my prince. He's my Star-Lord, and I can't even begin to understand how it happened.

"It's positive," he says, pulling back.

"What?" I'm slightly dazed and my lips are warm and well kissed.

"The Beatles song. It's positive. We should make more love. Then there's more love to take."

My nose wrinkles. "I can't believe you remembered that."

He reaches up to cup my cheek, and all signs of humor leave his face. "I remember everything about you . . . every minute, every laugh, every sigh, every moan. I love you, Rebecca."

He's never said my name that way, thick and heated. I have to blink fast. I don't want to cry, but . . . *Shit*, I'm going to cry.

His dark brow lowers. "What's wrong?"

Joy so strong it hurts fills my chest, expanding my lungs. "I've never known this kind of happy. I didn't know it existed . . ."

That dimple I love pierces his cheek as he smiles. He leans down and gives me another, longer kiss. I reach up to hold his face as we melt into each other, as our hearts move together in time.

His lips trace my cheek, brushing against my ear. "We should make more love now."

Laughter bubbles in my throat, and I stretch my body against his. "You won't get any arguments from me."

It's out of this world how life can change on a dime. I'd gone from frustrated, ready to give up, to one stupid, wasted night that turned out to be the luckiest break of my life . . .

With the last guy I ever expected . . .

Right here, on this planet, making all my dreams come true.

Epilogue

CADE

ONE YEAR LATER

I WAKE UP at the crack of dawn, way before I have to be at work, and Stone's curled up next to me, her soft naked body glued to mine. She's snoring delicately, and I grin and pull her even closer if that's possible. She'd moved in to the penthouse about six months ago and every single day when I wake up next to her, a sense of rightness settles in my chest.

She stretches out and mutters something about tacos, giving me a view of the curve of her hips and those luscious tits. My girl is so hot she could sell bikinis during a snowstorm. She's fucking perfect with her creamy skin and long wavy hair. With a light touch, my hand traces the line of freckles on her nose, and she waves her hand in the air like she's swatting a fly. She flips over on her stomach, and her arm flings out, smacking me in the face.

Still, she doesn't wake up.

I chuckle.

A bit zany, compassionate, funny, and crazy in the sack, I'm lucky she loves my ass—literally. She's *in love* with my tight, muscular backside, and me, of course. I grin again, my permanent expression since we'd made up and she'd finalized her contract with KHOT, making her the nightly co-anchor with Matt and me.

I think back to everything that's happened over the past year. Marv had been fired and is now working as one of those goofball consultants he loves to listen to so much. Lots of travel *and* he was low man on the totem pole. Fitting. Savannah had resigned and is currently working at the Gap.

Trent still works for Dad and is branching out to start new charities for other inner-city schools. He and Dad did some counseling to hash out the hateful things in their past. Their relationship isn't a miracle turnaround—I didn't expect it to be—but they do love each other and want to have each other in their lives.

Coach Hart and Cheetah won the high school football championships this past November, and part of me likes to think we all played a part in getting that trophy.

My phone buzzes on silent, and I scoop it up off the nightstand as I sit up on the side of the bed. It's Chas.

Morning, Killer. Hope your ass is awake. I'm tapping my heels in your lobby. Don't you think it's time you gave me a key?

Shit. She's early. Jerking up, I slip on last night's hastily discarded football shirt and a pair of flannel pajama bottoms I have to dig out of the drawer. It takes several minutes to find a pair because with Stone around, we're naked most of the time.

I slip out of the bedroom and head to the front door. Killer is nipping at my toes the entire way, but I ignore her and exit the apartment. I hop in the elevator and ride down to the lobby.

The door opens, and I see Chas leaning against a marble column. The doorman is eyeing her fishnet hose, spiked red heels, and mini-skirt with a steely gaze. She straightens and swishes toward me holding the ends of a black cloak with a high fur collar.

I wave at the doorman. "She's with me, Bobby. Next time send her on up if you don't mind."

"Of course, Mr. Hill." He gives me a short nod and turns back to the double-glassed doors, his expression blank.

"You're early—and very dramatic," I say.

She shrugs her tall frame in an effortless way as she makes her way over to me, the ends of the cloak flapping behind her. "Had to. Found out last night I have a face-to-face meeting with the bigwigs at Bloomingdale's. Happened rather suddenly to be honest."

"Makeup, I assume?"

She nods, a hint of nerves on her face—something I've never seen. "According to the voicemail they left me yesterday, they *adore* my new line of eye shadow."

I'm not surprised. Since we'd met, I've learned Chas's work ethic is mostly *work your ass off until you get someone to say yes.* "You deserve it," I say. "With those million hits on YouTube of you using your product, you can name your price."

She purses her lips. "Mercury *is* in retrograde again, and my horoscope did say I would make my fortune this month."

I laugh. Chas is Stone's number one friend, which is why I'd enlisted her help with picking up a special package for me yesterday when I'd realized I wouldn't be able to make the final pickup because I had to work late—with Stone.

"Do you have it?"

Chas nods and passes it to me. I take it, my hands suddenly sweaty. My heart somersaults as I peek inside.

"You gonna hurl?"

I tear my eyes off the gift—the one I'd carefully designed and selected months ago after Stone and I had come back from our spring break trip to Hawaii. "Maybe."

She studies me carefully and then after a few tics, her head does a quick bobble. "It doesn't take a palm reading to see you guys are written in the stars. I knew it the second you walked in the Pussycat Club. Forever and ever, Amen."

I feel light-headed but squash it down. "Yeah," I say and start backing toward the elevator. I'm anxious to get back to Stone. I don't want her knowing anything about what I have planned. "Uh, good luck today. Let us know how it goes."

She's already turning to the door and sending me a jaunty little wave. "Bye, Star-Lord."

I head back up to the penthouse, hop in the shower, and dress. Stone is still sacked out, and I know it's because we were up until the wee hours of the morning making love. I have a shit ton of work waiting on me, so I dress quietly, writing her a quick note before I walk out the door.

You look so peaceful I didn't wake you. See you at work.

Love, Cade.

It's brief, but it's all my brain can come up with.

Like Chas, I'm nervous and need some time to process what I'm doing.

I get to work, and the day drags by until Stone shows up around eleven.

By five thirty, I'm running from Vicky's office and texting Kevin at the same time. It's almost time for a huge story we've all been working on.

"Wait." I grab Stone's hand just before we take our chairs behind the modern-looking chrome and wood desk.

The cameraperson starts the countdown—sixty seconds until we're live.

I study her intently. She's wearing a royal blue pencil skirt and a V-neck sweater in a lighter color that's soft and fuzzy.

"What's up?" she asks.

I rub the back of my neck, searching for the right words. There are so many things I could say . . .

"Cade?" She tilts her chin and studies me. "What are you thinking?"

"Truthfully?" My gaze skates down her form. "How fucking great you'd look barefoot and pregnant."

That wasn't what I meant to say.

She blushes and smiles up at me. "That can be arranged."

I touch her face, my thumb sweeping across her cheek as my hand cups her nape. I'm dying to kiss her.

Twenty seconds.

The cameraperson is waving frantically at us, but I don't give a shit.

I gather myself, taking deep breaths.

"Cade?"

The words come out in a rush. "I want you to know that since I met you, I dig *The Little Mermaid*. Ariel and Eric have a great love story. In fact, you're *my* mermaid. I love Taco Bell because of you, which is saying a fucking lot because it's not good for you, and we all know it's not a hundred percent beef. I love jogging in the park with you. I love how you fall asleep, and your arm automatically curls around me. I love cooking for you." I pause. "I never thought I'd be this fucking consumed with a person every second—"

"Five seconds, people! I can't have empty seats!" Vicky calls, her voice a bit shrill. Matt is already seated, waiting patiently.

Stone is transfixed by my words and reaches up and kisses me on the cheek. "Ah, Star-Lord, I love you so much. Now let's go do the news."

I swallow, nod, and guide her to her seat. She's watching me the entire time, a bemused but baffled expression on her face. I take my seat on the other side of Matt.

The show's upbeat and peppy music comes on, and the camera is pointed straight at Matt as he reads from the teleprompter. He takes the first headline about a shooting while Stone jumps in with a story about a robbery of a local pharmacy. It's a normal news day.

"And now to Cade Hill for a rundown of the college games this weekend," Stone is saying.

The camera swivels at me, and I dig fucking deep to keep cool.

Put your game face on and stay calm.

I shoot a cocky grin at the camera. "College football can wait a few minutes, folks. First, here at KHOT, we'd like to celebrate an anniversary that's very special to us. It's been exactly a year since our very own Rebecca Fieldstone was promoted to anchor. Last month she was voted Favorite Anchor by the *Houston Herald*. It's a big day for her, and well"—I smile sheepishly and glance over at her—"we prepared a little surprise to commemorate how much the viewers and the staff at KHOT love her."

The view switches to film Kevin has spent the last two weeks shooting.

The first shot is of Petal wearing a sparkly tiara and a purple fluffy dress. "Happy anniversary, Miss. Fieldstone. I'm glad you're not on commercials anymore. Remember to read *To Kill a Mockingbird*!"

The next shot is of Albert from the children's zoo holding Pixie. "Say hi to the lady who made you famous on the internet," Albert tells Pixie. I hear Stone stifle a groan as Pixie reaches up and snatches his hat off his head then puts it on her own.

Phil and Sissy show up on screen. They're standing in front of Paulette's, the restaurant where we'd had our dates. "Thank you for introducing us, Rebecca!" Sissy calls. "We're engaged!"

Phil does a weird thing with his hands. "Qapla!"

Stone giggles and gives me a long look as the film rolls. "Did you come up with this?" she whispers.

I nod.

Her face softens and she gives me a look—*that look*—the one that tells me she loves me.

Then Trent and Chas take over the screen. They're standing arm-in-arm outside, just at the corner of the Pussycat Club. Thankfully Kevin had edited out the racy marquee.

There are other quick shots of people we work with blowing kisses and wishing her well—Vicky, Kevin, the beat reporters, my mom and dad.

Then, there's a montage of photos of us . . . at Christmas . . . in

Hawaii. It's pretty fucking good, and emotion wells up in my chest.

It fades, and the entire news crew erupts in applause. With her eyes misty, she's composing herself just as I stand and walk around the front of the desk to her side. I offer my hand and she takes it, her eyes looking around the room trying to figure out what's going on. I lead her a few feet away as the camera follows us. I get down on one knee.

She gasps as I pull out the velvet box Chas had delivered. I open it to reveal a three carat round diamond with an emerald nestled on each side to match her eyes.

I gaze up at her. "Rebecca Leigh Fieldstone, I love you. You brighten everything, and I can't imagine a day without you. Will you be the last girl for me and be mine forever?"

A tremulous smile spreads across her face. "Yes, yes, yes! A million times yes!"

I stand, and we kiss as the camera rolls.

Everything is full circle.

She's mine.

I'm hers.

Her last guy.

Forever.

THE END.

Read more …
BY ILSA MADDEN-MILLS

Fake Fiancée, 2017
Filthy English, 2016
Dirty English, 2015

Very Bad Things (Briarwood Academy #1)
Very Wicked Beginnings (Briarwood Academy #1.5)
Very Wicked Things (Briarwood Academy #2)
Very Twisted Things (Briarwood Academy #3)

BY TIA LOUISE

THE DIRTY PLAYERS SERIES
The Prince & The Player (#1), 2016
A Player for a Princess (#2), 2016
Dirty Dealers (#3), 2017
Dirty Thief (#4), 2017

THE ONE TO HOLD SERIES
One to Hold (#1—Derek & Melissa)
One to Keep (#2—Patrick & Elaine)
One to Protect (#3—Derek & Melissa)
One to Love (#4—Kenny & Slayde)
One to Leave (#5—Stuart & Mariska)
One to Save (#6—Derek & Melissa)
One to Chase (#7—Marcus & Amy)
One to Take (#8—Stuart & Mariska)

PARANORMAL ROMANCES

One Immortal, 2015
One Insatiable, 2015

Acknowledgments

TIA WOULD LIKE to thank Ilsa for having the vision for us doing this. I was a little nervous at first . . . I'd never co-written with anyone and wasn't sure my writing style would play well with others—LOL! (It's so scatter-brained and constantly evolving.)

We talked about doing something silly to take the pressure off. We talked about a lot of things. Then Rebecca and Chas appeared in my head so vividly.

Cade was only a fuzzy idea of a cocky jock who helped Rebecca out—in more ways than one (*wink*). Then you brought him to life so fully and beautifully. He's an amazing book boyfriend—the absolute best!

So THANK YOU, my friend, for believing in this little tale, for taking this crazy first step with me, for knowing we could do it, and for all the calls and chats and laughs and rants along the way. Here's to meshing.

I love you!

~T.

TIA, I LOVE your sweet heart, your goofy humor, and the silly emojis you send me because you know they make me giggle. Thank you for writing a short story that we shaped into a full-length, hilariously awesome book.

We've had so many great times together: stuck in a hot as heck elevator in Nashville, plotting funny storylines over breakfast in Dallas, and a weekend in Kiawah where you accidentally locked me out of our room. Watch out for alligators!

You're EPIC, and I love you! I can't wait to see where this adventure leads us next!

Love, Ilsa xoxo

SPECIAL THANKS TO Tara Sivec for reading the first half of our baby project and giving us our first huge kudos—or death threat if we didn't send the rest *STAT!* (same diff . . .)—and on your birthday! Love you, lady!

Thank you to Rebecca Freidman for running her eyes over the beginning (gotta have a hook) and offering feedback.

Thanks to our beta readers Ilona Townsel, Lisa Kuhne, Kylie McDermott, Lisa Paul, Miranda Arnold, and Joy Novel-Thoughts— you ladies are rock stars! Thank you for running your eagle eyes over our story and falling in love with the characters.

Thanks to Wander Aguiar for the gorgeous photography, to David Wills for bringing Cade to life, and to Shannon for the perfect design.

Thanks to all the amazing authors who made time to give us a read and a little praise. We appreciate you more than we could ever say!

Thanks to all the bloggers for sharing your love of our books. You ladies are the stars of our reading world.

Thanks to Lisa Hintz (The Rock Stars of Romance) and Jenn Watson (Social Butterfly PR) for coordinating our promo efforts.

Thank you to Caitlin Nelson for the great line and copyediting.

Huge thanks to Tia's Babes and Ilsa's Unicorns for the nonstop love and excitement, especially when we're in the cave bringing these characters to life. You're the reason we do it!

Thanks to Tina Morgan, Tammi Hart, Lulu Dumonceaux, Helene Cuji, and Elle Ramsey for helping Tia stay sane!

Thank you to Miranda Arnold, Suzette Salinas, Tina Morgan, Heather Wish, Pam Huff, Erin Fisher, Stacy Nickelson, Elizabeth Thiele, and Lexy Storries for keeping Ilsa focused.

Most of all, saving the absolute best for last, THANKS to our families for the love and support, the patience and the encouragement.

Mr. TL, Kat, and Laura; Mr. Mills, Eli, and Mia. We love you so much.

Stay sexy,
Ilsa & Tia

About the Authors

WALL STREET JOURNAL bestselling author Ilsa Madden-Mills and the "Queen of Hot Romance" Tia Louise are not a secret duo, but simply themselves.

Great friends, former English teachers, and southern gals in real life, they've teamed up to bring you laugh-out-loud naughty romances with strong leading ladies and sexy alpha males who know how to please their women—and who sometimes you just want to slap.

Keep up with them online:
www.IlsaMaddenMills.com
www.AuthorTiaLouise.com

Join **Tia's Reader Group** at *"Tia's Books & Babes"* **on Facebook**

Join **Ilsa's Reader group** at *"Ilsa's Racy Readers"* **on Facebook**

CPSIA information can be obtained
at www.ICGtesting.com
Printed in the USA
LVOW10s2209200518
577902LV00002B/193/P